RAVES FOR JAMES PATTERSON'S
SIZZLING SERIES!

NYPD RED 4

"IT IS EQUAL PARTS POLICE PROCEDURAL AND CAPER NOVEL...BOTH LOYAL AND CASUAL READERS OF THIS FINE SERIES WILL NOT WANT TO MISS THIS INSTALL-MENT."
                            —BookReporter.com

NYPD RED 3

"A GREAT EXAMPLE OF PLOTTING OUTSIDE THE BOX...PLENTY OF SUR-PRISES...PATTERSON AND KARP HAVE A WINNING FORMULA HERE [THAT] HOPE-FULLY WILL CONTINUE FOR SOME TIME TO COME."
                            —BookReporter.com

NYPD RED 2

"THE SECOND BOOK IN THIS FINE SERIES SHOWS PATTERSON AND KARP AT THE TOP OF THEIR CREATIVE GAMES, PRODUC-ING AN EXCITING STORY THAT TWISTS, TURNS, AND SHINES FROM FIRST PAGE TO LAST...Patterson and Karp bring a cinematic view-point to *NYPD RED 2*; this book and its predecessor could easily be the basis for a network television series. The action never really lets up, even when the characters stop to take (or steal) a breath. This is one of the better police procedural series out there today. Long may it run." —BookReporter.com

"'THRILLING!' 'EXHILARATING!' JUST PLAIN 'WOW!' These superlatives and more aptly describe the latest collaboration between Patterson and Karp...THERE ARE THRILLS GALORE, ALL PUNCTUATED BY KARP'S ACIDIC WIT AND SPOT-ON DIALOGUE. OR IS IT PATTER-SON'S? IN THE END, IT SCARCELY MATTERS WHEN A BOOK IS THIS ENJOYABLE."
—*Louisville Courier-Journal* (KY)

"Patterson and Karp spare no plot twist in this pageturning thriller...Love triangles, mafia ties, and political entanglements abound, expertly layering this character-driven mystery in such a way that no dull moment ever arises...*NYPD RED 2* IS JUST ONE MORE TRIUMPH FROM PATTER-SON'S LITERARY EMPIRE, AND CLEARLY WE CAN'T GET ENOUGH."
—*Hampton Sheet* magazine

"PATTERSON AND KARP ONCE AGAIN PROVE THAT THIS IS ONE CRIME SERIES THAT'S NOT TO BE MISSED—THE LITER-ARY EQUIVALENT OF YOUR FAVORITE SUMMER ACTION MOVIE...Patterson's proficient plotting gives the story its edge-of-your-seat action and suspense, throwing in one clever twist after another...With its entertaining mix of action and wit, *NYPD RED 2* is yet another up-all-night kind of read. Whether you're packing for a poolside getaway or planning a short staycation in your favorite reading chair, it's the perfect pick for literary thrill-seekers." —NightsandWeekends.com

NYPD RED

"[PATTERSON AND KARP] REACH NEW HEIGHTS WITH *NYPD RED*, A GREAT THRILLER…THE PLOTTING AND PACING ARE SPOT-ON…It is bravura storytelling, a grand example of the best the genre has to offer."
Louisville Courier-Journal (KY)

"IN THE CASE OF *NYPD RED*, THERE IS SIMPLY TOO MUCH FUN—IN THE FORM OF INVENTIVE MURDER, SEX, CHEMISTRY, IN-VESTIGATION, MORE MURDER, MORE SEX, AND THE LIKE. POTBOILER? YES. WON-DERFULLY TOLD? INDEED…Though the book is complete in itself, there are plenty of interesting characters who could carry this as a series for as long as Patterson and Karp will want it to go."
—BookReporter.com

"*NYPD RED* IS A FAST-PACED, ACTION-PACKED THRILLER WITH LOTS OF TWISTS AND FULL OF SUSPENSE—A REAL PAGE-TURNER." —AlwayswithaBook.blogspot.com

"WITH *NYPD RED*, THIS DYNAMIC DUO HAS ONLY GOTTEN BETTER…CRIME THRILL-ERS DON'T GET A WHOLE LOT MORE ENTERTAINING THAN *NYPD RED*. Patterson's eagle eye for action once again gives the story the kind of breakneck pacing that readers have come to expect from the beloved bestselling author...WITH ITS NONSTOP ACTION AND ITS WICKED WIT, IT'S AS MUCH FUN AS YOUR FAVORITE SUMMER BLOCKBUSTER—BUT IT'S STILL CHEAPER THAN A TICKET AND A TRIP TO THE CONCESSION STAND."

—NightsandWeekends.com

"IF YOU'RE A READER WHO THOROUGHLY ENJOYS A HIGH-OCTANE THRILLER WITH LOTS OF CHASES, EXPLOSIONS, A VILLAIN WHO'S A MASTER OF DISGUISE, AND GOOD-LOOKING HEROES WHO ALWAYS HAVE SNAPPY DIALOGUE AT THEIR COMMAND, THIS IS MOST DEFINITELY THE BOOK FOR YOU...If, like me, there are times when you want to pick up a book and just have fun, let me recommend *NYPD RED*." —KittlingBooks.com

"CHARACTERS SHOOT THEIR WAY THROUGH AN ENTERTAINING SCRIPT."

—*Kirkus Reviews*

"PATTERSON SERVES UP FAST FOOD LITER-ARY ADVENTURE...[HE] KNOWS HOW TO WRITE A DAMN THRILLER." —Breitbart.com

"WITH A RICH MIX OF CHARACTER AND ACTION, *NYPD RED* IS A HIGHLY ENTER-TAINING, FAST-PACED READ."

—ElizabethAWhite.com

RED ALERT

RED
ALERT

JAMES PATTERSON
AND MARSHALL KARP

VISION

NEW YORK   BOSTON

Copyright © 2018 by James Patterson

Hachette Book Group supports the right to free expression and the value of copyright. The purpose of copyright is to encourage writers and artists to produce the creative works that enrich our culture.

The scanning, uploading, and distribution of this book without permission is a theft of the author's intellectual property. If you would like permission to use material from the book (other than for review purposes), please contact permissions@hbgusa.com. Thank you for your support of the author's rights.

Vision
Hachette Book Group
1290 Avenue of the Americas, New York, NY 10104
grandcentralpublishing.com
twitter.com/grandcentralpub

Originally published in hardcover and ebook by Little, Brown and Company in March 2018
First oversize mass market edition: April 2019

Vision is an imprint of Grand Central Publishing. The Vision name and logo is a trademark of Hachette Book Group, Inc.

The publisher is not responsible for websites (or their content) that are not owned by the publisher.

The Hachette Speakers Bureau provides a wide range of authors for speaking events. To find out more, go to hachettespeakersbureau.com or call (866) 376-6591.

ISBNs: 978-1-4555-4351-9 (oversize mass market),
978-0-316-39558-8 (ebook)

Printed in the United States of America

OPM

10 9 8 7 6 5 4 3 2 1

*For Teresa Patterson, who keeps
getting better and better and better*

PROLOGUE

13,000 DEAD
AND COUNTING

ONE

THERE WERE ONLY four words beneath the tattoo of the Grim Reaper on Aubrey Davenport's inner left thigh. But they spoke volumes.

Death is my aphrodisiac

And nowhere in the entire city was her libido more on point than at the Renwick Smallpox Hospital, a crumbling three-story, U-shaped monster on the southern tip of Roosevelt Island.

Once a marvel of neo Gothic architecture, Renwick was now a rotting stone carcass, the final way station for thirteen thousand men, women, and children who had died a painful death.

For the city fathers, Renwick was a historical landmark. For the urban explorers, it was New York's most haunted house. But for Aubrey Davenport, it was a sexual Mecca, and on a warm evening in early May, she and a willing partner scaled the eight-foot fence, made their way into the bowels of the moldering labyrinth, and spread a thick quilted blanket on the rocky floor.

She kicked off her shoes, removed her shirt and bra, shucked her jeans, and stood there, naked except for a pair of aquamarine bikini panties.

Her nipples responded to the caress of a cool breeze that drifted over her breasts, and she inhaled the earthy scent of the decay around her, mixed with the dank overtones of river water.

She dropped to her knees on the blanket, closed her eyes, and waited for her partner.

She shuddered as he silently slipped the noose around her neck. His fingers were long and slender. *Piano player fingers,* her mother used to call them. *Like your father has.*

As a child, Aubrey wondered why a man blessed with the hands of a concert pianist never played an instrument, never even cared to. But somewhere along the way she came to understand that Cyril Davenport's long, slender fingers made music of another kind: the crescendo of sound that came from her parents' bedroom on a nightly basis.

Aubrey felt the rope pull tighter. Rope was a misnomer. It was a long strand of silk—the belt from a robe, perhaps—and it felt soft and smooth as he cinched it against her carotid arteries.

He took her shoulders and guided her body to the ground until her belly was flat against the cotton blanket below her.

"Comfy?" he asked.

She laughed. *Comfy* was such a dumb word.

"You're laughing," he said. "Life is good, yes?"

"Mmmmmm," she responded.

"It's about to get better," he said, tugging at the waistband of her panties and sliding them down to her ankles. His fingers teased as they walked slowly up her leg and came to rest on the patch of ink etched into her thigh. His thumb stroked the shrouded figure and arced along the scythe that was clutched in its bony claw.

"Hello, death," he said, removing his hand.

Crack! The cat-o'-nine-tails lashed across her bare bottom, burning, stinging, each individual knotted-leather strap leaving its mark. She bit down hard and buried a scream into the blanket.

Pain was the appetizer. Pleasure was the main course. Her body tensed as she waited for his next move.

In a single, practiced motion he bent her legs at the knees, tipped them back toward her head, grabbed the tether that was around her neck, and tied the other end to her ankles.

"Hand," he ordered.

Aubrey, her right arm beneath her stomach, reached all the way down until her hand was between her legs.

"Life is good," he repeated. "Make it better."

Her fingers groped, parting the pleats, entering the canal, tantalizing the nerve endings. The effect was dizzying: the man with the whip, the foul-smelling ruins, and the inescapable presence of thirteen thousand dead souls.

He said something, but she couldn't hear over the sound of her own labored breathing. And then—the point of no return. She felt the swell of gratification surging through her body, and with near surgical precision she gently lowered her feet toward the ground.

The silk rope around her neck tightened, compressing her carotid arteries. The sudden loss of oxygen along with the buildup of carbon dioxide made her light-headed, giddy, almost hallucinogenic. The orgasm came in waves. It left her gasping for air, but the euphoria was so powerful, so addictive, that she intensified the pressure around her neck, knowing she could go just a few more seconds.

If erotic asphyxiation were an Olympic event, Aubrey Davenport would have been a world-class contender. Her brain was just on the threshold of losing consciousness when she released the death grip, and brought her feet back toward her buttocks.

But the noose refused to relax. If anything, it felt tighter. Panic seized her. She thrashed, pulled her hands up to her throat, and clawed at the silk, fighting for air and finding none.

She never made mistakes. Something must have snagged. She reached behind her neck, desperately trying to find some slack, when her fingers found his hand. He jerked hard on the silk cord, and her arms flailed.

She slumped, too weak to struggle, all hope gone. Everything went black, and as the reaper stepped out of the darkness to claim her, tears streamed down her cheeks, because in the last seconds of her life, Aubrey Davenport finally realized that she didn't want to die.

TWO

THE COTILLION ROOM at The Pierre hotel bubbled over with New York's wealthiest—including a few who were wealthier than some countries.

They were the richest of the rich, the ones who get invited to fifty-thousand-dollars-a-plate dinners when one of their own wants to tap them for a worthy cause. In this case, the charity with its hand out was the Silver Bullet Foundation.

The thirty-foot-long banner at the front of the hall proclaimed its noble mission: FIGHTING FOR THE LESS FORTUNATE.

The man in the black tie and white jacket busing tables in the rear had boiled when he first saw the sign. *They haven't done shit for me, and I'm the least fortunate person in the room.*

They're like swans, he thought as he watched them glide serenely from table to table: *so elegant, so regal, but fiercely territorial and vicious when they feel threatened. And like swans,* he observed, *they are oh so white.*

He counted half a dozen black swans among them, but for the most part, the people of color were there to serve. He fit right in.

With his shoulders slumped, his jaw slack, and a cheap pair of clear-lens nerd glasses to dial down the intensity of his piercing black eyes, he was practically invisible, and definitely forgettable.

The only human contact he'd had in the three hours since donning the uniform was with a besotted old patrician who'd slurred, "Hey fella, where's the men's room?"

Shortly after nine, the lights dimmed, the chatter died down, and the commanding voice of James Earl Jones piped through the sound system.

"Ladies and gentlemen, please welcome the cofounder and chairman of the Silver Bullet Foundation, Mr. Princeton Wells."

The staff had been instructed to stop work during the presentation, and the busboy dutifully stepped into the shadows near a fire exit as Princeton Wells bounded onto the stage.

Wells was his typically charming, still-boyish-at-forty, old-moneyed self. And lest any man in the room suspect that someone that rich and that good-looking wasn't getting laid, Wells kicked off the festivities by introducing his current girlfriend, Kenda Whithouse, to a captive audience.

Ms. Whithouse stood up, waved to the room, and threw her billionaire boyfriend a kiss. She was only twenty-three, an actress who was not quite yet tabloid fodder, but who clearly had the talent to fill out an evening gown. Those who knew Princeton Wells had no doubt that the gown would be lying crumpled on his bedroom floor by morning.

Having trotted out his latest eye candy, Wells got down to the serious business of reminding all the do-gooders in the room how much good they were doing for the city's less fortunate.

"And no one," he decreed, "has been more supportive of Silver Bullet than Her Honor, the mayor of New York, Muriel Sykes."

The city's first female mayor, her approval rating still sky-high after only four months in office, was greeted by enthusiastic applause as she stepped up to the podium.

The busboy did not applaud. He slid his smartphone from his jacket pocket and tapped six digits onto the keypad.

One, two, two, nine, nine, seven.

He stared at it, not seeing a sequence of numbers but a moment in time that had changed his life forever: December 29, 1997. His finger hovered over the Send button as the mayor began to speak.

"I'm not a big fan of giving speeches at rubber chicken dinners," she said, "even when the chicken turns out to be grade A5 Miyazaki Wagyu beef."

Everyone but the busboy found that funny.

"On the second day of my administration, I had a meeting with the four founders of Silver Bullet. They showed me a picture of an abandoned old warehouse in the Bronx, and I said, 'Who owns that eyesore?' And they said, 'You do, Madam Mayor. But if you sell it to us for a dollar, we will raise enough money to convert it into permanent housing for a hundred and twenty-five chronically homeless adults.'

"I accepted their offer, framed the dollar, and am thrilled to announce that next month we will start construction. I'm here tonight to thank you all for your generous contributions and to introduce one of the four men who spearheaded this project. He is the brilliant architect whose vision will turn that dilapidated monstrosity into a beautiful apartment complex for some of our neediest citizens. Ladies and gentlemen, please welcome Del Fairfax."

Fairfax, architect to the one percent, stepped onto the stage to show off what wonders he could create for the indigent. Spot-on handsome and aw-shucks personable, he rested a laptop on the podium, flipped it open, and said, "I know how fond you all are of PowerPoint presentations, so I put one together for you. Only ninety-seven slides."

The half-sloshed crowd warmly gave him his due.

"Just kidding," he said. "Princeton told me if I showed more than five, you'd start asking for your money back. The new facility will be called Tremont Gardens. First, let me show you what it looks like now."

He picked up a wireless remote and pushed a button.

The explosion rocked the Cotillion Room.

Del Fairfax's upper torso hurtled toward the screen behind him, while the bomb's jet spray of ball bearings, nails, and glass shards chewed into his lower half, scattering bits and pieces across the stage like a wood chipper gone rogue.

Thick smoke, flying shrapnel, and abject fear filled the air.

The busboy, standing far from the backblast, slipped through the emergency exit, leaving in his wake sheer pandemonium, as four hundred New Yorkers found themselves caught up in the nightmare they had been dreading since September 11, 2001.

PART ONE

SEX, DRUGS, AND HIGH-STAKES POKER

CHAPTER 1

KYLIE AND I had never been attached to Mayor Sykes's security detail before, but once she agreed to speak at the Silver Bullet Foundation fund-raiser, she recruited us for the night.

The word came down from our boss. "The mayor wants to do a little fund-raising of her own," Captain Cates said. "She comes up for reelection in three and a half years, and as long as she's going to spend the evening rubbing elbows with her biggest donors, she wants to assure them that she's not just a champion of the unfortunate poor. She cares deeply about the disgustingly rich. And what better way to demonstrate her concern for their welfare than by trotting out a couple of poster cops from NYPD Red?"

"Thanks, but no thanks," Kylie said. "Doesn't she realize we already spend sixty hours a week over-protecting the overprivileged? Now she's inviting us to suck up to them at some—"

Cates cut her off. "Did I use the word *invite*? Because the last time I read the department manual I didn't see anything about *invitations* being passed down the chain of command. The mayor specifically instructed me to assign Detectives Kylie MacDonald and Zach Jordan to her security detail. Consider yourselves assigned. No RSVP required."

I figured it would be the most boring night of the week. And I was right—until the podium exploded.

It was one of those shock and awe explosions. The blinding flash, the deafening boom, the thick smoke, the chemical stench, and the flying chunks of wood, glass, metal, and Del Fairfax.

Mayor Sykes had just come off the stage and returned to her seat when the bomb went off. Kylie and I were only an arm's length away from her. We yanked her from her chair and, shielding her body with ours, bulled our way through the chaos toward our prearranged exit door.

At least fifty other frenzied people had the same idea.

I keyed my radio and yelled over the din, "Explorer, this is Red One. Vanguard is safe. Egress Alpha is blocked. We're making our way toward Bravo."

We did a one-eighty and shoved the mayor toward the kitchen. The path was clear, and the vast stainless steel hub of the hotel's multimillion-dollar banquet business was almost deserted. Except for a few stragglers, the staff had beaten a quick retreat through a rear fire door and down a stairwell to the employee locker rooms.

At that point, many of them decided that they were out of harm's way, and at least twenty of them were standing in the corridor, almost every one with a cell phone to his or her ear.

"NYPD. Get out of the way! Get out of the fucking way!" Kylie bellowed as we elbowed our way through the logjam.

A hotel security guard saw us coming and pushed

open a metal door that led to the outside world. As soon as she felt the cool night air and heard the sounds of her city, the mayor stopped.

"Please," she said. "I'm too old for this shit. Let me catch my breath."

"Sorry, ma'am," Kylie said. "Not here. We only have another hundred feet. Keep going, or Zach and I will carry you to the car."

The mayor gave Kylie an enigmatic stare that could have been anywhere on the spectrum from contempt to gratitude.

"Nobody..." she said, breathing heavily, "carries... Muriel Sykes...anywhere. Lead the way."

We single-filed down a narrow alleyway, past a row of Dumpsters, and I radioed ahead to her team.

The alley came out on East 61st Street between Madison and Fifth Avenues. Just as we got to the far end, the mayor's black SUV drove up onto the sidewalk. Her driver, Charlie, jumped out and swung open the rear door. I offered to help the mayor into the back seat, but she waved me off.

"This is as far as I'm going," she said.

"Ma'am, this is not the place for you to be," Kylie said.

"A maniac just set off a bomb in my city, Detective. This is *my* responsibility."

"Yes, ma'am, but maniacs have a bad habit of setting off secondary bombs targeting people who have just run from the first," Kylie said. "And it's our responsibility to get you to safe ground."

"Madam Mayor," Charlie said, "they're setting up a command center at the Park Avenue Armory. I can have you there in two minutes."

Crisis averted. The mayor got in the car, shut the door, and rolled down her window. "Thank you,

Detectives," she said. That was it. Three words, and the window went back up.

Within seconds, the oversize, bulletproof Ford Explorer peeled out and, with lights flashing and sirens wailing, whisked Muriel Sykes away to the longest night of her fledgling administration.

"I hate these boring babysitting jobs," Kylie said. "Let's go do some real police work."

The two of us ran back down the alley and up the stairs toward the smoke-filled ballroom.

CHAPTER 2

KYLIE AND I joined the influx of first responders who raced to help the injured. It was just cops and firefighters at first, but when a bomb explodes in a public place, it sets off a Pavlovian response. Law enforcement agencies everywhere start salivating.

By the ten o'clock news cycle, The Pierre was the most famous crime scene in America, and everyone—Feds, staties, NYPD, FDNY, even the DEA—wanted a piece of the action.

Fortunately, the turf war dust settled long before the acrid gray cloud in the Cotillion Room, and Kylie and I were thrown together with Howard Malley, an FBI bomb tech we'd run into before.

Malley is a hawkeyed post-blast investigator and a pull-no-punches New York ballbuster, but he can also get testy as a cobra when you disagree with him. In short, he was a lot like Kylie. Maybe that's why I liked him.

The two of us suited up—disposable Tyvek coveralls, sock boots, face mask—and we crossed the threshold to ground zero. The rear of the room was remarkably intact. Flower arrangements and wineglasses were still sitting on several tables, waiting to be cleared.

We walked toward the spot where Del Fairfax, Princeton Wells, and Mayor Sykes had stood less than an hour ago, wooing their wealthy benefactors. Windows were shattered, wood-paneled walls were peppered with shrapnel, and the floor was littered with the detritus of the blast: scorched drapery, sparkling chunks of chandelier crystal, overturned chairs, silverware, shoes, purses—thousands of puzzle pieces that had made a picture-perfect evening and now lay in tatters, covered in thick dust and splattered with blood.

At the center of it all was the man who was supposed to make sense of this seemingly senseless act. He was squatting at one end of the forty-foot charred swath that had been the stage. Agent Malley, a bald-headed, gray-bearded FBI lifer, was squinting at a pair of forceps in his right hand through a pocket magnifying glass. He looked up when he heard us coming his way. "Well, if it isn't Jordan and MacDonald," he said. "How's business at NYPD's Fat Cat Squad?"

"Booming," Kylie deadpanned. "You find something down there?"

"Maybe." He stood up. "If you think of this mess as a four-thousand-square-foot haystack, I may have just found a needle. Take a look."

Kylie and I took turns studying the prize dangling from Malley's stainless steel pincers. It was a piece of wire. Three pieces, actually—one red, one white, one blue—twisted together in pigtail fashion. It was as thin as a strand of angel-hair pasta and no more than two inches long.

"And that's significant?" I asked.

"Again, maybe. These bomb makers—we see them as mass murderers, but they like to think of themselves as artists." He gave the word a French spin so that it came out *arteests*.

"And like artists everywhere, they are compelled to sign their masterpieces. This little red, white, and blue twisty thing isn't something I've come across before, so the thought popped into my head that maybe it's our bomber's signature."

"Red, white, and blue," Kylie said. "So what does that mean—death to America?"

"The bomb says death. I think the wire is about the guy who built it."

"Red, white, and blue," Kylie repeated. "You think he's an American?"

"Or he could be a color-blind Lithuanian. It would be nice to know what it symbolizes, but what would be really helpful is if this is his trademark, and he's in our global database. I'll take it back to the office and see if we get a hit."

"So, what's your take so far?" I asked.

He bagged the tiny fragment of wire, marked it, and put it in an evidence bin. "It wasn't a terrorist attack," he said.

"You sure?"

"Hell, no. I'm just a humble underpaid government employee, not Harry Potter. But you asked what's *my take,* which kind of means my educated guess after snooping around for twenty minutes. It'll never stand up in court, but right now my take is that with only one dead and twenty-two injured, this is not the handiwork of a dyed-in-the-wool, trained-in-Syria jihadi."

"Not a terrorist?" Kylie said. "Howard, this guy took out twenty-three people with a bomb."

"You're not listening, Detective," Malley said, his defense mechanisms going on point. "I didn't say he wasn't a pro. This guy is top-shelf. But he was using a shaped charge aimed at killing one person. Those twenty-two other people were collateral damage, some from the blowback, but mostly from the stampede. I don't know nearly as much about dealing with zillionaires as you do, but I'm guessing this was an every-man-for-himself crowd. They'd have a lot fewer broken bones if they didn't panic. This guy was only after Fairfax. It wasn't terrorism. It was personal."

"If it were personal," Kylie said, "wouldn't it have been easier just to murder him in his bed?"

Malley shrugged. "I'm guessing he wanted to make a public statement. I just have no idea what he was trying to say." He winked. "But then, that's not my problem."

CHAPTER 3

MALLEY WAS RIGHT. Terrorism was Homeland's problem, but homicide—especially an A-list victim like Del Fairfax—was all ours.

Other than being witness to the final seconds of his life, we knew nothing about him. We needed to talk to someone who did. We tracked down Princeton Wells. He was still at the hotel, only he'd relocated to the thirty-ninth floor.

"Anything I can do to help," he said, opening the door to a suite with sweeping views of Central Park.

He'd traded his formal wear for a pair of wrinkled khaki cargo shorts, a faded gray T-shirt, no shoes, no socks.

The mayor had introduced us to Wells earlier in the evening. We'd given him our cards, and he'd joked about hoping he'd never need them. Yet here we were, only hours later, following him into the living room.

"Grab a chair," he said, heading for a well-stocked wet bar. "Drink?"

We declined. He tossed some rocks into a glass and added four inches of Grey Goose. Then he uncorked a bottle of white and poured an equally generous amount into a crystal goblet.

He took a hit of vodka, set the wine on the coffee table in front of us, and said, "What have you got so far?"

"We're sorry for the loss of your friend," I said, "but the fact that he was the only one killed points to the possibility that he may have been the primary target."

"That's insane," Wells said. "Who would want to kill Del?"

"That's what Detective MacDonald and I are here to ask you. How well did you know him?"

"We've been best friends since high school. We roomed together in college. Twenty years ago we co-founded Silver Bullet along with Arnie Zimmer and Nathan Hirsch. Del and I were like brothers."

"Did he have any enemies? Anyone who would want to see him dead?"

"This is fucking surreal," he said, tipping the glass to his lips and draining it. "I need another drink." He padded back to the bar.

The last thing Princeton Wells needed was more alcohol, which is something I would have told him if he were an ordinary citizen, and I were an ordinary cop. But he was a billionaire many times over, and I was a detective first grade trained to deal with the privileged class, be they shit-faced or sober. I watched as he ignored the ice and replenished the vodka.

"This is a beautiful place," Kylie said, backing off the raw subject of his murdered best friend.

He smiled. "Thanks. I've had it for three years now. The view is spectacular when it snows. Point the remote at the fireplace, open a bottle of wine…"

"Did someone say *wine*?"

Kenda Whithouse entered the room, her hair

wrapped in a towel, her body somewhat covered by a man's tuxedo shirt.

"Already poured," Wells said, pointing to the glass he'd left on the table.

She picked it up, sat on a sofa, and discreetly tucked her legs under her.

"Kenda," Wells said, "these detectives are from NYPD."

"Nice to meet you," she said. "Did you catch them yet?"

"We're working on it," I said.

"It was terrible. Like one of those disaster movies, only it was real. I was lucky I wasn't killed. Bad enough I got covered with all that crap flying through the air. I looked like one of those homeless women Princeton is building housing for. I had to wash my hair three times to get the smell out."

Wells sat down next to her, took another belt of the vodka, and shifted his body so he could square off with the two of us.

"You want to know what I think, Detectives? I think that bomb was meant for the mayor. I mean, she left the podium just a few seconds before it blew. That's the only thing that makes sense. There's always someone with a hard-on for politicians. But Del Fairfax? Everybody loved him. Hell, they love the four of us. We raise hundreds of millions of dollars. We provide food, shelter, and education for these people, but more important, we give them purpose, hope—"

He stopped, looked at the glass in his hand, and set it down. "Sorry. A couple of drinks and I go all humanitarian commando on you. My point is, nobody wants to kill the golden goose. Silver Bullet doesn't have enemies."

"What about Fairfax's personal life?" Kylie asked.

"Del was a player. Never married. And why would he? He was rich, he was good-looking, and the gals loved him."

"Did any of these *gals* have husbands?" Kylie asked.

"God, no. Del would never poach another man's wife. He was a hound, but he wasn't into drama."

My cell rang. It was Cates. I stepped into the foyer to take the call.

"Fill me in," she said.

"The blast investigator flat out said, 'It wasn't a terrorist attack.' He thinks it was a targeted hit at the victim. But Princeton Wells says the vic was a saint, beloved by all, so the bomb must have been meant for the mayor."

"I doubt it," Cates said. "Sykes was a last-minute addition to the program. This attack was planned, prepped—but I'll alert Gracie security. What else?"

"Nothing else, boss. There were four hundred people in the room, yours truly included, and we can't find a single witness who witnessed anything."

"How soon can you and MacDonald tear yourself away from the scene?"

"About twelve seconds. We're coming up dry here."

"Then get your asses out to Roosevelt Island. Chuck Dryden has a body he wants you to meet."

"Another homicide? For *Red*?"

"What can I tell you, Jordan?" Cates said. "It's a bad night for the rich and famous."

CHAPTER 4

"**NEVER UNDERESTIMATE THE** insanity of people with money," Kylie said.

"Did you just open a fortune cookie, or is this the beginning of a fascinating observation?" I asked.

We were in the car on our way to Roosevelt Island.

"I'm talking about Princeton Wells," she said. "Why in God's name would he buy a three-bedroom suite at The Pierre hotel when he owns a six-story town house on Central Park West less than a mile away? It's crazy."

"Why does Bruce Wayne dress up in a cape and a cowl and fight crime in Gotham City when he could just as easily sit back and have Alfred, the butler, wait on him hand and foot inside the stately Wayne Manor? Kylie, the rich have their own special brand of craziness."

"You'd think I'd have figured that out after working Red for almost a year, but when we called Wells, and he said he was on the thirty-ninth floor of the hotel, I automatically assumed he rented a room for the night."

"Guys like Wells don't rent rooms for the night," I said.

She grinned. "Just women. Poor thing had to wash her hair three times."

"I take it you don't approve of his choice."

"Just the opposite. She's perfect for the man who wants to devote his energy to being of service to the less fortunate."

I could tell by the glint in her eyes that she was just warming up, and she was ready to slice and dice Kenda Whithouse like a late-night comedian skewering the Kardashians. But her cell phone rang.

She checked the caller ID, smiled, and picked up. "Hey, babe, I didn't think you were going to call."

Babe? Personal call, I decided, my keen detective senses kicking in. I checked my watch and the look on Kylie's face: 11:47 p.m. Delighted. Very personal.

I couldn't hear the voice on the other end, but it went on for a solid minute. Finally, Kylie responded with, "Hey, you win some, you lose some."

A pause, and then she said, "I wish I could, but my partner and I just caught our second homicide of the night." A laugh, followed by, "Don't blame me. You're the one who thought it would be fun to date a cop. I'll talk to you tomorrow."

She hung up. "Damn it, Zach, these dead millionaires are killing my social life. I just had to turn down an invitation for drinks at Gansevoort PM."

She was baiting me, waiting for me to ask who she turned down.

Keep waiting. I'm not asking.

"I was there last week," she said. "The music is totally badass, but the bottle service prices in the Platinum Room are off the charts."

I refused to bite. I kept my eyes on the road and my mouth shut.

"Have you ever been to the Ganz?" she asked.

"Not yet," I said, "but if a dead body shows up, I'm there in a heartbeat."

That shut her up.

Normally, cops are happy to share the intimate details of their lives with their partners, but my relationship with Kylie was far from normal. We met a dozen years ago at the academy. She had just dumped her drug-addict boyfriend, and I turned out to be just what she needed to fill the void.

For twenty-eight days we couldn't keep our hands off each other. Somewhere along the way I fell in love with her. But on Day 29, the ex-boyfriend, Spence Harrington, came back, fresh out of rehab, begging her for one last chance. She gave it to him, and a year later they were married.

For the next ten years they were the perfect boldface couple. Kylie was a smart, beautiful, decorated NYPD detective, and Spence became one of New York's most prolific and successful TV writer-producers.

And then one day the drugs pulled him back in, and he began to spiral out of control. To her credit, Kylie did everything she could to save him from self-destructing, only to learn the hard way that you can't save an addict from himself.

Two months ago, Spence walked out on her, and when it was clear he wasn't coming back, Kylie slowly dipped her toe back into the dating pool.

There was a line of boys in blue hoping to get on her dance card, but she turned them all down.

"I'm not hooking up with any cops," she told me. "One was enough."

I didn't ask if that meant I had set the bar impossibly high or I'd ruined it for every other cop in the department.

For weeks she'd been dropping little hints about the new man in her life, egging me on to probe for details. But I was damned if I was going to ask.

All I knew for sure was that whoever this guy was, he could afford bottle service in the Platinum Room at the fucking Ganz.

I have no idea why he'd want to be surrounded by loud people and even louder music, and then spend thousands of dollars on a bottle of booze he could buy for fifty bucks at a liquor store.

But like Kylie said, "Never underestimate the insanity of people with money."

CHAPTER 5

ROOSEVELT ISLAND IS a two-mile strip of land in the East River. It's so narrow—barely eight hundred feet wide—that from the air it looks like a piece of dental floss in between two teeth called Manhattan and Queens.

Eleven thousand people live there. Most of the other eight and a half million New Yorkers have either never been or popped by once when they took the kids for a ride on the aerial tramway that connects the island to Manhattan.

I drove across the Ed Koch Bridge, made a U-turn in Queens, and then doubled back over a second bridge to Main Street on Roosevelt Island. The trip took twenty-seven minutes. The tram takes three.

We followed East Loop Road to the underdeveloped southern tip of the island, where there was a cluster of vehicles from various city agencies. One of them, an NYPD generator truck, lit up a gray stone hulk that looked like an abandoned medieval castle waiting for the wrecking ball.

"Good morning, Detectives," a familiar voice called out.

It was a few minutes after midnight, so technically it

was morning. And nobody is more technical than our favorite anal-retentive, obsessive-compulsive crime scene investigator, Chuck Dryden.

"It's my first homicide in 10044," he said, walking toward us.

I smiled as I imagined him racing home after work to color in another section of his Zip Code Murder Map.

"What do you know about autoerotic asphyxia?" he asked.

"As much as I know about Russian roulette," Kylie said. "It's a game you can win a hundred times, but you can only lose once. Who's our victim?"

"Caucasian female, thirty-eight years old. Driver's license in her purse ID's her as Aubrey Davenport."

That explained the Red connection. Davenport was a documentarian whose films focused on social justice: the impact of oil spills, wrongful medical deaths, gun violence in America—the kind of polarizing journalism that gets some people to write their congressman and others to send her hate mail.

We made our way over the rocky ground to where she was lying facedown on a blanket. She was naked except for a pair of panties around her ankles. Her back was covered with welts, and she'd been trussed with several lengths of blue fabric, one end knotted around her neck, the other attached to her ankles. I've seen hundreds of dead bodies, but I was unnerved by the grotesqueness of this one.

"Was she sexually assaulted?" Kylie asked.

"No evidence of penetration," Dryden said. "No sign of a struggle. She cooperated with whoever tied her up. She was as much a volunteer as a victim."

"You telling me she signed on for this?" I said. "Whiplashes and all?"

Dryden shook his head. "You have much to learn about sexually deviant behavior, grasshopper."

"All I know is what I heard from the missionaries. Feel free to enlighten me, sensei."

He cracked a smile, which for Chuck Dryden is the equivalent of a standing ovation. "AEA is for the most part a male sport—often people you'd never suspect. Family men, respected pillars of the community who get off by cheating death. They tie ropes around their neck and genitals, attach the other end to a pipe or a doorknob, and then masturbate, slowly lowering their bodies to cut off the oxygen to their brain, which I'm told gives them the best orgasm they've ever experienced…although sometimes it's also their last.

"Most of the recorded deaths are people who do it solo, but this woman didn't want to take chances. She had a spotter, most likely a man. His role was to tie her up and to help her if anything went wrong. Her biggest mistake was trusting him. Look at this knot."

He pointed to a loop in the middle of the sash. "It's supposed to be a slipknot, a fail-safe that she can pull at any time to set herself free. But he tied it so that instead of releasing, it tightened."

"A good lawyer will say it could have been an accident," Kylie said. "Not everyone has a merit badge in autoerotic knots."

"And that's exactly what the killer would like us to think," Dryden said. "But look at these ligature marks around her neck. If she had control over her oxygen flow, they would be on a downward angle toward her legs. But these are going in the opposite direction, and they're deep, which to me indicates he was standing over her, and pulling up hard. I'd like to see a lawyer talk his way out of that."

"What about the scratches on her throat?" I asked.

"Self-inflicted. She realized what the killer was doing, but it was too late. She didn't have the strength to put up a fight. Bottom line: Aubrey Davenport did not die because of kinky sex gone wrong. She was murdered."

"Thanks, Chuck," I said. "I'm looking forward to hearing you say those exact words in front of a jury. Who found the body?"

"A couple of fourteen-year-old boys with a twelve-pack who were planning a memorable evening and got more than they bargained for. They called it in at 9:36. Time of death is anywhere in the eight-hour window prior to that."

"What else was in her purse besides her ID?"

"Cash, credit cards, cell phone, a parking stub from a garage in Brooklyn time-stamped 4:52 p.m., and a SIG Sauer P238, which she unfortunately didn't get to fire."

"Prints?"

"This place is too rocky for me to come up with any usable fingerprints, but I do have three very telling footprints."

"Can you get a cast? A shoe size?"

"They're not the kind of feet that wear shoes." Dryden smiled. He enjoyed leading us up to the mountaintop, especially when he was the one who discovered the mountain.

He shined his flashlight on three equidistant circles in the dust a few yards away from the body.

"There was a tripod there," he said. "Whoever killed her filmed it."

CHAPTER 6

IT'S GOTTEN EASIER for people to get away with murder in New York City.

While the brass at One P P are quick to promote the fact that homicides in our city are at historic lows, there's one statistic they don't like to talk about. In four out of every ten cases, the killer isn't caught.

Other cities with the same problem can blame it on the rise of drug and gang homicides. When drug dealers or gangbangers start killing, the neighborhood goes blind. No witnesses usually means no arrests.

But New York has a singular reason for our less-than-stellar batting average.

9/11.

When the towers fell, Ground Zero became the emotional focal point of our national tragedy. But for NYPD, it was the biggest crime scene in the city's history. That morning, 2,749 men, women, and children were murdered, and every homicide demanded our full attention—one victim at a time.

The task of bringing closure to thousands of families fell squarely on the shoulders of our most seasoned detectives. It was physically and emotionally draining police work, and within two years of the attacks, three thousand of our best investigators pulled their pins. They retired, and an additional eight hundred detectives were reassigned to the new counterterrorism unit.

That left a hole that has never been filled. To this day there are precinct detectives working everything from petty larceny to major felonies who have hundreds of unsolved crimes on their plates. They catch new cases faster than they can clear the old, and there's no one available to share the load.

That kind of clearance rate won't cut it at Red. So when we need backup, we get it. At 1:45, while Kylie and I were still combing the grounds of the Renwick Smallpox Hospital, I got a call from Danny Corcoran, a detective second grade working out of Manhattan North.

I knew Danny from the One Nine. He's smart, thorough, and gifted with a wicked sense of humor.

"Zach," he said, "I heard you need some grunt work on a homicide, and I just got the good news that I'm your designated grunt."

I gave him a quick overview and told him to secure Aubrey Davenport's apartment and office, in Manhattan, and her car, which was in a garage in Brooklyn.

"And I need a next of kin," I said. "Kylie and I will do the notification."

"I'm on it," he said. "By the by, I'm breaking in a new partner. Tommy Fischer."

"And?"

"He's got his pluses and his minuses."

"What are the minuses?" I asked.

"Lactose intolerant. On the plus side, he's a great kisser."

I hung up, laughing. I realized it was the first time I'd laughed since I followed the mayor into The Pierre six hours earlier, and it was a welcome release. Kylie and I were looking at two very ugly cases, and it felt good to know that I could count on Danny Corcoran to break the tension along the way.

He called back twenty minutes later.

"Your vic has an older sister, Claudia Davenport Moretti. She works in the financial aid office at Barnard College. Her husband, Nick Moretti, is an air traffic controller out of La Guardia. Two kids. No record, no drama. From what I can tell, they're as normal as bumps on a gherkin."

He gave me an address on West 74th Street in Manhattan.

Ten minutes later, Kylie and I were back in the car on our way to break the bad news. She drove. I curled up against the passenger door, closed my eyes, and drifted off to the hum of our tires on steel bridge plates.

My cell woke me up. It was Cheryl.

Dr. Cheryl Robinson is the forensic psychologist attached to Red. Despite her predominantly Irish roots, she inherited the smoldering Latina looks of her Puerto Rican grandmother. When we met four years ago, Cheryl was married, so for me she was just another coworker who happened to be magnetically desirable, mind-numbingly beautiful, and totally unavailable.

Then she suddenly became an unmarried coworker, and I wasted no time trying to see if my fantasies could become a reality. Much to my amazement, they have. She's the first woman I've fallen in love with since Kylie, and I wake up every day hoping I don't torpedo my good fortune.

This was the fifth time she'd called me since the bomb went off at The Pierre. I picked up the phone.

"Don't you stalkers ever go to sleep?" I said.

"I was asleep," she said, "but I woke up, turned on the news, and they keep rerunning videos of the explosion. Zach, you could have been killed."

"But I wasn't. I'm fine. Just exhausted. Kylie and I are still out on the road."

"Call it a night, but don't go back to your apartment. Come over here. I need to give you a hug."

"We picked up a second case. We're on the way to notify the victim's family. Can I get a rain check on the hug?"

"You're in luck. My rain checks come with dinner and a sleepover. You interested?"

"I said I was exhausted, not dead. Tonight. I'll be there."

"I love you," she whispered.

"I love you," I said. I could have whispered it back, but I didn't. I wanted to make sure Kylie heard me.

CHAPTER 7

THEY SAY NEW YORK is the city that never sleeps. But at a quarter to three on a moonlit Tuesday morning in May, the stretch of Central Park West that we were driving on was crapped out like a cat on a porch swing.

Another hour or so, and things would start to stir: the predawn joggers, the early morning sanitation crews, and those age-old, break-of-day stalwarts, the *New York Times* delivery trucks, dropping off bundles of last night's bad tidings to every doorman along this strip of overpriced real estate.

Kylie and I also had some bad news to deliver. Only we couldn't leave it with the doorman and move on. We had to wake up a family in the middle of the night and change their lives forever. It's the suckiest part of our job, and it never gets easier.

Aubrey Davenport's sister, Claudia, and her brother-in-law, Nick Moretti, lived on the eighth floor of a prewar, redbrick building on a tree-lined street between Broadway and West End Avenue.

We had the doorman ring up first. It wouldn't

soften the blow for the Morettis, but it gave them a few minutes to brace themselves. By the time Kylie and I got to their door and showed them our badges, they were expecting the worst. We were there to confirm it.

"Is it Aubrey?" Nick Moretti asked.

"Yes, sir," Kylie said. "Her body was found on Roosevelt Island. She was murdered. We are both very sorry for your loss."

Claudia was wearing a lavender robe. Nick had thrown on a pair of jeans and a Jets sweatshirt. She fell into his arms and began sobbing into his chest. Holding her tight, he eased her onto a sofa, and they sat down.

We stood.

It took five minutes before either of them looked up. Finally, Nick asked the inevitable. "Do you know who did it?"

"Not yet, sir," Kylie said. "But we will."

Claudia leaned over and whispered something in her husband's ear.

He shook his head. "Don't go there, Claudia."

"How could I *not* go there?" she said, pulling away and turning to me. "I warned her. Over and over and over. I was the pushy big sister—the voice of doom— but I was right, and now she's dead."

The people who are closest to the victim are the ones who can help us most in the investigation, but usually they are too numb to answer questions immediately, so we try to schedule an interview as soon as they get past the initial shock. But Claudia Moretti seemed to have answers that couldn't wait.

"You warned her about what?" I asked.

"Janek. I said, 'Get a restraining order. Get a gun. He'll kill you.'"

"Tell us about Janek."

"Janek Hoffmann, her cameraman. Her *protégé*. She hired him out of film school. He was a kid— maybe twenty-two—and she was thirty-eight. She said he was talented, but who knows? She was sleeping with him."

"But what made you tell your sister to get a gun?" Kylie asked, trying to get Claudia back on track. "Why did you think Janek was going to kill her?"

"They fought all the time. One minute they'd be like two lovebirds, and the next minute they were like cats and dogs. He was unpredictable. And scary. The man has a terrible temper."

Nick jumped in. "Temper, my ass," he said. "It was straight-up 'roid rage. He was always juiced up. One time they were at a restaurant, and Janek got pissed at the waiter, so he smashed him in the face with one of those oversized pepper mills. Sent the guy to the hospital with a broken jaw."

"Did he ever hit Aubrey?"

"Plenty," Nick said.

"Did she call the police?" Kylie asked.

"Aubrey wasn't the type to do anything like that," Claudia said. "She always needed to solve things her own way, in her own time. She fired him a couple of times, but she always took him back. I could never understand why."

"Jesus, Claudia. Take the blinders off. That muscle-bound dick was always belting her around. She kept coming back for more because that was a turn-on for Aubrey. She was a total sex—"

"Stop! Stop! Stop!" Claudia screamed.

Nick reached out to put his arms around her. "Sweetheart, I'm sorry. I didn't mean to—"

She shoved him aside. "She's dead. Stop judging

her!" Claudia shrieked, and ran out of the room in tears.

Nick took a few steps after her, stopped, and then turned to us. "I'll be back," he said. "Don't go."

We didn't move. With or without his invitation, we had no intention of going anywhere.

CHAPTER 8

CLAUDIA DIDN'T HOLD back her anguish. The crying that was coming from behind a closed door escalated to a full-blown wail as she tried to come to grips with the news of her sister's murder. Before long, her voice was joined by a younger, more piercing one, and Nick, whose patience and compassion had broken down rapidly, yelled out, "You happy? Now you woke the fucking baby."

It took fifteen minutes before things settled down and Nick emerged from one of the bedrooms.

"Sorry about the ruckus," he said. "Claudia never could deal with her sister's *issues*. She's from the if-you-pretend-the-problem-isn't-there-it-will-eventually-go-away school of denial."

"But she told us that she warned Aubrey about Janek Hoffmann," I reminded him. "That doesn't sound like she was pretending the problem wasn't there."

He shook his head. "You're missing the point. Janek wasn't the problem. I'm not saying he didn't kill her. Maybe he did. But it could also have been any one of a thousand other guys. The real problem was Aubrey. She was one of those women—they used to call them nymphomaniacs. I think the politically correct term these days is sex addict. But with Aubrey…"

I thought he was groping for words, but he wasn't. He'd clammed up.

"You want something to drink?" he asked. "Water? Or I could make coffee."

"Nick," I said, "we're investigating a murder here. Finish what you were going to say."

He plopped into a cushy armchair and immediately stood up again. "You guys have to sit down. I can't talk if you're going to stand there hovering over me like a couple of dark clouds."

Kylie and I sat on the sofa. Nick reclaimed his spot in the chair.

"Aubrey was a sex addict, but she wasn't like one of those party girls who really likes screwing. It was different for her."

"Different," Kylie repeated. Her body shifted on the sofa, and she turned toward him. "How so?"

She asked the question offhandedly, but I recognized the tone. Kylie is a hunter, a puma lying in wait for the gazelle.

Nick sat back in his chair. "She only got off if the guy was dishing out physical pain or putting her through abject humiliation."

"That's very helpful," Kylie said. "And your wife has trouble dealing with that fact?"

"*Dealing?* I don't know if Claudia even has a clue."

"Then how do you know so much about your sister-in-law's sexual preferences?" Kylie asked, her fierce green eyes locking into his limp brown-eyed gaze.

"Whoa, whoa, whoa," Nick said, holding up his hands. "Back off, lady."

"I'm not a lady. I'm a homicide detective, and if I

even smell that you're holding out on me, I will slap a pair of cuffs on you and haul you in for obstructing justice."

Nick looked at me for help.

"She'll do it," I said. "And I'll back her up. Answer the question: how do you know what your wife's sister got off on?"

He looked at me like I'd just handed him a shovel and told him to start digging his own grave.

"This is between us, okay? If Claudia ever knew…"

"If it's not directly related to our investigation, then it's our secret," Kylie said. "We don't tell your wife, and we don't even put it in our report."

He nodded. It wasn't exactly an ironclad guarantee, but he knew it was the best he was going to get.

"It happened five years ago," he said, easing into his story. "Claudia had just given birth to our first kid. It was a C-section, so she was in the hospital for a couple of days. It was the second night, and visiting hours were over, so Aubrey and I left together. It started out innocent enough. We were just going to have a couple of drinks and get something to eat."

He paused, hoping we could figure out the rest on our own. I decided to help him out.

"And one thing led to another?" I said.

"Claudia had complications during the pregnancy. She cut me off in her sixth month. I was horny as a stallion and plenty drunk. Aubrey was even drunker and plenty willing. We went back to her place."

"And?"

"And the girl was a total freak show. Hey, I'm all in favor of getting a little kinky—leather, role-playing, the kind of shit you read about in those

'Spice Up Your Sex Life' articles in magazines—but when a chick begs me to put a cigarette butt out on her nipple, I draw the line."

"Did you ever consummate the relationship with her?"

"No. I guess I sobered up in a hurry. When I realized what a hot mess she was, I got out of there."

He leaned forward in his chair. "You must think I'm a real hypocrite. I would've fucked my wife's sister, but I wouldn't paddle her, whip her, or piss on her. But trust me, there's a city full of guys who would, and she knew where to find every one of them."

"How many other names can you give us besides Janek Hoffmann?"

"None. Zero. I swear. I never asked. I didn't want to know. The only reason I knew Janek was that he was her cameraman, and they had this serious on-again, off-again relationship for over a year. I saw a lot of him. And I saw the bruises on her. I didn't have to ask him if he did it. He's the kind of guy who has to beat the shit out of someone, and Aubrey was the kind of woman who needed the beating. It was a match made in sadomasochist heaven."

"Do you know where Janek Hoffmann lives?" I asked.

His body sagged, and he slumped down in his chair. "I don't know," he mumbled. "Somewhere in Brooklyn."

Somewhere in Brooklyn turned out to be a block from where Aubrey's car was parked.

CHAPTER 9

IF NEW YORK CITY is a melting pot, then Brooklyn is the cultural hodgepodge that gives the stew its special kick. Throw a dart at a map of the world, and no matter where it sticks, the odds are there's a mini-version of that country in Brooklyn.

Janek Hoffmann lived in Little Poland, a microneighborhood in Greenpoint, the northernmost section of the borough.

Kylie and I drove across the Pulaski Bridge, past alphabetically organized streets—Ash, Box, Clay, Dupont, Eagle—until we hit a working-class enclave where the mom-and-pop pharmacies are called *apetkas,* the butcher shops stock dozens of varieties of kielbasa, and the restaurants have hard-to-pronounce and impossible-to-spell names like Karczma and Lomzynianka.

Hoffmann lived in a five-story walk-up, across the street from a Catholic church and a short walk from where Aubrey Davenport had parked her car.

Rule number one when you're making a house call: Don't let the suspect know you're coming. We entered the building, and I rang the super's bell.

He buzzed us in and met us in the vestibule. It was

only 5:15, but he was already dressed and working on a mug of coffee.

Rule number two: The super doesn't have to unlock an apartment door just because a cop wants to question a tenant. You'd better give him a good reason to let you in.

"NYPD," Kylie said. "We've been sent to check on Janek Hoffmann. His girlfriend was found murdered, and we're concerned that it could be a double homicide. We need to make sure he's all right."

Rule number three: The super almost always knows you're full of shit, but if you give him what he needs to cover his ass, he'll usually cooperate.

This one did. "Four B," he said, flipping through the oversize key ring attached to his belt. "Follow me."

He led us to the fourth floor, unlocked Hoffmann's door, and left in a hurry.

The first thing that hit me when we entered was the smell. Correction: smells. Sweat-stained gym clothes piled up in a corner, rancid food containers on the kitchen table, and the nasty, burnt-plastic stench of crack cocaine.

The second thing I noticed was the body lying facedown on the living room floor. He didn't smell that sweet, either.

Kylie looked at me, pointed at the human heap, then reversed her finger and tapped her chest. Translation: *This prick beats up women. He's mine.*

I nodded, and she drew back her foot and gave him a not-so-gentle nudge under his rib cage.

He groaned, rolled over, and looked up at us. "Who the fuck are you?"

"We're from *Better Homes and Gardens*. We're here for the photo shoot." She flashed her badge. "Who did you think we were, asshole?"

She kicked him again, and he instinctively clenched his fists.

"Come on. Get up and hit me," she taunted.

He stood up as far as he could go, which was only about five foot six inches high. But what he lacked in height he made up for in bulk. His biceps looked like they came off the label on a tub of whey protein powder, and his skintight muscle shirt showed off every pec, delt, and ab on his upper torso.

"Janek Hoffmann?" she said.

"Yeah, I live here. How did you get in?" he asked, staggering over to a tattered lime-green sofa that even the Salvation Army wouldn't try to salvage.

"Your cleaning lady left the door open. Do you know Aubrey Davenport?"

That got his attention. He struggled to fight his way through a substance-induced fog.

"I work for her," he said. "Well, technically, she fired me. But she'll take me back. She always does."

"When did you last see her?"

He closed his eyes and squeezed out an answer. "Friday."

"You sure you didn't see her last night?"

The eyes popped open, angry, challenging. "I told you: she fired me. The bitch makes me repent for a week before she calls and gives me another chance. It's all part of her twisted dance."

"Where were you last night?"

He gave a nod at his ravaged apartment. "Party for one."

"I don't think so," Kylie said. "Aubrey's car is parked around the corner. We know she was here last night."

That stumped him. He scrunched his eyes tight again, rummaged through his muddled memory bank, and came up with insufficient funds. "She was?"

"You tell us, Janek."

He sat forward on the edge of the sofa and massaged his temples. "I don't know. Maybe she was. My brain is a little fuzzy since Friday. Why the hell don't you ask *her* if she was here?"

Kylie squatted, leaned in so close that she was practically eyeball to eyeball with him, and whispered, "I can't ask her. She's dead."

"Dead?" The wheels inside his steroid-addled head were turning now, and I could see that he was finally on the verge of being able to put two and two together. "And is that why you're here? Do you think I killed her?"

"We don't think you killed her," I said, tired of letting my partner have all the fun. "We *know* you killed her. She parked her car nearby, then the two of you took your car to Roosevelt Island, where you tied her up, whipped her, choked her to death, came home, and fired up your amnesia pipe, hoping it would all go away. It won't. The only thing going away will be you."

He stared at me with his high beams on. "Roosevelt Island? Near the big old haunted house?"

If we had taken him into custody, we would have had to warn him that anything he said could be used against him. But we hadn't arrested him, and cops are not required to stop a chatterbox from incriminating himself.

"Now it's coming back to you, isn't it?" I said. "That's where we found her body. You're in deep shit, Janek, but we can help. Tell us everything now, and we'll see to it that you get brownie points with the DA's office."

Silence.

Kylie sat down on the sofa next to him, put a hand on his shoulder, and spoke softly. "Get it off your chest, Janek. Tell us the truth. Did you kill her?"

He shook his head, and began to sob. "I don't know. I don't remember."

CHAPTER 10

THERE ARE TWO ways to search a suspect's apartment: get a warrant, which would take hours, or con the tenant into giving us permission, which in Janek Hoffmann's case would take seconds. Kylie took the lead.

"Let's go easy on him, Zach," she said, her hand still on our prime suspect's shoulder. "So he can't remember anything. That doesn't make him guilty. Maybe he didn't do it."

That's the genius of Kylie MacDonald. A few minutes before, she was kicking the guy when he was down, trash-talking him, using every trick in the Bad Cop's Handbook to goad a confession out of him.

Now she was Detective Mother Teresa, and it was my turn to put on the Bad Cop pants.

"*'Maybe he didn't do it'?*" I bellowed. "And maybe when he wakes up tomorrow morning he'll be six foot two." I kicked my voice up an octave. "He's a juicer, a crackhead, and now he's a murderer. All the DA has to do is get up in front of a jury and say two words—*'roid rage*—and this sackless wonder will spend the next forty years doing drop sets in the prison yard at Green Haven."

"At least give him a chance to prove he's innocent." She turned to Hoffmann. "Can you do that, Janek? Can you prove you were here last night?"

He gave it his best shot. "I might have had some friends over. I could call around and see if any of them—"

"Friends lie," Kylie said. "You have to do better than that."

He shook his head, his reservoir of ideas dried up.

"What about take-out food?" Kylie said. "Did you get a delivery last night?"

"Probably. I mean, I order in all the time." He pointed with pride at the array of pizza boxes, Chinese food containers, and other roach bait rotting on the kitchen table. "We can call and see if any of the delivery guys remember."

"It won't fly," Kylie said. "The DA thinks delivery guys lie even more than friends. Let's look around and see if we can find a receipt with the date on it."

Janek thought that was a stellar idea and was grateful when we offered to help search the apartment for his meal ticket to freedom. We neglected to tell him that if we happened to stumble on a tripod, it would be admissible evidence.

Since it took us less than a minute to find a couple of crack pipes and a bag of weed in his dresser drawer, we realized that hiding shit from the cops wasn't his strong suit. After ten minutes, we knew the tripod wasn't in the apartment.

"My ex was in the film business," Kylie said once we'd come up empty-handed. "I'm surprised this place isn't cluttered with camera equipment."

"It all belongs to Aubrey," Janek said. "She keeps it in her office. Did you find any receipts yet?"

"No, which means you still don't have an alibi,"

Kylie said. "Give me your cell. The GPS might tell us if you were here last night."

Without missing a beat, he passed her his phone, and I wondered why the hell an intelligent photojournalist like Aubrey Davenport would spend more than ten minutes with this brain-dead Neanderthal.

If we had any doubts that Janek was a narcissist, they were put to rest when we opened his photo app. There were gigabytes of selfies of him oiled up and stripped down to nothing but the classic ball-cupping posing thong.

And then we found what we thought was pay dirt: a series of pictures of Aubrey, fully clothed, standing in front of the Renwick Smallpox Hospital.

"What are these?" Kylie asked him.

"That's the place," he said.

"What place?"

"The creepy place on Roosevelt Island where you said you found her."

"What were the two of you doing there?"

"Aubrey thought she might want to do a documentary about it. A lot of people died there, and death really turned her on. She'd rather have sex in a cemetery than a five-star hotel."

"Did you have sex there?" I asked.

"Shit, man, we had sex everywhere."

"These are dated last October," I said. "Have you been back there since?"

"A couple of times. But not in the winter. And definitely not last night."

We delved into his contacts, his phone log, his browser history, his text messages, and dozens of unappetizing sexts between him and Aubrey, but other than finding out that they had a twisted long-term love-hate-work-sex relationship, there was no evidence to link him to her murder.

My text alert beeped, and I checked my phone. It was Malley.

I know who made your bomb. Meet me at 26 Fed.

It took me a beat to put it together, and then it all came flooding back. The Silver Bullet dinner. A smiling Del Fairfax suddenly ripped in half. A tiny pigtail of red, white, and blue wire. I'd become so immersed in the narrow world of Janek Hoffmann that for a few glorious minutes I'd totally forgotten that Kylie and I had another homicide to solve.

CHAPTER 11

I SHOWED THE text to Kylie.

"At least the FBI's got their act together," she said. "We're not getting anywhere with this lunk. How are we supposed to figure out if he killed Aubrey if he can't figure it out himself?"

Janek was out cold on the sofa, snoring like a bear. "I doubt if he's a flight risk," I said.

"I doubt if there's a risk of him getting out of the apartment."

The sun was up when we left the building, and the air was thick with the heady aroma of something sweet and irresistible. We followed our noses to a tiny bakery on the corner of Java Street.

The sign on the window said RZESZOWSKA, which I decided meant the best place in New York to get cheese babka, poppy seed rolls, blackberry Danish, and if you want coffee, find a Starbucks.

We did, and we drove back to Manhattan restoring our souls in the grand tradition of cops everywhere: wolfing down sugary pastries and deconstructing the events of the past twelve hours.

The Jacob K. Javits Federal Building at 26 Federal Plaza on Foley Square is forty-one stories of steel, glass, and red tape. It houses a multitude of government agencies, including Homeland, GSA, Social Security, Immigration, and, on the twenty-third floor, the New York field office of the Federal Bureau of Investigation.

Howard Malley was waiting for us in his office.

"Do you accept bribes?" Kylie asked, dropping what was left of the Polish goodies onto his desk.

"It's the first thing they teach us at Quantico," Malley said, digging into the bag and pulling out a piece of apple cake. "I found your bomb maker. He's a master. One of the best in the business."

"Name?" Kylie said, pen and pad in hand.

"Real name is Flynn Samuels, but Interpol gave him a code name: Sammy Six Digits."

"Six Digits? He doesn't sound that masterful."

"That's that wacky French sense of humor. The guy has all ten fingers, but he always uses a symbolic six-digit date to trigger his bombs. So, like, if he wanted to blow up Independence Hall, he might go with July 4, 1776, and use 741776."

"What numbers did he use to set off this one?"

"Impossible to tell," Malley said, putting away half a square of cake in a single bite, "but last night's blast has his signature all over it. His specialty is shaped charges designed to take out a single target. And remember the red, white, and blue wires? You thought that meant he was American. You were close. He's Australian, and guess what colors their flag is."

"Do you have a mug shot? We'll put out a citywide BOLO."

"Don't bother. He's in a prison in Thailand. Fifteen years ago he built the bomb that killed their minister of justice. It was neat, clean, and did the job without any collateral damage. But the people behind the assassination were stupid and got caught. They were facing the death penalty, so they made a deal. They gave up their bomb maker in exchange for a lighter sentence. The cops arrested Samuels at the Bangkok airport just as he was about to get on a plane for Australia. The next morning, the bozos that hired him were executed by machine gun. Samuels wasn't so lucky. They decided to let him rot in a Thai prison."

"Then he must have a disciple," Kylie said. "Someone he taught the tricks of his trade."

"I doubt it. Samuels commanded top dollar to create one-of-a-kind bombs. Blowing people up was his livelihood. He didn't have disciples. He was too smart to share his secret sauce recipe."

"Do you have any idea when he gets out of prison?" I asked.

Malley reached into the bag and plucked out a gooey Danish. "Good question, Zach. Let me check my calendar. Oh, wait: it's Thailand. Never."

CHAPTER 12

WE DROVE BACK to the precinct, where I showered, shaved, and grabbed a change of clothes from my locker. By the time I got to my desk, Kylie had already cleaned up and was checking her email.

"We got a gratitude note from Mayor Sykes." She tapped her computer screen. "Take a look."

My mind was too preoccupied with Cheryl for me to care about reading an attaboy from the mayor. "How about you just give me the executive summary?"

"Sure," she said, swiveling her chair away from the screen. "'Blah, blah, blah, Jordan and Mac-Donald, quick thinking. Blah, blah, blah, Jordan and MacDonald, excellence and valor.' Plus four more paragraphs of 'Blah, blah, blah.' Bottom line: we are the flavor of the month."

"I'm not sure if that's a blessing or a curse."

"That's the beauty of politics, Zach. It's both— all wrapped up in a digital love letter, with copies to Cates, the chief of d's, and the PC himself." She stood up. "We should get out of here. Our backup team is waiting for us at the diner."

"I'll meet you there," I said. "Give me five minutes

to stop on the second floor and say hello to the department psychologist."

She looked at her watch. "*Five* minutes? Really?"

"Maybe ten. I might think of something else to say besides hello."

I took the stairs down to Cheryl's office. She was at her desk, reading, dark brown eyes fixed on the thick binder in front of her, wavy jet-black hair framing her face and resting on her shoulders. I stood in the open doorway and thought, *God, she's gorgeous*.

Or maybe I said it out loud, because she raised her head, sang out my name, came around to the other side of the desk, pulled me into the room, closed the door, grabbed me in her arms, and gave me a long, slow, lingering kiss. She looked, smelled, felt, and tasted like heaven.

"You're alive," she said.

"And becoming more alive by the second," I said, as she dug her hips into mine. I backed off reluctantly. "Let's not start anything we can't consummate. I've got two fresh homicides to work. Can we pick this back up again at dinner?"

"Oh, we will," she said, letting me go. "But fair warning: I know you didn't get any sleep last night. Don't expect to get much tonight, either."

She kissed me again, and I left the room happy and horny. I double-timed it around the corner to Gerri's Diner and found Kylie at a booth in the rear with our backup team.

Danny Corcoran is second-generation NYPD who did his twenty and is two years into his next five. As usual, he was well-dressed, sporting a gray off-the-rack suit from one of the city's better racks. Hair-challenged, he topped off the look with a gray newsboy cap.

Always on the wrong side of the body fat index, his round Irish face lit up when he saw me, and he tore himself away from a stack of pancakes with a side of sausage to give me a fierce bear hug.

"Still on that health kick?" I said, pointing to his lumberjack breakfast, and Danny responded by not so subtly scratching the tip of his nose with his middle finger. Then he introduced me to Tommy Fischer, who, like all of Danny's partners over the years, was the quiet type.

"Foreplay is over," Kylie said. "Cut to the chase, boys."

"We hit the garage at about three a.m. and found her car," Danny said. "The attendant who punched her in was long gone, so we got his home address and paid him a visit."

"Did he remember her?" I asked.

"Oh yeah. She greased him twenty bucks to keep her car up top in one of those golden spots reserved for good tippers. She said she'd be back soon, but of course she never showed."

"Had he seen her before?"

"She wasn't a regular, but she'd park there from time to time. Mostly overnight. A few times he remembers her driving in with some yobbo half her age. He called him 'a young Arnold Schwarzenegger.'"

"Sounds like the boy we like for the murder," I said. "Name is Janck Hoffmann. He's her cameraman. Where's the car now?"

"Impounded. The lab guys are dusting and probing."

"How about her apartment?" Kylie asked.

"It's like the Barbie Dreamhouse for the terminally oversexed." He handed Kylie his cell phone. "Scroll through some of the highlights."

Corcoran had taken pictures of a closetful of sex paraphernalia that for most people would be taboo, but for Aubrey Davenport was the norm. I looked over Kylie's shoulder as she flipped through the pictures in a hurry. By now we knew enough about Aubrey's world not to be surprised.

"Drugs?" Kylie asked.

Fischer flipped open a notepad. "Ecstasy, coke, poppers, weed, plus scripts for Paxil and Zoloft," he said. "The prescribing doc's name is Morris Langford. Here's his number." He tore off a page and handed it to me.

"We're looking for her video cameras and her computer," I said. "You find any in her apartment?"

"Nothing."

"How about her office?"

"It was closed, so we left a pair of uniforms in front of the door," Corcoran said. "They called a few minutes ago. Her assistant just opened up. His name is Troy Marschand. They're holding him. You want us to talk to him?"

"We'll take it," I said. "I'd rather you go back to the parking lot attendant and show him a photo lineup of six young Arnold Schwarzeneggers. One of them should be Janek Hoffmann. You can dig out five more from the files."

Danny stuck his fork back into the stack of hot-cakes and grinned. "I only need four more," he said. "The fifth one can be a selfie."

CHAPTER 13

AUBREY'S OFFICE WAS on West 17th Street in the Flatiron district near Union Square. A squad car was parked outside. The directory in the lobby said Davenport Films, 303. We took the elevator to the third floor and found a uniformed officer standing outside the door.

"Officer Hairston," I said, reading her name tag. "You were here when the assistant showed up?"

"Yes, sir. He wanted to know what was going on, so my partner and I told him that his boss was found dead. Was that okay?"

It wasn't, but I decided to let it go. Kylie, on the other hand, is a lot less forgiving.

"No, it's not okay," she snapped. "Detectives can learn a lot just by watching how people react when they're told someone is dead. Now we have to rely on secondhand information. How'd he take the news?"

"He freaked out."

"People freak out when they hit the lottery, officer. If you're going to play detective, do a better job of it."

"Sorry, ma'am. He was all broke up when we

told him. Not crying, but very upset. Devastated. Heartbroken."

"Heartbroken like he was banging her?"

"No, ma'am. More like his boss was dead, and he's out of a job. He kept saying, 'What am I going to do now?' Anyway, I doubt if he was banging her. He's gay."

"Oh really?" Kylie said. "And how did you jump to that conclusion?"

"He asked if he could call his fiancé for moral support, and we said yes. The fiancé turns out to be another dude. It came up gay in my book."

It was a small victory for Hairston, and to her credit, she kept a straight face. She opened the office door, gestured for her partner to step out, and Kylie and I stepped in.

Except for a few light stands and a twenty-foot roll of seamless background paper covering one wall, the room was nothing more than a wide-open, high-ceilinged photo studio. There were two desks, a makeup vanity with a lighted mirror, a stylist's chair, and a kitchenette where two men in their early thirties were sitting at a table, each with a coffee mug in front of him.

They say opposites attract, but not in this case. The two men looked a lot alike. Each was slender with a patch of thinning dark hair on his head and the dark shadow of designer stubble on his face. One was wearing a blue shirt; the other one was in yellow.

Blue shirt stood up. "I'm Troy Marschand, Aubrey's assistant. Do you know who killed her?"

"Not yet, but we're working on it." I turned to yellow shirt. "And what's your name, sir?"

"Dylan Freemont. I didn't know her. I mean, I met her a few times, but that's all. I'm just here to help Troy get through this. Hey, can I ask you a question?"

"It works better when we ask the questions," Kylie said.

"Yeah, I watch a lot of cop shows. But I just want to know: is it true what they're saying about Aubrey on the Web?"

"What are they saying?"

"Some real kinky shit was going on before she got killed."

"And where did you hear that?"

"As soon as Troy called me, I did a search for Aubrey's name on social media and a couple of those celebrity news feeds. They say she was found at some haunted house on Roosevelt Island, and that there was some weird sex going on before she died. Is it true?"

"NYPD doesn't comment on internet gossip," Kylie said.

"I wouldn't be surprised if it was true," Troy said. "All her life, Aubrey was obsessed with two things: sex and filmmaking. How ironic if that's how she died."

"Gentlemen," Kylie said, "we're trying to catch a killer, and you're wasting valuable time. Mr. Marschand, the first thing we need from you is your boss's computer. You can either give it to us or we can get a court order."

"I'd give it to you if I had it, but I don't. Aubrey always had her laptop with her. It's probably in her apartment."

"It's not. Can you think of anybody who might be holding it for her? We really need to get a look at all her files."

Troy shook his head. "Aubrey wouldn't trust

anybody with her computer. Maybe it's in the trunk of her car."

"It's not," Kylie repeated.

"It doesn't matter," Troy said. "She backed everything up religiously. I can retrieve the files from the cloud. It'll take me a couple of hours."

"Thank you," Kylie said. "When you're done, give them to the two officers outside. They'll get it to us. We also need to look at her camera equipment."

"This way," he said, walking us toward the rear of the studio. "It's not very impressive. It's mostly old crap that she can't throw away. If she's shooting anything important, she rents."

He unlocked a closet door. Inside there were metal storage racks cluttered with cameras, lenses, cases, and, most promising of all, tripods.

"Lock it up," I said. "We'll send a team to go over it. Who else besides you has a key?"

"Just Aubrey."

"How about her cameraman?"

Troy made a face. "Janek? Hell, no. This stuff may not be worth a lot, but give him a key, and it would wind up on Craigslist."

"You don't think highly of Mr. Hoffmann?"

"The guy's a loser. I never understood what she was doing with him. He's probably the one who—"

My cell rang, and he stopped. I recognized the number on caller ID. The phone rang a second time, but I didn't pick up. "Go ahead, Mr. Marschand."

"Don't you have to answer that?"

"It can wait. Finish your thought, please."

"Janek Hoffmann is a brute, an addict with a violent temper. He always scared the shit out of me. I'm not saying he killed her, but if it turns out he did, I wouldn't exactly be surprised."

I nodded and mentally added Troy Marschand's name to the list of witnesses for the prosecution. Then I turned away and answered the phone on the fourth ring.

"Madam Mayor," I said, trying to sound as upbeat as I could. "And how are you this fine morning?"

CHAPTER 14

MADAM MAYOR WAS anything but fine on this fine morning. She was pissed to the gills, and she let loose a stream of profanity, which, while unbecoming of her office, was totally in keeping with her gritty Hell's Kitchen roots.

The good news was that her anger was not aimed at her flavor-of-the-month cops. She went off on Arnie Zimmer, one of the three surviving founders of the Silver Bullet Foundation.

"The son of a bitch called me—at home, no less," she said, seething. "He told me he didn't like the way I—*or my overhyped police force*—was handling the vicious attack on his charity and the brutal murder of his partner."

"Ma'am, Kylie and I just met with the FBI bomb expert, and we're working as fast as—"

"Zach, don't get defensive. I didn't call to ask why you haven't solved a major crime twelve hours after it happened. All I need right now is for you to get this cocksucker off my back."

One of the first things you learn as a cop is that if it's important to your hook, it's important to you. And there are not too many better hooks than the woman who runs the city. Defusing Arnie Zimmer shot straight to the top of my things-to-do list.

"Where can I find him?" I asked.

"He's rounded up the other two partners. They're at Princeton Wells's place. They're expecting you." She hung up.

Fifteen minutes later, Kylie and I pulled up to a magnificent brick and limestone beaux arts facade on Central Park West. In a city full of ridiculously expensive real estate, there aren't many private homes that can be called mansions. "Princeton Wells's place," as the mayor had called it, was one that could.

I rang the doorbell, expecting to be greeted by a butler wearing a proper black morning coat, gray striped trousers, and a white wing-collar shirt. Instead, Wells himself came to the door, dressed like he was ready to pose for the cover of the J. Crew catalog.

"Sorry about this," he said, shaking his head. "Arnie is on a tear."

"It's understandable," I said, using some of the language they taught me in NYPD Red charm school. "He may just be getting over the shock of last night."

"I doubt it," Wells said, walking us through a sprawling foyer and up a sweeping marble staircase. "Arnie is a notorious micromanager. It ain't soup unless he's stirred the pot."

"The mayor said he's not happy with the way we're handling the case. We'll do what we can to reassure him that—"

"Save your breath," Wells said. "Arnie already tore the mayor a new one. You're just here so he can vent to the cops."

Kylie gave me a subtle nod. One of the qualifications

for joining a police force dedicated to working with the uber-rich is being able to put up with their verbal abuse while you're busting your ass to help them. It's the shit part of the job, and I'm much better at it than Kylie is. The nod was a message. It was my turn to stand between her and the bullets.

On the other hand, one of the best parts of the job is getting a taste of the mind-boggling creature comforts that unlimited wealth can buy. But this time, we hadn't been invited to soak up the grandeur. We were there to take our lumps.

"They're in my office," Wells said when we got to the second floor. He opened a mahogany door, and we stepped into a vast room with wood-paneled walls, a soaring ceiling, leather furniture, and all the trappings of an old-school private men's club. I took a few seconds to fantasize what it must feel like to sit down at the end of a tough day and enjoy a well-earned snifter of single malt whiskey. The fantasy fizzled as soon as Wells made the introductions.

I'd done a quick background check on the players before we got there. Nathan Hirsch was a thousand-dollar-an-hour banking and finance attorney with an Ivy League pedigree and a blue-chip résumé. He was a lot less impressive in person. Overweight and straining the good graces of his designer suit, he smelled of cigar. His handshake was clammy, and his eyes never made contact with mine. My cop radar kicked in, and I wondered if he was still reeling from last night, or if he had another reason to be twitchy.

Arnie Zimmer, who owned the Zim Construction Group, was taller and thinner and wasted no time taking on the mantle of designated bully. "Do you know how much I gave to Muriel Sykes's election campaign?" he asked, ignoring my extended hand.

"No, sir," I said.

"Enough money so that I shouldn't be paying for hind tit. If Sykes expects a nickel out of me when she runs for reelection, she better put the two of you on this case 24/7."

"Sir, we're sorry for the loss of your friend, but we *are* on the case. We haven't slept since the bomb exploded."

"Don't bullshit a bullshitter. I've got friends in the department. You're splitting your time between a page one terrorist attack and some page thirty-seven sex crime."

"Mr. Zimmer, we understand your frustration, but I can assure you that Mayor Sykes has made this our number one priority. And we're not working alone. The FBI has already helped us identify the person who built the bomb."

"I don't care if *Lockheed Martin* built the fucking bomb. Your job is to figure out who set it off. Del was in construction. Did it ever dawn on you that contractors use explosives? Why don't you start there? It was probably some pissed-off asshole who lost out on one of Del's jobs."

And with that, the pissed-off asshole left the room.

"Meeting adjourned?" I asked Wells.

He smiled. "Arnie called it; Arnie gets to pull the plug on it. I'll tell the mayor you represented her admirably."

"I'd much rather you just gave Mr. Zimmer my phone number," I said, holding out my card.

"Detective, you saw what he can be like. Are you sure you want him badgering you?"

"Anytime—as long as he stops badgering the mayor."

He took the card reluctantly. "Nathan and I will

do what we can to keep him at bay, but Arnie's a pit bull. He's going to give you problems."

I shrugged off the comment, but it turned out to be an understatement. Arnie Zimmer gave us more problems than anyone ever anticipated.

CHAPTER 15

I WAS READY to leave, but Kylie, who hadn't said a word since we got there, wasn't. "One question before we go," she said to Wells. "Which one of you knew the real Del Fairfax? You or Mr. Zimmer?"

Wells looked confused. "I'm sorry, Detective. The four of us have been friends since high school. I don't understand the question."

"Last night we told you that the blast analysis indicated that Mr. Fairfax was the primary target, and we asked you if he had any enemies. Do you remember what you said?"

"Not word for word, but the answer is no. People liked him."

"I took notes. Last night you said, 'Everybody *loved* him. Hell, they love the four of us.' Then you suggested that the bomb was intended for the mayor. Now, this morning, Mr. Zimmer has a different perspective. He's saying it's a disgruntled contractor out to settle a score, but he stormed off before we could ask him if there were any specific contractors he might point us to. So let me repeat what I asked you last night. Can you think of anyone—especially in the building trades—who *didn't* love Mr. Fairfax and would want to see him dead?"

"All right, I get it," Wells said. "I painted a pretty rosy picture last night. But you're right. We give away a lot of money, but we can't give it to everybody. We can't support every cause. We can't award jobs to everybody who bids on one. We make some people incredibly happy, and we can disappoint the shit out of others. That's life. That's business. It's not a motive for murder."

Kylie turned to Hirsch. "Counselor, we need all the help we can get. Do you have anything you can add?"

If he did, he didn't look anxious to share it, but Kylie hadn't made it easy for him to say no.

"Arnie means well, but I think he's...wrong," Hirsch said, choosing his words carefully. "Last night's insanity wasn't payback for some kind of a business grudge. I want you to solve Del's murder as much as anybody, but please don't waste your time looking for vindictive contractors."

"Who should we look for? According to Mr. Wells, everybody loves the four of you."

Hirsch forced a smile. "Detective, I'm a lot more cynical than Princeton. We live in a city of haves and have-nots. I'm sure there are plenty of people out there who were happy to hear that somebody blew up a roomful of rich white do-gooders. I hope that helps."

It helped more than he realized. We thanked the two of them and didn't say a word till we were back in the car.

"Nicely done, partner," I said. "Did you suspect Hirsch had something to hide, or did you just go fishing and get lucky?"

"A little of both. Did you notice where he was sitting last night?"

"Yeah. He was at a table close to the front, slightly off to the left."

"And did you notice what he did when Princeton Wells introduced his girlfriend to the crowd?"

"No, but I imagine he was doing what most men in the room were doing: admiring Ms. Whithouse and thanking the cleavage gods."

"He wasn't. And while your eyes were honed in on Kenda's boobs, I watched Nathan Hirsch quietly get up from the table and leave the room."

My cell phone rang. I was about to let it go to voice mail when I saw who was calling. I picked up. "This is Detective Jordan."

"Detective, this is Dr. Langford. I'm returning your call. I'm…I was Aubrey Davenport's psychiatrist. I'm in shock over her death. The reports on the internet say it was homicide. Is that true?"

"Yes, sir. My partner and I would like to talk to you. We could come to your office immediately."

"That's impossible," he said, and I braced myself for the usual doctor-patient confidentiality resistance. "I'm at a medical conference in Albany. I couldn't possibly get back to the city till tomorrow morning. I realize time is of the essence, but we can't do this over the phone. Most of my notes are in my office."

"But you'll help us?" I said.

"Of course I'll help you. The law forbids me to share information about my living patients, but Aubrey's death frees me to help you in any way I can. I'll gather her files, and we can meet in my office tomorrow at ten a.m."

He gave me the address and we hung up. "Good

news on the Davenport case," I told Kylie. "Now where were we on Fairfax?"

"You were ogling Kenda Whithouse's tits, and I was wondering why Nathan Hirsch would go to the men's room instead of waiting a few more minutes until the mayor got up and said her piece. But now I'm thinking, *What a lucky coincidence—Nathan left the room right before the bomb went off.*" She smiled. "And you know how cops feel about luck or coincidence."

CHAPTER 16

IT WAS TIME to dig deeper into the lives of Del Fairfax's surviving partners. Fortunately, there was no shortage of material.

"These guys generate a lot of ink," Kylie said.

"People with no money love to read about people who have mountains of it," I said. "The world is full of hermits, loners, and recluses, but Howard Hughes was a billionaire, so the press made him famous for it."

We were looking for a motive for the bombing, but in article after article, interview after interview, the four founders came across as model citizens. Princeton Wells had summed it up the night before: "Nobody wants to kill the golden goose. Silver Bullet doesn't have enemies."

By 1:00 p.m. we had raked over their public persona, and there wasn't enough Red Bull on the planet to get us started looking under their private rocks.

After pulling a thirty-hour shift, we punched out. I went home, slept five hours, showered, and showed up at Cheryl's apartment at seven. The heady aroma of jambalaya hit me as soon as she opened the door.

She had a wooden spoon in her hand, so I gave her

a quick kiss, and she hustled back to the stove while I made straight for the open bottle of Chardonnay on the counter.

"Can I violate one of our cardinal rules tonight?" she asked, spooning mounds of chicken, shrimp, sausage, rice, and chopped vegetables into a serving bowl.

"Just give me half a minute to inhale some of this wine, and you can violate anything you want."

"Reel it in, lover boy. I'm talking dinner table rules."

"You mean the one where Zach can't use his phone at the table, but Cheryl can, because she's a doctor?"

"That one is chiseled in stone, but I'd like to bend the no-cop-talk-at-dinner rule. I've been getting secondhand news about the bombing all day, and I want the unsanitized version."

We sat down to dinner, and in between forkfuls of spicy Creole bliss and sips of chilled, fruity Chardonnay, I took her through it all—glossing over the carnage and milking absurdities like Kenda Whithouse's post-explosion bad hair for all the laughs I could get.

By the time I got to the verbal drubbing we'd taken from Arnie Zimmer, the bottle of wine was empty. "You must be exhausted," she said, opening another. "And you haven't even come up with a motive for the bombing yet."

"Plus I still have a second high-profile murder on my hands. Which reminds me: did you ever hear of a shrink named Morris Langford?"

"Morey Langford? Yes, he's the go-to doc on psychosexual disorders. Why do you ask?"

"Kylie and I are going to see him tomorrow."

"Oh, sweetheart, that's wonderful," she said, re-filling my wineglass. "It's about time you and Kylie came to terms with your issues. I'm sure Morey can help you."

"Thanks, but I get all the therapy I need from Gerri at the diner. It's free with breakfast whether I ask for it or not. My other homicide victim, Aubrey Davenport, was a patient of Langford's, and he agreed to help. Didn't throw any of the standard HIPAA bullshit at us."

"That sounds like Morey. He's a no-bullshit kind of guy. I had a consult with him a few months ago."

"Are you serious? You went to see a sex therapist a few months ago, and you didn't say anything to me?"

"Get a grip, Romeo. It wasn't about you. I'm a department shrink. You think I only deal with PTSD and alcohol abuse? Cops have at least as many sexual impulse disorders as congressmen. It's none of my business until they either bring it to me on their own, or someone from on high asks me to evaluate how it could impact their job."

"Why did you consult with Langford?"

"I had a transit cop who was suffering from frot-teurism, and I had zero experience with it. Langford knew it chapter and verse."

"I never even heard of it."

"Good, and please promise me you will continue to remain blissfully unsophisticated."

"*Unsophisticated?* Come on, Doc—how can you say that? You've seen my moves—all three of them."

"Hmm," she said, her eyes locked on mine, her fingers twirling a lock of raven hair. "There were three?"

I stood up, took her by the hand, and put my arms

around her. "You know, I think I'm coming down with a case of sexual impulse disorder myself."

She began kissing my neck. "I'm a doctor," she whispered. "Why don't you step into my office and take off your clothes? I may be able to help."

"I think you're helping already," I said, rotating my hips in time with hers.

"Are you sure there were three?" she said, leading me to the bedroom. "I think I'm going to have to sign up for a refresher course."

CHAPTER 17

BY THE TIME I got to the precinct the next morning, Kylie was already at her desk. "How was your evening?" I asked.

"Stellar," she said with a gleam in her eye that challenged me to ask for the juicy details. When I didn't, she came back with, "And how was yours?"

"Educational," I said. "I learned a new word."

"Educate me."

"Frotteurism. It means—"

"Zach, I know what it means. I arrested a guy for it. It happened a few years ago on the number 6 train. It was rush hour, the car was packed, and this dirtbag started rubbing his junk up against the woman standing next to him."

"Most of these pervs don't get caught. Lucky for the woman, there was a cop on the train."

She grinned. "Actually it was unlucky for the perv that the ass he decided to rub against belonged to a cop."

Her phone rang, and she picked it up. "Hey, Jason, what've you got?"

Jason White is a recent transfer from NYPD's

Real Time Crime Center and our back door into the private lives of private people. He's the Big Brother who can track anyone's digital footprints. Yesterday, after we'd come up empty-handed, we recruited him to see what he could find on Wells, Hirsch, and Zimmer.

"Thanks," Kylie said, hanging up. She turned to me. "Nathan Hirsch lives with his wife and three kids in Forest Hills Gardens, Queens, but he also rents an apartment on Hudson Terrace in Fort Lee, New Jersey. And his E-ZPass has him going over the G. W. Bridge every Thursday around three p.m."

"Maybe the apartment is for his ailing mother, and, good son that he is, he visits once a week."

"According to Jason, Mom is black, has implants the size of disco balls, and goes by the name of Tiffany Wilde."

"How the hell does he dig that shit up so fast?"

"I'm curious, too, but it would be unwise of us to ask. The less we know, the more honest we can be on the witness stand."

"So Nervous Nathan's got himself some shugah on the side," I said. "That's grounds for divorce, but it's not a motive for murder. And it's definitely not enough to convince the DA to give us the green light to run trap and trace devices on three philanthropists who fight for the less fortunate."

"But you know the rich," Kylie said, holding up a finger. "One dirty little secret is the tip of the iceberg, and if Nathan is into sex for money, Thursdays in Jersey won't be enough. And thousand-dollar-an-hour lawyers who are into hookers don't cruise Twelfth Avenue looking for bargains."

"No, they don't," I said. "Those who can afford the best invariably reach out to New York's number one purveyor of quality female companionship for gentlemen of breeding and taste."

"Get him on the phone and see if he knows any or all of the three amigos."

Q Lavish, who was born Quentin LaTrelle, knows enough about the sex lives of the rich and famous to write a book. But since he's also the one who fulfills their kinkiest fantasies, he's as discreet as a mute in a monastery. With one exception: he'll share certain secrets with us. We, in turn, have been known to help him navigate the unfriendly waters of justice when one of his wealthy clients winds up handcuffed to a cop instead of to a bedpost.

I called Q and put on the speaker so both Kylie and I could listen.

"Detectives," he said. "How can I be of service to New York's Finest?"

"We have three persons of interest, and we were hoping you might know something about their mating habits."

"This is truly a fortuitous moment," he said. "As luck would have it, I was going to call you, although I planned on waiting for a more civilized hour. But who am I to complain about some lost sleep when the quid pro quo gods are smiling so brightly down upon us? May I tell you my conundrum?"

"We go first," Kylie said. "Princeton Wells, Arnie Zimmer, Nathan Hirsch—do you know any of them?"

"What child of the ghetto hasn't heard of the illustrious benefactors of the Silver Bullet Foundation? I'm guessing this is connected to the unfortunate incident at The Pierre hotel."

"No comment. Do you know them?"

"The first two only by reputation, but Macanudo Nate is a valued client. He has a fine appreciation for women of color."

"What do you hear?"

"Apart from the fact that he smells like the inside of a humidor, none of my girls have ever said an unkind word about him."

"Ask around," Kylie said.

"Happily. But first let me ask if you can reason with someone on my behalf."

"Who?"

"He's a judge. And before you say no, he's also a client."

"Then what's the problem?"

"He's accused me of blackmailing him."

"Are you?" I said.

"I will take that question as a lapse of judgment on your part rather than a condemnation of my character, Detective Jordan."

"Get over it, Q. I'm a cop. It's how I roll. Who's the judge?"

"The Honorable Michael J. Rafferty."

"What's the matter—you couldn't pick a beef with Attila the Hun? Rafferty is the biggest prick in the entire judiciary. Nobody likes him, and nobody can reason with him."

"I'm sure that once you know the particulars, you'll find a way."

"Lay them on us."

"That can only be done face-to-face. Can I have Rodrigo drive me over to the One Nine?"

"We have a meeting off campus at ten. If you can be here by—hold on."

Cates's door flew open, and she came storming toward us, her heels echoing on the tile floor.

"Get moving," she yelled, still at least fifty feet away. "A bomb went off at Sixty-Eighth and York."

"What's there?"

"A construction site. The blast was contained to a small field office. One person is dead."

"Who?" I said, but I knew the answer before I asked the question.

"The owner of the company. Arnold Zimmer."

CHAPTER 18

"LOOKS LIKE ARNIE Zimmer got what he was asking for," Kylie said as we made our way to the blast site.

"That's harsh," I said. "The guy was a jerk, but he didn't deserve to die."

"Jesus, Zach, I didn't say he got what he *deserved*. I said he got what he was asking for. Us."

"Not quite," I said. "He wanted us exclusively. Technically he's still got to share us with Aubrey Davenport."

"Right now, Arnie Zimmer has our undivided attention. Aubrey is going to have to wait. Why don't you call Dr. Langford and tell him we're going to be late for our sex ed class."

Langford's calendar was jammed from eleven on, so we rescheduled for 8:00 p.m., which was the earliest he could see us. It was going to be another long day.

The explosion took place on the campus of Rockefeller University, which is tiny as institutions of higher learning go, stretching only five blocks along York Avenue. But what it lacks in size it makes up for in worldwide renown. Devoted to research in biomedical science, Rockefeller produces Nobel Prize laureates the way some schools turn out point guards for the NBA.

Zim Construction was one of several contractors hired to add state-of-the-art laboratories and other buildings to the campus, and their field office, a steel box about eight by twenty feet, was tucked into a corner away from most of the foot traffic.

Howard Malley was waiting for us with a damage report.

"One dead: Arnold Zimmer, the owner of the company. As far as we can ascertain, nobody else was injured," he said. "From what I can piece together, the victim arrived about seven thirty, unlocked the door, walked over to the air conditioner, and the bomb vaporized him."

"Did he trip it when he turned on the AC?" Kylie asked.

"No. It was triggered wirelessly from outside. He would have been clearly visible from the street as he approached the window where the AC unit was mounted. The bomber just watched and waited."

"Same bomb maker?"

"Same blast pattern, a shaped charge, but we still have to sift through the rubble and see if we can find some of the same signature elements."

"Is there a crew boss or somebody in charge around here from the construction company?" Kylie asked. "We've got a few questions that you can't answer."

"I like to think I can answer any and all questions, but if you're looking for the general superintendent, he was just here. I told him NYPD would want to talk to him. He works out of a second field office near the Sixty-Fourth Street gate, but that's off-limits till we get a K-9 unit to go through it. He's easy to spot.

Big guy, about six four, work clothes, yellow hard hat. His name's Bill Neill."

"Thanks," Kylie said. "How soon can you let us know if we're looking at the same bomber as the hotel?"

Malley grinned. "Now that's a question I can't answer."

Kylie and I walked across the campus and saw Bill Neill standing under a tree, talking on his cell phone. Malley was right—he was easy to spot. And with our badges on chains around our necks, so were we.

"Barbara, it's the police," he said into the phone. "Let me call you back. I love you, too."

He hung up the phone. "That was my wife," he said. "She heard on the news that a bomb went off in a construction office at Rockefeller University, and she panicked. The FBI agent said you wanted to ask me some questions, but I was four blocks away when it happened. I heard the explosion, but I didn't see anything."

"That's okay," I said. "You can still help. How many people had keys to that office?"

"Arnie, me, and I don't know who else, but it doesn't matter. It's just your basic pin and tumbler lock. Anyone can open it with a paper clip and a tension wrench. A key is optional."

"It's the boss's office," Kylie said. "Wouldn't you have tighter security?"

"There's nothing in there worth securing. A desk, a couple of file cabinets, a fridge, a microwave, a coffeepot, and that's about it."

"Surveillance cameras?"

"The university has cameras on the gates and peppered around the campus, but Arnie's office was in no-man's-land. It'd be easy enough for someone to scale the fence, pick the lock, and get away without anyone noticing."

"Did Mr. Zimmer have any enemies?" Kylie asked.

Neill shrugged. "Sure, but not the kind that would blow him up. Arnie pissed a lot of people off. If something wasn't going the way he wanted, he was quick to get in people's faces. You guys ought to know."

"Why would you say that?"

"Yesterday afternoon Arnie told me he laced into the mayor, then he read the riot act to a couple of her supercops because they weren't looking hard enough for whoever killed Del Fairfax. I figured that was you."

"We're not supercops," I said.

"But you're trying to solve the first bombing, and now you're on the second one. Do you have any leads?"

"We're working on it," I said.

And as soon as the words came out of my mouth, it dawned on me. That was the same promise I'd made to Arnie Zimmer just twenty-four hours earlier.

CHAPTER 19

KYLIE AND I thanked Bill Ncill and started walking back toward our car, which we'd been forced to abandon on 70th Street because York Avenue had been clogged with emergency vehicles.

By the time we got back to the blast site, some semblance of order had been restored. At least half of the fire trucks and patrol cars had been released, news vans were relegated to the side streets, and all civilian traffic from 61st to 72nd had been diverted to First and Second Avenues. That left two lanes open on York for official vehicles. I immediately recognized the black SUV parked in front of the 68th Street gate. It was the most official vehicle of them all.

"Detectives!" a voice boomed.

It was Charlie, the mayor's driver. He waved us over to the car, opened the back door, and Kylie and I slid into the back seat next to Muriel Sykes.

"Yesterday, when I called you and asked you to get Arnie Zimmer off my back, this is not what I had in mind," she said. "He has now managed to become a bigger pain in the ass to me dead than he was alive. I realize that the dust hasn't even settled, but do you have anything? One murder is a tragedy. Two is a conspiracy."

"Madam Mayor," Kylie said, "when Zach and I met with the three surviving Silver Bullet founders yesterday, Arnie Zimmer tried to convince us that Del Fairfax was killed by a disgruntled contractor. If there's a conspiracy against them as a group, I'm sure it came as as big a surprise to Zimmer as it did to us."

"So you have nothing. No suspects. No leads."

"Not yet."

"What about Aubrey Davenport? She got bumped off the front page because of the bombing, but she's a big-name filmmaker, and the whole autoerotic asphyxiation thing is going to sell a lot of newspapers. Where are you on that?"

We told her.

"So this Janek Hoffmann," she said, going over the high points, "he's her cameraman, and there's evidence of a tripod at the crime scene. The brother-in-law tells you that the guy is mentally and physically abusive. Davenport's car is parked a block from Hoffmann's apartment, and he has no alibi for the time of the murder. It sounds to me like you have an incredibly viable suspect."

"But we can't arrest him," I said. "We don't have enough evidence to take to the DA."

"Zach, I know the rules. I was a U.S. attorney, and when I ran for mayor, I pushed every law-and-order hot button I could. How is it going to look to the voters if I have two unsolved high-profile cases hanging over my head in my first four months? I need an arrest, and you're closer on this than you are on the bombings."

"Madam Mayor, if we go to Mick Wilson and tell

him we want to charge Janek Hoffmann, he'll kick us out of his—"

"I've got two words for our illustrious district attorney," she barked.

I braced myself for the inevitable mayoral f-bomb.

"Selma Kaplan."

"Ma'am?"

"Selma is the smartest ADA in New York County. If anyone can help me get a win on the front page, it's her. Plus she's got the balls to stand up to Wilson, and she's loyal—we went to Brooklyn Law together. Talk to her and see what she can come up with." She leaned over and yanked the door handle. "Please..."

Thirty minutes later, Kylie and I were in the Louis J. Lefkowitz State Office Building, reconnecting with one of the best prosecutors in the business.

Kaplan came around from behind her desk and shook our hands. "Detectives, I wish we could spend twenty minutes together rehashing past glories," she said, "but the villagers are breaking the law faster than I can lock them up. The only reason you got past the wolf at the door is because my old friend Muriel has my cell number, and she's not ashamed to beg. She gave me an overview, but tell me what you've got on this Janek Hoffmann."

Kylie and I filled her in, and when we were done, Kaplan shook her head and frowned.

"If I'm going to get a conviction, I need more than some juicer playing Fifty Shades of Weird with the victim and no alibi," she said.

"We told the mayor we didn't think you could hang a case on it," I said.

"I can't." She paused. "*But*—and this is a big but— my gut tells me you've got enough circumstantial evidence to convince a grand jury to lock him up. Especially once they're told he's a flight risk who could hop a plane to Warsaw at any minute. Bring him in. I can get an indictment. That'll buy you enough time to either build a case against Hoffmann or, to quote O.J., 'find the real killer.'"

"Thanks, Selma," Kylie said. "We owe you one."

"No, sweetheart," Kaplan said. "Muriel owes me one. And make sure you let her know that I plan to collect."

CHAPTER 20

THE MIRANDA WARNING is eloquent in its simplicity. And yet a few seconds after we advised Janek Hoffmann that anything he said "can and will be used against you in a court of law," he assured us that he understood his rights and then blurted out, "I didn't kill her. But if I did, I didn't mean it."

Kylie tossed me a grin that summed up what we were both thinking: *We may not have enough evidence to convict this idiot, but with a little luck, he'll hang himself.*

In short order, he was assigned a lawyer from Legal Aid, arraigned, and remanded without bail. The mayor's spin doctors did their best to drum up media buzz for the arrest, but in a city whose mantra is "If you see something, say something," the two unsolved bombings dominated the airwaves.

By six thirty we'd wrapped up the paperwork. Since Dr. Langford's office was across town, we welcomed the opportunity for some new dining options and drove to Pizzeria Sirenetta on Amsterdam Avenue for some rustic Italian fare.

Ninety minutes later, we parked at a hydrant on a tree-lined stretch of West End Avenue outside

Langford's apartment building. Kylie and I had Googled him before we left the office. He was forty-seven and had written five books, and with his thick mop of ginger hair, surfer-blue eyes, and camera-ready smile, he was the guy the TV stations called when they needed an expert.

"Just our luck," Kylie said. "Another pain-in-the-ass celebrity shrink."

The two of us had faced off with our share of A-list psychiatrists in the past, and humility is not their strong suit. Rule of thumb: the more famous they are, the more arrogant they can get.

"Cheryl likes him," I told her. "She says he's a no-bullshit kind of guy."

"Cheryl's a lousy judge of character," Kylie said. "Look at who she's dating."

It turned out that Cheryl was right: Langford was likable from the get-go. Two minutes after we entered his waiting room, he stepped out of his office, walked his patient to the front door, and introduced himself.

"Morey Langford. I've heard quite a bit about you both. I'm sorry to meet you under such tragic circumstances. I've been in a news-free zone since this morning. Have you made any progress?"

"Not enough," I said, and left it at that. I didn't want Hoffmann's arrest to color any of Langford's comments.

He shook his head and escorted us into his office. It was warm and inviting, with curtained windows, upholstered furniture, and a deep red Persian rug, and in lieu of the usual ego gallery of framed diplomas and degrees, the walls were decorated with vintage movie posters. I stopped to admire the one behind his desk.

"Ah," he said. "The proverbial elephant in the room."

It was indeed an elephant—Walt Disney's Dumbo, to be specific. "I saw the movie as a kid," I said, "but for the life of me, I can't figure out what a flying elephant has to do with sex therapy."

He laughed. "Not all my patients are dealing with sexual dysfunction, but virtually every one of them has self-esteem issues. I hung the posters because I'm a film buff, and they cheer the place up. But *Dumbo* turned out to have a not-so-subliminal message. He symbolizes the power of belief. If we believe, we try; if we don't believe, we give up."

"What can you tell us about Aubrey?" Kylie asked.

"Here are her files," he said, sliding an envelope across his desk. "But a doctor's notes can be dreadfully clinical. I can probably be more helpful if you ask me some questions."

"For starters, you prescribed Paxil and Zoloft," I said. "What were you treating her for?"

"Both drugs are SSRIs—in layman's terms, antidepressants—and if you check the dates on the bottles, you'll see that I prescribed them months apart. I started her on the Paxil, but she complained that it was making her gain weight, so I transitioned her to Zoloft."

"Did it help with the depression?"

"Depression wasn't her problem. Aubrey had compulsive sexual thoughts and behavior that led her into liaisons that could have had life-threatening consequences. One of the most common side effects of SSRIs is diminished sexual desire. I used the pills to try to squelch her libido, but that was a Band-Aid. The real work was being done in our weekly sessions, yet clearly I failed her."

"Doc," I said, "cops know a thing or two about survivor guilt trips. You were trying to help her. Somebody strangled her to death. Not your fault."

"You're good, Detective," he said. "And you're right. Aubrey was deeply mired in her addiction when we first met. For her, sex had to be loveless and punishing, and like any addict, she kept chasing bigger and better highs. The men she had sex with became more dangerous. She stopped saying her safe words. Twice she was left for dead. She wanted to end the madness, but she couldn't. That's why she came to me. I won't say I failed, but I accept that I didn't succeed. The best thing I can do now is help you catch the bastard."

"The file you gave us should help," I said. "Does it name names?"

"Detective, Aubrey lived in a netherworld where men and women freely exchange bodily fluids, but not identities. If she saw the same men on more than one occasion, she would help me keep track of them by saying things like 'the one from Queens who breathes like Darth Vader,' or 'the Puerto Rican guy I picked up on the L train who gave me the black eye.' However, there is one real name in the file. She mentioned him often. Janek Hoffmann. He was her cameraman."

"What can you tell us about him?" Kylie asked.

"Nobody terrified her more than Janek."

"Why? What did he do that the others didn't?"

"You may find this hard to understand, but after years of having men treat her like she was a worthless, unlovable piece of shit, Janek did the unthinkable." Langford inhaled deeply and exhaled slowly. "He told her he loved her."

CHAPTER 21

A STILLNESS FELL over the room as we processed Dr. Langford's last statement. Psychiatrists, of course, are totally comfortable sitting in silence. Kylie is not.

"So let me get this straight," she said. "Aubrey told you that Janek Hoffmann physically and mentally abused her."

Langford nodded.

"And she kept going back for more."

Another nod.

"But when he told her he loved her, *that* scared the hell out of her?"

"Welcome to the world of psychosexual disorders, Detective MacDonald. I've written several books on the subject. Would you like one?"

"I'll pass, thank you, but we've arrested Janek Hoffmann. There's no smoking gun, so the DA will need your testimony to help make a case."

"Absolutely. But make sure the DA knows that I never met Mr. Hoffmann. I have no idea if he's guilty of murder, but I can testify that from everything Aubrey told me about him, he was certainly capable."

We thanked him. He walked us to the door, and we went back to our car.

"I liked him," Kylie said. "Cheryl's a better judge of character than I thought. Tell her she's now batting five hundred."

I ignored the dig.

"Do you know what he gets paid to testify as an expert witness in a sex trial?" she said.

"No, but I'm sure it's plenty."

"There was a piece online about a case in Dallas. The defense flew him down and paid him a hundred fifty thousand dollars."

"That's insane."

"Pricey, but it wasn't crazy. The defendant walked. Sex is free, Zach. Sex therapists are expensive."

Her cell phone rang. It was sitting between us, and we both saw the caller's name come up on the screen. Shelley Trager, Spence's former boss.

Kylie tapped the Speaker button. "Shelley, I'm in the car with Zach, and you're on speaker. Is this about Spence?"

"No, it's about me. I thought you'd be off shift by now. You and Zach are still working?"

"Around the clock."

"Good. I need a cop. Better yet, I need two cops. I've been robbed."

"We'll be right there. Where are you—the apartment? The studio?"

"The Mark hotel on Seventy-Seventh and Madison. I was hosting a private poker game when two guys with guns broke in and got away with eight hundred thousand dollars."

"My God, Shelley, are you okay?"

"No. None of us are okay. We can all afford the money, but none of us can afford the publicity. The

News and the *Post* will have a field day with a story about eight rich assholes pissing away a hundred K apiece while millions of real New Yorkers are eating Big Macs and buying lottery tickets. We wanted to keep it quiet, but before they broke in, they chloroformed Bob Reitzfeld, who was on security duty outside the door."

"Is Bob okay?"

"He's fine—more embarrassed than anything. He said they're amateurs and he never should have gotten suckered. Anyway, they duct-taped his mouth shut and tied him to a pipe in the stairwell. We could have kept it under the radar, but some goddamn Good Samaritan saw Reitzfeld trussed up like a Christmas goose and called 911."

"Are there uniforms on the scene now?"

"Damn right there are. They're coming out of the woodwork!"

"Well, then it sounds like NYPD's got it under control."

"It's not under control, Kylie! Why do you think I'm calling you? We've got a bunch of cops walking around asking us questions we don't want to answer."

"I understand. But what can Zach and I do?"

"Get over to the Mark hotel and get rid of these goddamn nosy cops."

CHAPTER 22

"**THE HOTEL IS** two blocks from your apartment," Kylie said as we headed east across Central Park. "This is a nonevent. Why don't I drop you off and spare you the bullshit?"

"Better yet," I said, "why don't you find the turnip truck you think I fell off and throw me back on? Do I look like I woke up stupid this morning? Since when is an eight-hundred-thousand-dollar armed robbery a nonevent?"

"Come on, Zach, you heard what Shelley said. He'd be embarrassed if this went public. He wants it to go away."

"And if this were 1987, I'm sure we could make that happen. But if we try it today, we'll be lucky if we get to spend the rest of our careers writing parking tickets in the Bronx."

"Shelley's been like a father to me and Spence. I'm willing to risk it—just me—on my own. If I get caught, your ass won't be in a sling."

"Sorry. I already have one partner I can't stand. Why would I want to break in a new one?"

She gave me the finger, and we drove the rest of the way in silence.

There were two squad cars in front of the Mark. I flashed my shield at the doorman, who nodded and softly spoke a single word: "Fourteen." It was the essence of five-star discretion.

We took the elevator to the fourteenth floor and walked to the far end of the corridor, where Bob Reitzfeld was standing with four uniformed officers from our precinct.

"You're too late, Detective," one of them said. "We're ninety-one, ninety-eight here."

Kylie grinned. I stood there dumbfounded. Ninety-one is radio code that informs the responding officers that no crime has been committed. Ninety-eight orders them to resume patrol.

"Just in case my captain asks," I said, "who called this a ninety-one?"

"The lieutenant," he said, pointing at Reitzfeld.

Reitzfeld was *not* a lieutenant. True, he'd spent thirty years with NYPD and retired with medals on his chest and gold bars on his shoulders. But now he was a civilian—the head of security for Shelley Trager at Silvercup Studios.

The four cops said good-bye and walked off to the elevator.

"Zach, Kylie," Reitzfeld said, "I'm sorry you got dragged into this."

"Into what?" I asked. "Ten minutes ago, Shelley called us and said it was an armed robbery. Now it's a noncrime, and you sent the troops packing. What's going on?"

"Nothing I can't handle," Reitzfeld said.

"Bob, someone made a 911 call. This isn't like the old days. They follow up on this shit."

"Relax, Zach. Nine one one got a call that a man was tied to a pipe in the stairwell. I told the cops it was a misunderstanding: the guy who phoned it in didn't realize Shelley is a film producer and we were shooting a movie."

"And they believed that?"

"No, it's complete horseshit. But when their CO asks why they walked away without taking a report, they'll have an answer that will fly."

"In that case, thank you," I said.

"For what?"

"For lying. Kylie was about to do the same thing, but she can't get away with it. You can."

"I hated lying to them, but Shelley's in there with a suite full of high rollers, none of whom would think twice about losing a hundred grand, but all of whom would be very unhappy to see this little incident spin out on social media."

"You want to tell us what really went down?" I said. "We're off the clock, and we're here as friends, one of whom was willing to throw herself under the bus for Shelley."

"What do you know so far?"

"Shelley said something about two armed men, an eight-hundred-thousand-dollar haul, and his head of security trussed up like a Christmas goose, but I don't believe he used the phrase *little incident*."

Reitzfeld laughed. "The old man hosts a one-hundred-thousand-dollar buy-in game every other week. Same cast of characters, about a dozen, all told, but they rotate. He always rents the same two adjoining suites. One is for the game; the other is the losers' lounge. We have hot and cold running room service, but they never get in the room with the players—or the money. I'm posted outside both doors. Cushy gig. Never had a problem."

"What happened tonight?"

"I see this blind man feeling his way down the hallway with a cane, and as he gets closer, my instincts kicked in. Why is a blind guy wearing an Apple Watch? So I stand up, square off, and then...I never saw the second guy. He must have come through the fire exit behind me. Before I knew it, he had the chloroform rag over my face, and when I came to, I was in the stairwell, my hands zip-tied to a water pipe and my mouth duct-taped."

"Could you ID him?" Kylie asked.

"No, but he's sloppy—I made him from thirty feet away. Amateurs can get lucky, but they don't get smart, and I'll bet that somewhere there's a couple of mooks with loose lips tossing around cash like Floyd Mayweather. I'll find them."

"We have some good people working the streets," Kylie said. "We can help you get the word out."

"No thanks. Much appreciated, but you're not invited, and if you've got a problem with that, talk to the boss. I'll let him know you're here."

CHAPTER 23

REITZFELD OPENED THE door for us. I was about to walk in when Kylie grabbed me by the elbow and whispered in my ear. "Don't say anything."

"About what?" I said.

"I'll explain later," she said, the whisper even more urgent. "Just be cool, and don't say anything about anything."

"Vow of silence," I said, and I mimed zipping my lips.

We entered the suite. One look around the room, and I understood why Shelley wanted to keep the robbery under wraps. Most of the poker players were familiar faces. I recognized a retired NBA player turned ESPN commentator, a stand-up comic, a director, an actor, and an aging rock legend. There was another man sitting on a sofa at the far side of the room with a cell phone to his ear, but I'd never seen him before.

As soon as we walked in, Shelley Trager, a sixty-year-old bundle of kinetic energy with a receding hairline and an expanding waistline, came bounding toward us, wrapped his arms around Kylie, and planted a big kiss on her cheek. Shelley is a film producer and a studio overlord, but he's not one of those Hollywood air kissers. Shelley is Big Apple to the core, so the smooch was pure New York: loud and genuine.

"Thank you for coming," he said.

"You call; we come," Kylie said. "Any day, any time."

"And I couldn't have picked a worse day or a worse time. I know how busy you are with those bombings. Plus I heard you're working on the Davenport murder. By comparison, this is small potatoes."

"Maybe so," a voice said, "but a hundred thousand bucks' worth of small potatoes still adds up to a lot of fucking spuds." It was Rick Button, the comic. He was sitting at the bar. "I came here figuring I'd lose a hundred grand tonight. I just didn't expect to be cleaned out so fast. But those guys had guns, and I could tell they weren't bluffing."

"You want your money back, Rick?" Shelley said. "I'll write you a check."

"I don't need your money. I could write this whole crazy poker game into my act and make a fortune."

"You do that, and you'll be dead before you can spend a dime," Shelley said. "And my two friends here will have seven suspects."

Kylie put a hand on Shelley's arm. "I realize you guys have the ability to joke about this," she said, "but there are two armed robbers walking around the city thinking they're the baddest asses in town, and they're not going to quit while they're ahead. They're going to do it again, and the next time, the outcome might not be something to laugh about. Are you sure you won't reconsider reporting this to NYPD?"

"I can't," Shelley said. "Do you see the guy on the couch talking on the phone? His name is Eitan

Ben David. *Doctor* Eitan Ben David, plastic surgeon to the rich and wrinkled. If you think these show business assholes would be embarrassed for this to get out, imagine how a respectable citizen like Eitan would feel. Look, you guys did your job. You ran right over, and you stopped the cops from making a federal case out of this."

"We didn't do anything," Kylie said. "By the time Zach and I got here, Reitzfeld had it under control."

"Then it's over and done with."

"Shelley, it's *not* over and done with. Bob Reitzfeld is going to go after these guys, and he's a damn good cop with a lot of resources at his disposal, so I wouldn't be surprised if he caught them. Then what? You can farm out the police work, but once these felons are apprehended, they still have to be prosecuted through the city's criminal justice system."

"I know, but that can happen quietly. No hoopla, no newspapers, no other victims besides me, and no trial, because we'll make it worth their while to cop a plea."

"And maybe you'll get your money back."

"I don't care about the money."

"Then why bother?"

"First, to do what you want: get these bastards off the streets. And second, to do what Reitzfeld wants: get even with the two punks who snookered him."

Kylie shrugged. "Two noble goals. Call if you need our help."

"Thank you both for coming," Shelley said. "One question before you go. Have you heard from Spence?"

Kylie shook her head. "Not a word. You?"

"Nothing."

The door to the adjoining suite opened, and a man entered, carrying a plate of shrimp and a beer. He saw us talking to Shelley, put his food and drink on a table, threw his arms up in the air, and yelled, "Kylie!"

He headed straight toward her, took her in his arms, and kissed her. This was a far cry from the father-figure, happy-to-see-you kiss Shelley had given her. This was a full-on mouth kiss that could easily have escalated into something a lot more passionate if there hadn't been eight other men in the room.

Quick-witted detective that I am, I immediately figured out two things.

One: I now knew what Kylie meant when she said "Don't say anything."

Two: I was about to meet Kylie's new boyfriend.

CHAPTER 24

HIS NAME WAS C. J. Berringer. Kylie knew, of course, that he'd be at the poker game, which is why she offered to drop me off at home and spare me the tedium of an eight-hundred-thousand-dollar *nonevent*.

Failing that, she got me to promise *not to say anything about anything,* a promise I kept until she was forced to introduce me to C.J.

"I can't believe I finally get to meet Kylie's partner," he said, pumping my arm and acting like he was as thrilled to see me as he was to see his girlfriend.

I sized him up: about my age, slightly taller, and annoyingly handsome. He was also a talker, and for the next ten minutes, which I could only hope were excruciating for Kylie, he bent my ear.

He was born in Hawaii to a native Hawaiian mother and a white father. He struggled through his freshman year in college because he spent more time playing cards than cracking books. And then he had an epiphany: who needs college? He dropped out and carved out a life for himself as a professional gambler.

He asked me if Kylie had told me how they met. *Why no, she hadn't.* He was happy to fill me in.

"It was a few weeks after her husband…" He didn't finish the sentence. I guess I was supposed to fill in the blank. *Flew the coop? Took a hike? Dropped her like a hand grenade?*

"Anyway," he said, "she hopped a plane down to the Bahamas for a quick getaway. I was going down there for a blackjack tournament. We were on the same flight, but we didn't meet until the baggage carousel. Then we split a cab to the Atlantis. I couldn't believe it when she told me she was Five-O. I didn't think cops could be that…I mean, look at her. Anyway, I lost fifty K, but it was the luckiest weekend of my life. After that…well…" He gave me another blank to fill in.

"Great story," I lied. "How do you know Shelley?"

"Kylie introduced us. She told me she had a friend who hosted a biweekly Texas Hold'em game, and she got me an invite. This is only my third time here. The other two times I got played under the table by a plastic surgeon."

Knowing Kylie, I figured she hadn't told him anything about our past. And then he said, "Enough about me. I want to hear all about you. Come on over to the losers' lounge, and let's throw down a few drinks."

The losers' lounge. Of course she had told him, and now the fucker was sticking it to me.

"Another time," I said, looking at my watch. "I've got to get back home and shoot the cat."

He stared at me, dark eyes curious, a bright white smile and a crown of black hair on a copper canvas.

"I have a diabetic cat," I said. "I've got to give him an insulin shot every twelve hours."

"Ah, *shoot the cat,*" he said. "Cop talk. Funny."

I left him laughing.

My apartment was only two blocks east. I walked slowly, but my mind was racing.

I understood why Shelley didn't want NYPD to investigate the robbery. It's not just the publicity. There'd be interviews, digging into the private lives of the victims, and then if there was an arrest, there would be depositions, subpoenas, a trial. It was far too time-consuming for these high rollers. Like the comic said: he had expected to lose the money anyway, so why get tied up in a criminal investigation?

And yet the criminal investigator in me couldn't let it go.

The details of Shelley's high-stakes poker games are a well-kept secret. It's by invitation only. Reitzfeld said the two guys with guns were amateurs. So how did they know where and when the game was being held? And how did they know to sneak up on Reitzfeld from behind?

I knew the answer in two words: *inside job*.

Someone on the inside tipped them off. It could have been someone at the hotel—a manager, a reservation clerk, a room service waiter—or it could have been someone at the table.

According to Reitzfeld, most of the players were regulars. Same cast of characters, he said. About a dozen all told, but they rotate. But there was one new guy, an engaging rogue who had lost a hundred grand to the plastic surgeon in his first two sit-downs at the table. C. J. Berringer.

I got to the corner of 77th and Lexington and looked up at my apartment building. I was in no hurry to get home. It's not like I had a cat to take care of.

I began walking south on Lex. The precinct was only ten blocks away. I knew Shelley wanted NYPD to back off, but it was too late. I already had a prime suspect, and I wanted to sit down in front of a department computer terminal and do some digging.

For starters, I wanted to know what the *C.J.* stood for.

PART TWO

THE BANGKOK HILTON

CHAPTER 25

THERE WAS FRESH hot coffee in the break room. I took that as a positive omen, poured myself a cup, and logged on to the Interstate Identification Index, a catalog of criminal histories in the U.S. If C. J. Berringer had a rap sheet, it would pop up on Triple Eye. It didn't.

I tried two other law enforcement databases. No luck. Either he wasn't a crook or he hadn't been caught yet.

"You can run, C.J.," I said as I booted up the LexisNexis Accurint Virtual Crime Center, "but you can't hide." I dove into the bottomless pit of public and not-so-public records, and there he was—Clyde Jerome Berringer, a Hawaiian-born college dropout who traveled the world playing cards. He had an excellent credit rating, impressive reported earnings, and no criminal history.

But I did find something almost as damning. Clyde Jerome was married.

My first instinct was to pick up the phone and tell Kylie. My second instinct was to play out that phone call in my head. *Hey, Kylie, you'll never guess what I stumbled on when I was running your boyfriend's name*

*through the system to see if I could find something that
would put him behind bars.*

I needed a better plan. Normally when I'm con-
fronted by challenging interpersonal situations like
this, I go to Cheryl for advice. But telling my new
girlfriend that I felt compelled to investigate my old
girlfriend's new boyfriend had all the earmarks of
a bad soap opera where the Zach character winds
up losing his new girlfriend, his old girlfriend, and
his balls.

My motives for digging into C.J.'s past may not
have been pure, but now that I knew the truth, someone had to tell Kylie that her handsome gambler
was gambling on the fact that she'd never find out
about Nalani, his wife of seven years, who lived five
thousand miles away in Honolulu.

And I knew just the someone who could do it.

The next morning at 5:45, I arrived at Gerri's
Diner. The sign on the door says NO SHIRT, NO SHOES,
NO SERVICE. There should be a second sign that says NO
BOUNDARIES, because as soon as you walk through that
door, your private life belongs to Gerri Gomperts.

She's one part short-order cook and one part Internal Affairs. The difference between Gerri and IA
is that cops are happy to share their deepest, darkest
secrets with her.

"Good morning, Zachary," she said. "What'll you
have this morning?"

"Greek omelet, rye toast, coffee, and five minutes
of your time."

"Would you like to sit at the counter, or would you
like a private confessional in the back?"

I smiled and found a quiet booth at the rear of
the diner.

"I see you made an arrest in the Davenport case,"

she said when she delivered the food. "But that's probably not what you want to talk about."

She sat down across from me, and in between bites of my breakfast, I gave her the highlights of last night, starting with the phone call from Shelley and ending with what I had learned about C.J.

She didn't blink.

"Aren't you going to say something?" I asked.

"What's the question?"

"Someone should tell Kylie that the guy she's dating is married. I can't do it, so I thought maybe—"

"She already knows he's married, Zach. She told me a week ago."

"She...she *told* you?"

"You think you're the only cop who comes to me for relationship advice? That week before Valentine's Day I have to open up early and close late just to handle the seasonal demand."

"And she doesn't care that she's sleeping with a married man?"

"In case you forgot, Kylie is married, too. She doesn't live with her husband, and C.J. doesn't live with his wife. Consenting adults, Zach. Let it go."

"I could use some more coffee," I said.

"And a side order of antipsychotic drugs," she said. "Why the hell are you doing this?"

"Doing what?"

"Trying to solve a crime that isn't your crime to solve. Or maybe you're just trying to prove to Kylie that she's making the same mistake all over again by picking some jerk whose name is *Not Zach Jordan*."

"Forget the coffee," I said. "I'll just take the check."

She leaned across the table and put her hand on mine. "That's what I love about you, Zach. You're always so open to good advice...until you hear it."

She stood up. "Breakfast is on me."

"Thanks...for everything."

"Is there anything else I can do for you?"

"Yeah. Don't give up on me."

"Don't worry, kiddo," she said. "I love a challenge. Stay where you are. I'll bring you some more coffee."

She headed back toward the kitchen, and I checked my watch: 6:05. Kylie would be in by 6:15. I had time for one more cup before we tackled another impossibly long day.

"Just wait right here," I heard Gerri say from the front of the diner. I looked up, and she was headed straight for me. No coffee. All business.

"Zach, someone up front is looking for you," she said.

"Who?"

"Never saw him before. Civilian. Overweight. Jumpy as grease on a griddle. Smells like a cigar factory. Do you know him?"

"Hell, yeah. Send him back."

A few seconds later, Nathan Hirsch, the happily married dad from Queens with the high-priced hooker in Jersey, loomed over me.

"Sorry to bust in on your breakfast," he said, "but I went to the precinct, and they said you'd probably be here."

"No problem. Kylie and I were going to call you this morning. We are so sorry about Mr. Zimmer. We've been on the case since it happened."

"Well, I can tell you who did it," he said. "It was the same guy who killed Del."

He shoved his body into the booth and sat across from me. His breathing was labored, and his hands were trembling. He leaned forward and whispered, "And I'm next."

CHAPTER 26

I CALLED KYLIE and filled her in. By the time I brought Hirsch back to the house, she was waiting for us in an interview room.

As soon as I opened the door, he balked. "Lose it," he demanded, pointing at the video camera.

"It's just for internal use," Kylie said. "Our captain's not in yet, and she's been very involved in the—"

"Can it, Detective," he said. "I'm about to give you the name of a mass murderer. If he finds out I'm the one who gave him up, he'll have me killed even if he's rotting away in prison. The only way we're going to do this is if I have total anonymity."

Kylie nodded and capped the lens. He took a seat at the table, and she sat down across from him. I stood.

"In your own words, Mr. Hirsch," she said.

"Look, I broke a few laws when I was a kid, but whatever I tell you, the statute of limitations ran out long ago."

"Statutes run out," Kylie said. "Grudges are forever. Who's coming after you?"

"Did you ever hear of Zoe Pound?"

After years of dealing with the superrich, I've

come to appreciate a certain subtle sophistication about them. They live inside a bubble, and the veneer of privilege and class always seems to remain intact, even when they're caught up in the most nefarious crime imaginable.

There is nothing subtle or sophisticated about Zoe Pound. Spawned in the Little Haiti section of Miami in the nineties, they've evolved from a violent street gang into one of the most ruthless and feared criminal enterprises in the United States. I couldn't imagine how this middle-aged, puffy, pasty white man could be a target of an organization known for drug trafficking, arms dealing, robbery, and contract killing.

"Zoe Pound," I repeated. "The Haitian drug cartel out of Miami."

"Their New York branch runs a thriving drug business out of Brooklyn," Hirsch said.

"And why would they want to kill you?" Kylie asked.

"The *grudge,* as you called it, goes back twenty years. We were in college."

"We?"

"The four of us: me, Del Fairfax, Arnie Zimmer, and Princeton Wells. We were...let's say customers in good standing." He paused. "That's an understatement. The reality was, we bought a shitload of coke from them."

"To sell?"

"To snort. And to share with our friends—especially our lady friends. I wasn't blessed with the fine patrician features of Princeton or Del, but you'd be amazed how easy it is for a fat boy with unlimited blow to wind up in a threesome, a foursome, or whatever the hell else I wanted.

"We were spending a fortune on dope, but our parties were legendary. We were kings. Then one day Princeton has this brilliant idea. We were flying off for winter break—senior year, our last big hurrah. We'd smuggle some heroin back into the country for Zoe, and they'd pay us off in cocaine.

"Princeton set up a meeting with Dingo Slide. He was the undisputed boss back then. Dingo thought it through like he had a PhD in economics. On the downside, he'd be losing some good customers, but he knew no matter how much coke he gave us, we'd go through it fast. On the upside, the Feds had just shut down one of his supply channels, and he needed product. Malique La Grande, one of his lieutenants, was against it, but it was Dingo's call. The cartel fronted us a hundred grand, and we took off on an all-expenses-paid drug run."

"You were mules," Kylie said.

"Rich mules with a corporate jet at our disposal. Princeton's father had three of them, and if a plane was just sitting around, he'd ask Daddy for a flight crew, and off we'd go. It was before 9/11. Private aircraft like that were almost never searched." He paused. "Emphasis on the word *almost*."

"You got busted," I said.

"Big-time. I've never been so scared in my life. Luckily, cops and judges are as corrupt as drug dealers. We bribed our way to freedom, only to find out that Malique wanted to kill us when we got back to the States. More money changed hands. Princeton cut a deal with Dingo. We paid them two hundred fifty thousand dollars and Dingo told Malique to stand down."

"That was a long time ago," I said. "Why would they suddenly change their mind and come after you now?"

"Dingo Slide died last month. Malique La Grande is running the show now. He doesn't have any of Dingo's business instincts. He's a born killer."

"And you think he's out to settle a twenty-year-old grudge," I said.

"Yes. And I need you to stop him before he kills me."

"What about Princeton Wells?" I asked.

"What about him?" Hirsch snapped.

"If what you say about La Grande is true, then Wells is on his hit list, too."

"Not my problem."

"He's your friend. Don't you think you should at least warn him?"

"Fuck him. He's the *friend* who got us into this mess in the first place. Besides, if I tell him that Zoe Pound is out there looking for revenge, he'll hop on his private jet and disappear on an extended business trip to God knows where."

"But—"

"There is no *but,* Detective. Malique is picking us off one by one. I'm trying to save my own ass, and the last thing I'm going to do is help him get to me faster by thinning out the herd."

CHAPTER 27

"**THE SILVER BULLET** boys have come a long way in a short time," Kylie said as soon as Hirsch left.

"How so?" I said.

"When we first met them, they were friends for life and beloved by one and all. Now two of them are murdered, and Survivor One is willing to throw Survivor Two under the bus to save his own skin."

"I guess you never know who your real friends are until you come face-to-face with a Haitian drug lord who's threatening to put a bomb under your ass."

My landline rang.

"Speaking of bombs," I said, "it's Howard Malley." I put him on speaker. "Agent Malley, you've got us both. What did you come up with?"

"No surprises. The two bombs were identical. The second one has the same Flynn Samuels signature touches as the first."

"But Mr. Samuels couldn't have built the bombs because he's still in a prison in Thailand," I said.

"He's got a lifetime commitment, and as far as we know, he's never taught anyone the tricks of his trade."

"Any chance he may have a secret Haitian apprentice?" Kylie said.

Malley laughed. "An Aussie bomb maker in a Thai prison with a Haitian groupie. Sounds like you guys have cracked the code."

"You're not funny, and you're not helping, Malley," Kylie said.

"Then my work is done. As we say at the Bureau, 'We're not happy till you're not happy.'"

He hung up.

"There may not be a connection between Malique La Grande and Flynn Samuels," I said, "but Hirsch's story about a twenty-year-old drug deal gone south is the first time we've even heard a viable motive for these killings."

"Or it could be the delusions of a paranoid lawyer. The only one who can confirm or deny what Hirsch said is La Grande, and guys like him pay lawyers a lot of money to keep guys like us from asking questions."

"It couldn't hurt to give it a try," I said, reaching for the phone.

"Great. Do you have him on speed dial, or did you Google *heroin distributors Brooklyn?*"

"It's a long shot, but I think we have a connection," I said, dialing the landline and keeping it on speaker.

"Who are you calling?"

"Danny Corcoran."

He answered on the first ring.

"Danny, we need a favor."

"Name it."

"You worked Narcotics in Brooklyn, right?" I said.

"Five glorious years."

"Kylie and I need a sit-down with Malique La Grande."

"No problem, Zach. Malique is having dinner with me, Angela, and the kids tonight. Why don't you guys swing by?"

"Danny, I know this is a big ask."

"Bigger than you think. Malique and I have an ugly history. I can't exactly pop by and ask if he wants to chat it up with two of my cop buddies."

"You bust him?"

"Just the opposite. I could never get him dirty, so I spent years fucking with him. Booting his car, hauling him in on every candy-ass charge I could come up with, and one time I got a snitch to tell me where his stash was, and it cost him a bunch of guns and eighty ten-dollar bags. We're not exactly Facebook friends, Zach. When did you start talking to drug dealers?"

"He may have a connection to the multiple-bombing case we're working."

"Bombs aren't Malique's style."

"Zoe Pound is the only lead we have."

"I wish you had called me a month ago. I had a better relationship with his former boss, Dingo Slide."

"I heard Dingo is dead, and Malique took over."

"Whoever told you that left out some details. Dingo died of natural causes: lung cancer. His heir apparent was a nephew, Kervin Blades. But Blades died three days after Uncle Dingo—unnatural causes: lead poisoning. *Then* Malique took over."

"Work your magic, Danny. We need this."

"It would be easier if you needed an audience with the Pope or Springsteen tickets, but give me a day, maybe two. I'll see what I can do."

I thanked him and hung up.

"I'm impressed," Kylie said.

"Hey, every now and then I have a good idea," I said.

"Not with you. I'm impressed that Corcoran can score Springsteen tickets."

A rookie opened the door. "Detectives, there's a guy out front who wants to see you—both of you—but he won't come in the building."

"Did he give you his name?" Kylie said.

"No, ma'am. He just said he'd be waiting for you in his car."

"What kind of car?"

"A Benz. Silver S550. Totally badass."

"Q," I said to Kylie. "Judge Rafferty accused him of blackmail, and we never got back to him."

"Tell the guy in the badass Benz that we'll be down in a few minutes," Kylie said to the rookie. "It's not like we have anything else to do."

CHAPTER 28

THE BENZ WAS double-parked, engine idling, rear door cracked open. As soon as we joined Q in the back seat, Rodrigo, his driver, started rolling. Q is too circumspect to conduct business in front of a station house.

"Detectives," Q said, "I know how busy you are, so I took the liberty of showing up without calling you."

"We *also* know how busy we are," I said, "so even though you've got an angry judge on your hands, we took the liberty of not calling you."

"I'm hurt," he said, putting both hands to his powder-blue cashmere sweater and pressing them to his heart. "Do you know why I'm here this morning?"

"Yes. You're here to call in a favor."

"Zachary," he said. "That's harsh. I thought your unit had the sensitivity training to deal with New York's most affluent citizens. Certainly you know that I'm one of them."

"Red was created to serve and protect New York's most affluent *taxpayers,*" I said. "Are you one of *them?*"

"I plead the Fifth," he said.

"But I'm sure the Cayman Islands cops are very sensitive to your needs."

"Allow me to get to the purpose of my visit," Q said. "Yesterday you asked me to see what information I could gather on the Silver Bullet Foundation."

"And did you find anything?"

"Since we spoke, a second one of them was blown up. It was in all the papers, so I'm sure you're aware of it."

"Thank you very much," Kylie said. "It's on our radar."

She looked at me, her eyes smiling. Q Lavish enjoyed dicking around with us, but only when he had something we needed. If he was only here to call in a chit, he'd have asked by now. He knew something, and the more he jerked us around, the bigger the prize.

I played along. "Did you come up with anything else on the Silver Bullet case?" I said.

"Alas, not a thing."

He looked out the window and then tapped his driver on the shoulder. "Rodrigo, we're almost done here. Why don't you swing up to Fifth and head back downtown."

There was a black briefcase on the seat next to him. He picked it up and put it on his lap. "Ostrich," he said, stroking the leather.

He opened the case and pulled out a silver MacBook Air. "You remember yesterday I told you that a member of the judiciary accused me of blackmail?"

"Judge Rafferty," I said.

"He's a longtime client who enjoys role-playing. What I have here on my computer is a video of His Honor doling out some *punishment* to a lovely felon, who apparently showed up in his chambers wearing nothing but a pair of handcuffs. It's only a three-minute clip, apparently just a trailer for the feature presentation. Would you like to see it? Spoiler alert: Rafferty is, like, a hundred years old, and as ugly as he can be in court, he's even more grotesque without his robes on."

"Spare us," I said. "Just tell us what we can do."

"The flash drive with the video was delivered to Rafferty anonymously with a note—'$100,000 or it goes public.' He immediately rushed to judgment and accused me of being the blackmailer."

"That's not your style," I said.

"That is precisely what I told His Honor. In addition, the woman in the video is not one of my girls. I didn't know who she was, and I didn't care who she was. Until this morning when I picked up the *Post*. I know you don't want to screen the video, but I do have to subject you to a single screenshot."

He tapped a key on the laptop, and a picture popped onto the screen. It was definitely not the kind of porn anyone would pay for. It was a naked couple going at it doggy-style. The man, his chalk-white skin wrinkled, sagging, and liver-spotted, had rear-mounted a much younger woman.

"Holy shit," Kylie said. Not because she recognized Michael J. Rafferty. We'd been prepared for that. What we hadn't expected was the woman bent over the judge's desk, cuffs around her wrists.

"I take it you recognize her," Q said.

"Hell, yeah," Kylie said. "We met her a few nights ago on Roosevelt Island. Her name is Aubrey Davenport."

CHAPTER 29

"MEN AND THEIR dicks," Kylie said after we'd screened a dupe of the Rafferty-Davenport sex video.

"Yeah, well, women and their..." I groped for a passable retort.

"Evil, scheming, blackmailing ways?" Kylie said, helping me out.

"Technically, Aubrey's not the blackmailer," I said. "She was probably going to use it as leverage against the judge, but he didn't get the extortion demands until a full day after she was found tied up in knots."

"So Janek killed her, took her computer, found the video, and saw an opportunity to cash in."

"No," I said. "His brain is too fried to pull this off. Plus Q told us that the judge got a phone call late last night with instructions for delivering the money. By that time, Janek was already in lockup."

Kylie took a few seconds to let it sink in. "So either Janek is our killer, and somebody else is our blackmailer, or...someone else is behind it all, and we arrested the wrong man."

"Let's not take all the credit," I said. "Mayor Sykes and ADA Kaplan helped."

"We better take this to Cates. I'll grab the video. Why don't you make us some popcorn?"

"Shit floats up," Cates said as soon as we stuck our heads into her office. "And from the looks on your faces, you're here with a lapful."

"Have you got a couple of minutes to screen a short film?" Kylie asked.

"What's the subject?"

"Geriatric porn."

We filled her in on our meeting with Q and then ran the video.

"Good Lord," Cates said when it was over. "If that old buzzard won't pay the hundred thousand, we should pass the hat around the department just to keep young people from ever seeing it. If I were a teenager, I think it would scare me into a lifetime of abstinence."

"He's pretty scary from the bench, too," Kylie said. "I've testified in front of him more than a few times. He's got this lecherous stare that creeps women out. He's smarmy, and he doesn't try to hide it."

"It looks like he doesn't care about hiding anything," Cates said. "He was right there in his chambers, going to town on that woman like a rutting pig."

"According to Q," I said, "Rafferty confines all of his sexual dalliances to the courthouse after hours. It's not as crazy as you might think. A hotel is public, very high-risk. His office is safe. At least that's what he thought."

"So clearly he had no idea he was being recorded," Cates said.

"None. Aubrey must have hidden a minicam in her purse."

"And we know she didn't shoot it so she could

post it on Instagram," Cates said. "This has *classic extortion racket* written all over it."

"Except that in this case, somebody murdered Aubrey before she could ask for hush money," Kylie said, "and either the killer or someone else saw the value of the video and decided to cash in."

"Worst-case scenario, this may be the tip of the iceberg," Cates said. "If Davenport made one hidden-camera video of her having sex with an unsuspecting man, there may be more. And whoever is doing the blackmailing is going to go after every one of them. Have you looked at all her video files?"

"Yes and no," I said. "Her computer is missing. Her assistant told us that she uploaded everything to the cloud, and he gave us total access. But there were no sex videos. Not even the one we just saw of the judge."

"Then you better come up with that computer in a big hurry."

"We've got people looking for it," Kylie said, "but maybe the best way to find the computer is to find the blackmailer who's using it."

"And how do you propose doing that?"

"The plan the blackmailer laid out for the drop is smart," I said. "We won't be able to pay him off in phony money or dye packs. So first we have to get the DA to sign off on fronting the hundred thousand."

"I'll give Mick Wilson a call," Cates said. "He wouldn't put up that kind of cash for Joe Citizen, but what prosecutor doesn't want a sitting judge to owe him one?"

"Thanks. Once we know we've got the money, all we have to do is convince Judge Rafferty to deliver it. Then we surround the drop zone with undercover cops and wait for someone to make the pickup."

"Do it," Cates said.

We started to leave.

"One more thing," Cates said. "How old is this old coot, anyway?"

"Seventy-five and change."

"I thought the retirement age is seventy."

"It is," I said. "But Rafferty is a supreme court justice, and he can get three separate two-year extensions if a panel of appellate judges decides his services are needed and a doctor thinks he can still do the job."

"It wasn't pretty," Cates said, "but it looked to me like His Honor was getting the job done."

"Another testimony to the miracle of performance-enhancing drugs," I said.

"Well, somebody should warn him that Viagra can play fast and loose with his blood pressure," Cates said. "At his age, the only performance-enhancing drug he should be using is Metamucil."

CHAPTER 30

"SO YOU'RE TELLING me she's *not* from the escort service?"

"No, Your Honor," I said. "She's not."

"Conniving bitch. She said she was my Christmas present."

We were in Judge Rafferty's chambers. He was sitting behind his desk in a leather armchair that looked to be at least as ancient as he was. Kylie and I were standing. Once again she'd asked me to do the talking.

"I'm not sure I understand, Your Honor. What do you mean she was your Christmas present?"

He tipped back in his chair and rested a pair of large, craggy hands on the substantial paunch that hung over his belt. "It was Christmas Eve last year. The courthouse was cleared out for the holiday. I was just sitting here, nursing a twenty-five-year-old single malt when she knocked on my door."

"How did she get through security?"

"How the fuck should I know, Detective? She could have come in with the rest of the Great Unwashed anytime during the day. What difference does that make? Because if you're trying to hang my court officers out to dry—"

"I apologize, Your Honor," I said. "It was a stupid question."

It was especially stupid since I knew that an attractive woman paying an after-hours call to Judge Rafferty would be quietly waved through security. Even if the guards had noticed a camera in her bag, they wouldn't have asked questions. It was just another play toy for His Honor's evening merriment.

"Anyway, she comes in, shuts the door behind her, and she stands there. Not a bad looker—a solid seven, maybe an eight. She's wearing a trench coat, and there's this little tiny red bow on the belt. And she says, 'I've got a gift from your secret Santa. He wants to know if you've been naughty or nice.'"

He chuckled and looked at me. "I guess you can imagine what I said."

I took the high road and didn't say a word.

"Jesus, you're slow on the uptake. What do you *think* I said? 'Unwrap the present, and let's find out.'"

I took a sideways glance at Kylie. Her face was stone cold, but I knew that just below the stoic exterior, she was inflamed with disgust and rage.

"And then," he went on, "this is a hoot—it was like one of those soft-core pornos. She opens the coat wide, and all she's wearing is a bra, panties, and a pair of stilettos. Can you figure out what I did next, *Detective* Jordan?"

"Yes, Your Honor. I saw the video."

"Go to the head of the class. So now the bitch wants to blackmail me? Well, fuck her. I'm seventy-five years old, my wife is dead, I've got six months left on the bench, and if she thinks I give a shit about a video on YouTube of me getting it on with a woman half my age, she's wrong. I'll send the link to my friends. They'll all be jealous."

"She's dead, Your Honor," I said. "Murdered."

That stopped him. But not for long. "So who the hell is putting the squeeze on me for a hundred thousand dollars?"

"We don't know, sir. It could be someone who stumbled on the video and decided to go into business for himself. Or it could be the person who killed her."

"Well, I'm not paying him a red cent."

"District Attorney Wilson is willing to front the money."

"I don't care whose money it is. You can tell Mick Wilson that Michael J. Rafferty doesn't negotiate with terrorists."

"Sir, you may not be the only victim."

"Really? Are you saying there are more horny bastards out there who got caught with their dicks in their hands? That's their problem, not mine. So stop confusing me with someone who gives a shit. Are we clear?"

"Yes, Your Honor."

"Good. Now go back and tell your commanding officer—never mind. You're an idiot." He turned to Kylie. "You. You've got to be smarter than your partner. You be the messenger."

"Yes, sir."

"What are you going to tell them?" he said.

"I'll tell them that you have no issues being immortalized on YouTube for accepting free sex for Christmas, but you're far too principled to help NYPD catch a murderer."

Rafferty didn't have a gavel, but that didn't stop

him from jumping out of his chair and pounding his fist down on the desk.

"And what the hell is your name?" Rafferty bellowed.

"Detective First Grade Kylie MacDonald, NYPD Red, Your Honor."

"You realize I could hold you in contempt, MacDonald."

"I'm trying to solve a homicide, Your Honor, not make friends with the court. I apologize if I offended you, but I believe what I just said is an accurate replay of this meeting."

He eased himself back down into his chair. A faint smile crossed his lips, morphed into a grin, and then erupted into a full-blown laugh.

"Your partner certainly has got a pair there, doesn't she, Jordan?"

"You don't know the half of it, Your Honor."

He shook his head. "I'm sure you're aware that I'm not the most beloved magistrate in the shire," he said. "I've got one of the best legal minds in the business, but people will remember me as a lecherous old curmudgeon with no patience, no tact, and absolutely no humility. And now you want me to wrap up forty-one years on the bench by being your bagman?"

"Without you, sir, we don't have a prayer," Kylie said. "Will you do it?"

"I'm wavering, Detective MacDonald."

"What'll it take to put you over the top?"

He rested his chin on one hand and whispered, "Dinner."

"It would be an honor, Your Honor," Kylie said, turning on a smile that can transform glaciers into puddles. "Dinner. Just the three of us."

"Hold on. You seriously don't think I invited this bozo to tag along," he said, pointing at me.

"No, sir. That's not the threesome I had in mind."

His eyes popped. "What were you thinking?"

"Just you, me, and my friend Mr. Glock," she said, patting the 9mm automatic on her right hip.

"You won't need it," he said. "I'm taking you to the Harvard Club. You'll get a damn good dinner out of it, and I'll get to drive every other man in the room batshit crazy."

CHAPTER 31

KYLIE'S DINNER DATE with the judge was at seven. I didn't hear from her until eleven. "Rafferty's on board," she said.

"It took long enough," I said. "How was dinner at the Harvard Club?"

"We decided to skip dinner and rented a hotel room. I'll send you a link to the video."

"You're enjoying this, aren't you?" I said.

"Yes. And I'm guessing you're not, because it's never fun for the bozo who didn't get to tag along. I'll see you at seven a.m. Get some sleep."

It was good advice, but my head was too filled with crap, and C. J. Berringer was at the top of the pile. I searched the internet for any skeletons that might have escaped the law enforcement databases, but after an hour all I had learned was that C.J. was a professional gambler who won some, lost some, and photographed devilishly handsome no matter what the outcome.

At midnight I turned off the computer and sat down to meditate. It helped, although I was struck by the irony of using a meditation app to do what people without iPhones have done for thousands of years.

I drifted off about twelve thirty. The phone jolted me awake at three. I pawed it off the night table and grumbled my name into it.

"Zach, it's Danny Corcoran."

"What's up, Danny?"

"I got through to Malique. He's willing to talk to you."

"Nice work, Danny, but Jesus, did you have to call me in the middle of the night?"

"Yeah, I kind of did, Zach. Malique just called. You have until four a.m. to meet him in Brooklyn."

I sat up in bed. "You're serious."

"It's a power play. He knows you're not charging him, so it's his rules, his turf. He'll give you ten minutes of his time. Take it or leave it."

I took it. I rousted Kylie, dressed, and was in front of my building in five minutes. She picked me up three minutes later, and we made the hour-long trip to the Canarsie section of Brooklyn in thirty-seven minutes.

The Karayib Makèt on Rockaway Parkway was a half-block-long supermarket catering to the largest Haitian population in America outside Florida. Kylie pulled up to the front at 3:54 a.m. We were greeted by a welcoming committee of four men, all large, all tattooed, and all in need of dental work. The store was closed, but a fifth man opened the front door, and we were ushered past aisles of produce, meats, and groceries you don't find on the Upper East Side of Manhattan.

We walked through a steel door into a vast cold room. There was a second door on the opposite side. One of our escorts tapped out a code on a keypad. The door was opened from the inside, and we were led in.

The far wall was covered with a large flag: two horizontal bands, one blue, one red, resting on top of large gray letters that spelled out Zoe Pound. The final letter, d, was spattered with the same blood-red color as the bottom band. In the center was a white panel bearing a multicolored coat of arms proclaiming L'UNION FAIT LA FORCE. I didn't know Haitian Creole, but I spoke enough French to understand: Unity makes strength.

In the center of the room was an oversize scarred wooden desk. Six armed men stood at key points around it. A seventh sat behind it.

"I am Malique La Grande," he said.

"I'm Detective Zach—"

"I know who you are, and I know why you're here," La Grande said. "You think Zoe Pound is responsible for the deaths of Fairfax and Zimmer. I am delighted that they are dead, but Zoe does not blow people up."

"So you're saying you didn't kill them," I said.

"Trust me, Detective. If we had killed them, it would have taken them a lot longer to die."

"But you did have a motive. They ran drugs for you, and it went south."

"They did not run drugs for *me*. It was my predecessor's call. I warned Dingo against it. I told him mules should be desperate. These were spoiled rich kids. I was right. They came back to New York empty-handed."

"Did they give you a reason?"

"They said they made the buy, and were about to fly back to the U.S., when the police stopped them at the airport and confiscated the drugs."

"Heroin," I said.

"Four kilos. Dingo fronted them a hundred large.

When they came back empty-handed, I knew they were lying, and should have been put to death, but Dingo said it would be bad for business if we killed four rich white boys. So he settled for a payout of two hundred and fifty thousand dollars, even though the shit would have been worth five times that once we cut it and put it on the street."

"You don't believe the drugs were taken by the authorities at the airport?"

"No."

"What do you think happened?"

"I think they set us up. They bought the dope, planted some of it on that Guatemalan kid, let him take the fall, paid off the cops, and flew back to New York with a couple of kilos of Zoe Pound heroin. But we couldn't prove—"

"Excuse me," Kylie said. "What Guatemalan kid?"

"The one they took with them on their fucking private jet. He was dirt-poor, but he got a scholarship to their fancy white school, so they took him along for the ride. And then they hung that little brown boy out to dry."

"There was a fifth kid on the drug run with them?" I said. "Do you know his name?"

Malique nodded. "Segura. Geraldo Segura." He looked at his watch. "Your time is up."

"Thank you," I said. "You've been a big help, Mr. La Grande. One more quick thing: We'd like to talk to this Mr. Segura. Do you know where we can find him?"

Malique laughed. A few of his bodyguards cracked smiles as well.

"Geraldo Segura is in the same place he's been for the last twenty years," La Grande said. "The same place he'll be for the next thirty."

"Where's that?"

"The Bangkok Hilton."

My mind started to race, and I repeated the word in my head. *Bangkok. Bangkok. Bangkok.*

As in Thailand.

CHAPTER 32

WE'D BEEN BLINDSIDED, and Malique knew it.

"Well, well," he said. "It seems that the do-gooders from Silver Bullet failed to mention that they left their boyhood friend rotting away in a hellhole in Thailand."

I nodded. "Do you think Segura could be connected to the bombings?"

"What do you mean *connected*?"

"Could he be orchestrating the hits?" I said.

"Strange question, Detective. I don't know what would make you think that a man chained to a prison wall in Thailand could be responsible for setting off bombs in New York. Unless..." Malique ran a hand under his chin and stroked his wiry beard. "Unless there's something *you* failed to mention."

Danny Corcoran had warned me about Malique. "You can fuck with him," he had said, "but don't try to con him."

"There is something," I said. "But I didn't *fail* to mention it. I just wasn't going to walk in here with my kimono wide-open. But now that I know there's good faith, I'll tell you."

I looked around the room, and then turned back to Malique. "Do we need this big a crowd?"

He barked a command in Haitian Creole, and five of the six bodyguards left the room. The sixth man didn't budge. "That's my son," Malique said. No further explanation was necessary.

"The bombs that killed Fairfax and Zimmer had an identical signature. They're both the handiwork of an Australian named Flynn Samuels. The problem is that Samuels has been in prison for the past fifteen years."

Malique La Grande had perfect teeth. And I could see almost every one of them as a wide smile crossed his face. "Let me guess. The prison is in Bangkok."

"Small world," I said.

"So they're cellies?"

"We don't know that yet. The Thai government isn't exactly forthcoming with details on their prison pop."

"Does Segura have a network here in the city?" Kylie asked. "People who might be willing to exact revenge for him?"

"He's got his Guatemalan grandmother and a couple of aunts. That's his *network*. But I doubt if these ladies know much about blowing shit up, because if they did, they wouldn't have waited twenty years to get even."

Malique looked at his watch. "You got one more minute. It's not good for my reputation to have a cop car camped out in front of my market."

"It's unmarked," Kylie said.

"People in this neighborhood don't need the big blue letters. They can smell a cop car."

We got in a few more questions before our time ran out. We thanked him and left. As soon as we were on the road I called Cates at home and told her we had a new development in the Silver Bullet case.

"Another bomb?" she asked.

"Metaphorically speaking, I guess it is."

Kylie and I stopped in a coffee shop in Queens, where the breakfast waitress didn't know anything about our lives and didn't care. I put in a quick call to Howard Malley at the FBI, and by 6:20 we were in Cates's office telling her about our middle-of-the-night ride to a Haitian supermarket in Canarsie.

"Was Segura in on it?" she asked.

"Malique thinks he was clueless. The heroin was found in Segura's bag, but all five boys were hauled off and locked up by the Thai cops. About ten hours later, an emissary from a Bangkok bank paid a visit to a senior police official, and the four rich kids hopped on their private jet and flew home. Segura is still there. Malique swears up and down that they only brought him along to take the fall."

"So the guy who took the rap for the drug deal is locked up in the same country as your bomb maker," Cates said. "Do you have any idea if their paths ever crossed?"

"According to Howard Malley, there are 144 prisons in Thailand, with a combined male population of over two hundred thousand," I said. "It seems unlikely that the two of them met and even more unlikely that Flynn Samuels would ever give up his trade secrets, but we're looking to see if we can make a connection."

"Where are you on the Davenport murder?" Cates asked.

"Closing in," Kylie said.

"That's not an answer I can pass up the food chain, MacDonald. I need details."

"Sure. As soon as we're done here, Zach and I are going to pick up a hundred thousand dollars in cash from the DA's office, hand it over to a seventy-five-year-old man of dubious ethics, and have him deliver it to a blackmailer who may also be a murderer. Then we'll hold our breath, keep our fingers crossed, and hope for the best."

Cates has no patience for lame cop jokes. But this time she didn't say a word. She knew Kylie wasn't joking.

CHAPTER 33

TWO HOURS LATER, we were back in Judge Rafferty's chambers along with Jason White, our tech guru. Kylie gave His Honor her most endearing smile, and I gave him an attaché case packed with cash.

"There's a microchip embedded in the bottom, so we can track the money," I said.

"That won't work," Rafferty said. "There's been a change of plans. This was delivered this morning along with some instructions."

He held up a plastic bag that was identical to the ones we use at crime scenes to collect and preserve evidence. It was transparent, about the size of a sheet of typing paper, and, most important, it was tamperproof. Once the bag was sealed, if anyone attempted to open it, the adhesive strip at the top would read VOID.

The bags we use at NYPD are imprinted with data fields to be filled in with details relevant to a crime and the chain of custody. The printing on this one was more like a bank deposit slip. It was used by millions of small businesses to make secure cash bank deposits. The blackmailer could have picked it up at any Office Depot in the country.

"This is where he wants me to put the money," the judge said.

"He's smart," Kylie said. "There's more than enough room for twenty stacks of Benjamins, at five thousand dollars per stack, but there's no place to hide a tracking device."

"Your Honor," I said, "you said it came with instructions."

"Yes. He wants to watch me count out the money to make sure it's real and untraccable."

"Tell him he can pop by your office and look over your shoulder," Kylie said.

"He'd rather Skype. Apparently, he doesn't trust me."

"I can trace a Skype call," Jason said.

"Somehow I bet he knows that. This guy is not stupid," the judge said. "He also sent this."

He handed me a small brown paper shopping bag with a Starbucks logo on it.

"What's that for?"

"He didn't say, Detective. Maybe he wants me to deliver some fucking coffee along with the money."

"Did he give you any other instructions?"

"Come alone. No cops."

"That's not going to happen, Your Honor," Kylie said. "You'll be surrounded by cops: me, Zach, and half a dozen undercover detectives who've worked operations like this before. We can't tail you too closely, but you'll be wearing an earpiece that will let us communicate with you, and a tracking device that will tell us exactly where you are."

"That's good," the judge said, "because if you're

right, and this guy is also a murderer, you'll be able to locate my body." He lifted his arms in the air. "Wire me up."

"It's wireless," Jason said, holding up a black audio-video transmitter that looked like a smartphone. "Just tuck it in the top pocket of your jacket, and we'll be able to see what you see, hear everything you say. And when you get a call, keep your phone close to your jacket pocket, and we'll be able to pick up everything the caller says."

"Excellent plan," the judge said, "but as you can see, I'm wearing this black turtleneck. I thought it was very James Bond, but alas, it has no pockets."

"No problem," Jason said. "The department has a fine line of menswear for every occasion. Do you have a color preference, Your Honor?"

"Surprise me," Rafferty said, sliding into the leather chair behind his desk. He picked up a folder, began to read, and tuned us out.

He didn't look up until his cell phone rang forty-five minutes later. He took the Skype call, which, as expected, was one-sided. The caller could see the judge, but the camera was off on the other end.

Surprisingly, the seventy-five-year-old justice was completely at ease with technology. He positioned the phone so the caller could watch, and, following instructions to the letter, he removed the band from a stack of five thousand dollars and counted out fifty one-hundred-dollar bills. Then he replaced the band and slid the five thousand into the plastic bag.

The caller picked out three more stacks at random. When they came up clean, he told Rafferty to "bag it all and seal the bag."

By that time, Jason White had traced the Skype account and the phone the call was coming from.

He pulled me to the far side of the room and whispered in my ear, "It belongs to a high school math teacher on the West Side. I called the school security guard. She's in class."

"Can you pinpoint where the call is coming from?" I whispered back.

Jason shook his head. "I can narrow it down to a three-block area two miles from the school. But pinpointing is impossible. The caller is on the move."

I looked at the judge. The hundred thousand was in the bag, and he ran his fingers over the tape, sealing it. Any thought we'd had of tracking the money was out the window. We had to rely solely on the eyes and ears of our undercover team.

"It's still your show," the judge said to the black screen on his side of the video call. "What now?"

"Put the money inside the Starbucks bag, take a cab to Twenty-Third Street and Tenth Avenue, get out on the southwest corner, and wait for my next call. And Judge," the man who was calling the shots added, "at the risk of repeating myself, no cops, or I'll kill you."

That was followed by the familiar *whoop* sound of the Skype hang-up.

The judge gave the dead phone the finger.

Jason handed him a tan corduroy jacket with the camera peeking just above the breast pocket.

Rafferty put on the jacket and dropped the sealed packet of money into the Starbucks mini–shopping bag. "Come on," he said, looking at Kylie and me and heading out the door. "Let's go catch this flaming asshole."

CHAPTER 34

MALIQUE LA GRANDE was right. Street-smart New Yorkers, especially those who are looking to steer clear of the law, can practically smell an unmarked police car. That's why NYPD has a mini-fleet of Ford Interceptors that are painted yellow and tricked out to look exactly like the city's thirteen thousand licensed taxis.

We call them cop cabs, and they're perfect for running surveillance in heavy crime neighborhoods, where a squad car, or even an unmarked, would be a dead giveaway. They also come in handy when you're tailing a blackmail victim on his way to make a hundred-thousand-dollar ransom drop.

Judge Rafferty left the courthouse and hailed a legitimate taxi, and Kylie got behind the wheel of the decoy. I was about to get in the front passenger seat when she stopped me.

"Sorry, dude," she said, "but if you want this to look authentic, you're going to have to sit in the back."

"If I wanted this to look authentic, I'd get someone a little less blond and a lot less hot to do the driving. Guys will be flagging you down, even if they have no place to go."

"Please don't hate me because I'm beautiful," she purred, her green eyes wide and soulful, her lips in a mock pout. Then came the more familiar Kylie MacDonald wiseass smirk. "Now get in the back, or find another taxi."

I got in the back, and she pulled onto Centre Street. A few blocks later she turned onto Canal, and we blended into the rolling sea of yellow cabs.

His Honor had a knack for undercover work. A few minutes into the ride, he engaged the driver in classic idle taxi chitchat. *Where are you from? How long have you been driving? How 'bout those Mets?* Then he aimed the pocket cam at the man's hack license. By the time they reached their destination, we knew all we needed to know about the driver. Most important, he wasn't part of the shakedown. It had been a random pickup.

The judge got out of the cab and stood on the corner of Tenth Avenue and 23rd Street.

"I don't like it," Kylie said, parking in a bus stop on the opposite side of the avenue. "The nearest subway is on Seventh, which is a solid half-mile walk from here. That means whoever is coming for the money is going to be on wheels."

"So what part don't you like?"

"The judge is too vulnerable standing there. We should move in on foot and get closer to him just in case a van swoops in and tries to pick up the old man along with the money."

I was about to get out of the cab when Rafferty's cell phone rang. Kylie and I listened as he took the call.

"I'm on the damn street corner," he barked at the caller. "Now what?"

"Walk west on Twenty-Third," the voice said.

We watched as the judge headed west. "I've got a bum knee," he said. "How far do I have to walk?"

"Half a block. That big green box in the middle of the sidewalk is an elevator. Take it up to the second floor."

"Son of a bitch," Kylie said, pointing at the trestle thirty feet above the street. "He's meeting the judge on the High Line."

The High Line is one of New York City's most inspired public parks. It's the brainchild of two men who saw an unused elevated railroad spur and helped convert it into a mile-and-a-half-long aerial garden that winds above the city from Gansevoort Street in the meatpacking district to Hudson Yards on 34th Street.

I radioed Danny Corcoran. "The drop is on the High Line at Twenty-Third. We need to block off the closest exits so the perp can't get back down to street level. Kylie and I have this one covered. Get a team to cut him off at Twentieth and another at Twenty-Sixth."

"Box him in," Corcoran said. "I'm on it."

"One more thing," I said. "Get a bird up there. We need eyes in the sky."

I turned to Kylie. "Take the stairs. I'll meet you up top."

I ran toward the elevator. It was the slowest way to get where I wanted to go, but I had to make sure that the money that had just gone up wasn't already on the way down.

It wasn't. The elevator was empty, and I got on. Kylie was waiting for me at the top. Even though I was in full-blown cop-in-pursuit mode, I couldn't help but be dazzled by the beautiful greenway float-ing above Manhattan's west side. It was a triumph of urban development that attracted five million tourists a year. I took Kylie by the hand, and we pretended to be two of them.

"Start walking north," the voice on the judge's phone ordered.

His Honor, who was only fifty yards away, saw us, nodded, and started walking. We did the same, walking at his pace, pretending to admire the vegetation as we went.

"Red Leader," Danny said over the radio. "Aviation is on the way, and backup is in place. Do you want them to close in?"

"Not yet," I said. "Judge is headed north. Keep a tight lock on the exit at Twenty-Sixth. Backup at Twentieth can start moving uptown."

The judge was almost at 25th Street when the voice came back. "There's a bench up ahead. When you get there, I want you to set your little shopping bag on it, and keep walking."

Not only could Kylie and I see the judge from a safe distance, but we could also look at my iPhone and see exactly what his pocket cam was seeing. There was a beautifully crafted teak bench nestled in front of a thick patch of greenery. The judge slowed down as he approached the bench, lowered the bag with the extortion money onto the seat, and then kept walking.

I radioed Danny, gave him the exact drop location, and told him to position his remaining backup team on the avenue directly below us.

"Do you see anybody?" Kylie asked.

I looked around. Not many people. And those who were there were strolling, oblivious to the mini–shopping bag sitting on a bench, tucked into a quiet nook, surrounded by nature.

"Nobody," I said, looking left, right, north, and south.

What I didn't do was look up. So I didn't see the quadcopter as it stealthily moved in on its target. I didn't hear the buzz of the tiny rotors slicing through the air until it was too late.

The drone swooped down from the sky and hovered over the bench. Within seconds, a grappling hook that was suspended from the landing gear latched onto the handles of the Starbucks bag, lifted it up, and banked west.

"Aviation!" I yelled, keying my radio. "Red Leader on the High Line. Where are you? We need air support, and we need it now!"

"Zach, what's going on?" It was Danny Corcoran.

"We got sucker punched," I said as I watched a hundred thousand dollars of district attorney Mick Wilson's money fly low over the Hudson River and make its way uptown.

CHAPTER 35

ORDINARY MORTALS WATCHING all that cash disappear into thin air might shake their fists at the sky and give up.

Not cops. Especially not me or Kylie.

We ran after it. Instinctively we both headed toward the 26th Street exit. It wasn't where our car was, but it was the fastest way to the ground.

By the time we got there, Judge Rafferty was surrounded by six cops: Danny Corcoran; his partner, Tommy Fischer; and four uniforms.

"I've got the chopper pilot on the radio," Corcoran said. "He's tracking the drone. It looked like a flyspeck at first, but he finally got his camera locked in on it."

"We're going after it," I said. "You and Tommy get the judge out of here fast."

"I'm fine, Detective," Rafferty said. "Don't worry about me."

"I'm not worried about you, Your Honor. I'm worried about your picture being all over the internet in the next five minutes." I swept my hand in an arc around the growing crowd that had come to take in the beauty of the High Line and got the extra added bonus of being in the middle of a police action. Most of their cell phone cameras were still pointed skyward, but some of them started to advance on the cluster of cops at the top of the stairs.

"We need wheels," Kylie yelled. "Who's got an RMP?"

One of the uniforms reached into his pocket and pulled out a key fob. Contrary to what you see in the movies, cops don't bolt from their cars and leave their motors running. The vehicle is their responsibility, so when it's unattended, most of them lock it.

He tossed Kylie the keys, clearly not happy about giving up his ride. "And who are you?" He grinned. "Get the name, share the blame, Detective."

"Kylie MacDonald, Red unit. I've got a decoy cop cab parked at Twenty-Three and Ten. It's all yours"—she read the name on his uniform—"Officer Pendleton." She gave him her keys, and the two of us flew down the stairs.

Within seconds we were tear-assing up Tenth Avenue. I got the chopper pilot on the radio. "Aviation, this is Red Leader. What's the twenty on that drone?"

"The UAV—unmanned aerial vehicle," he said, correcting me, "is about eight hundred feet over Thirtieth and Ninth and headed east. He's only poking along at about twenty miles an hour. My kid has one that goes faster."

"This one is carrying a hundred thousand dollars in cash," I said.

"That wouldn't slow my kid down, but…Red Leader, do not—repeat, do not—turn onto Thirtieth. There's an eighteen-wheeler backing into a loading dock. He's jamming up the whole street. Head east on Thirty-Fourth."

Kylie slowed down just enough to hang a hard right onto Thirty-Fourth. It's a wide, busy crosstown thoroughfare, four lanes with two-way traffic. But at least it was moving. Cars, trucks, buses, and pedestrians all got out of our way as she barreled down the street, lights flashing, siren wailing, creating a center lane of her own.

"UAV is descending," the pilot said. "That will cut his speed dramatically. He's at Thirty-First and Seventh Avenue. I have you in the RMP at Thirty Fourth crossing Eighth."

By the time he finished his sentence, Kylie had whizzed past an accordion-fold articulated bus, and we were halfway to Seventh.

"Red Leader, the UAV is at three hundred feet and dropping," the pilot said. "Looks like he's going to set it down. The avenue is crowded. I may lose him. You're going to need eyes on the ground."

I radioed Central, told them the drone was hovering over Penn Station, and asked for every cop in the area to start looking up. "It's carrying a hundred thousand dollars of department funds," I added. "Arrest anyone who touches it."

"Turn right, turn right," our eyes in the sky said.

The traffic in front of us was stopped for a red light, so Kylie yanked the car to the left and hopped over the double yellow line into the westbound lane. Then she blasted a couple of *whoop-whoop*s on the siren, made a sharp right across two lanes of eastbound traffic, and skidded onto Seventh Avenue.

I bent down low in the front seat and looked up through the canyon of skyscrapers. Nothing. "Aviation, I still don't have a visual," I yelled into the mic. "Where is he?"

"He's at your twelve o'clock headed straight

toward you over Penn Station and still descending. He's at fifty feet, forty, thirty, and...camera lost him. He's gone."

"What do you mean *gone*?"

"He dipped under the canopy at Thirty-Second and Seventh—the one over the entrance to Penn Station that cuts through to Madison Square Garden. Stop your car. Right there by that taxi rank."

Kylie jammed on the brakes, stopping the RMP in the middle of one of the busier crosswalks in Manhattan. We jumped out of the car. Several uniformed officers who had seen the drone go down came racing toward us.

"The white drone," one of them said. "Is it carrying a bomb?"

"No," Kylie said. "Stolen money. Did you see where it went?"

"It flew under this overhang and disappeared," the cop said.

"Find it," Kylie barked at the growing cadre of men and women in uniform.

The lot of us stampeded down the steps into the massive underground catacomb that sits below Madison Square Garden. Unlike its east side sister, Grand Central Terminal, Penn Station is devoid of charm. Its main claim to fame is its capacity.

I looked up at the departures board. Trains were coming and going minutes apart. Over half a million passengers a day pass through the vast space, tens of thousands of them with rolling suitcases, any one of which could have contained the UAV and the ransom money.

"Detective," our eyewitness cop said, "I saw that drone fly in here, and I know for sure it didn't fly out. It's got to be somewhere inside the station."

"Somewhere inside the station," Kylie said, looking at me. "That's good news. Now all we have to do is find something the size of a couple of coat hangers inside the biggest transportation hub in the Western Hemisphere."

CHAPTER 36

SUCCESS HAS MANY fathers. When a police action goes down perfectly, there's never a shortage of people ready to take credit for it. That's why there's always a crowd of high-ranking cops standing behind the podium when the PC holds a press conference announcing the department's latest triumph over crime.

Failure, on the other hand, is an orphan, and the top brass is notorious for pointing fingers and assigning blame.

One of the things that makes Delia Cates a great boss is her willingness to stand back-to-back with her team—even when the wheels come flying off the wagon.

She was at her computer when we got to her office. The door was open, and Kylie rapped on the glass. "Captain, can we have—"

"Sit down," Cates said without looking up from the keyboard. "I'm just answering my fan mail. It's amazing how my inbox fills up when a hundred thousand dollars of the DA's money flies off into the sunset."

"Ma'am, you don't have to fall on your sword for

us," Kylie said. "We lost the money and the perp. We'll take the heat."

Cates lifted her head up. "MacDonald, in case you haven't noticed, I'm black, I'm a woman, and I'm on the fast track. I don't have to fall on swords. There are plenty of white men in white shirts who are happy to throw me on the nearest one if they think it will help a horse they have in the race."

She slid the keyboard tray under her desktop. "Besides, as the DA's latest email just reminded me, I'm the one who called, asked for the money, and practically promised him we'd all live happily ever after."

"How did you respond?"

"My first draft said, 'Dear Mick, Shit happens.' The version I ultimately sent said the same thing, but it benefited from time well spent during my youth in the writing program at Columbia."

"Have you heard from the chief of d's or the PC?" Kylie asked.

"All of the above and many of those below. Listen to me, MacDonald: Running a high-profile squad is like coaching in the Super Bowl. Everybody is rooting for you until you make one bonehead play. I can go from deep shit to high glory overnight, then back to the crapper before lunch. But that's *my* job. *Yours* is to catch bad guys. So stop asking about the politics and start clearing cases."

"That's why we're here," I said. "We need your approval to put Troy Marschand and Dylan Freemont on round-the-clock surveillance."

"And who are they?"

"Marschand was Aubrey Davenport's assistant. Mr. Freemont is his fiancé."

"What do you have on them?"

"Nothing yet," I said. "Marschand has been very helpful. If you remember, Aubrey Davenport's computer was missing, and he's the one who retrieved her files from—"

Cates held up a hand. "I remember the missing computer all too well, Jordan. Catch the blackmailer; find the computer. We all know how that worked out. Get to the part where you explain why you want to tail these two men."

"The day we met Troy Marschand he told us that Aubrey was obsessed with two things: sex and filmmaking. When he retrieved her files from the cloud, we figured there'd be dozens of explicit videos, but it was all vanilla. Naked selfies between her and Janek don't exactly qualify as an obsession with sex and filmmaking."

"What about Aubrey's romp with the judge?" Cates said. "I'd say that qualifies."

"Yes, ma'am, but we got that video from Q. There were no sex films in any of the files Marschand gave us."

Cates sat back in her chair, and I could see the realization spread across her face. "Then how did Mr. Marschand even know that these dirty movies existed?" she said.

"That's the lightbulb that just went off in our heads. We think Marschand and Freemont got hold of Aubrey's computer and decided to go into the blackmail business."

"They could be a lot more than blackmailers," Cates said. "Do they have an alibi for the night of the murder?"

I responded with half a shrug. "We…um…we never asked."

"Why the hell not?"

"Captain, you saw the photos from Roosevelt Island," Kylie said, jumping in. "It was a sex crime. Chuck Dryden, who almost never goes out on a limb without hard evidence, said that the killer was 'most likely a man.' I guess we made the natural logic leap to heterosexual man."

"So you profiled them," Cates said, "and you decided that being gay was an alibi."

"Not our finest moment," Kylie said. "But in our defense, it was the end of a grueling night that started out with a bomb blast and went downhill from there."

"If you're right," Cates said, "and the blackmail scheme was a crime of opportunity, then it makes sense that Marschand and Freemont are the opportunists who pulled it off. They've already had one major score, and since the judge probably isn't the only one caught on camera with his pants down, they'll probably go after the other potential blackmail targets next."

"Yes, ma'am," Kylie said. "So can you approve a budget to tail them?"

"I'll pay for the manpower," Cates said. "But it doesn't warrant round-the-clock. One team, twelve hours a day. And when the ransom demands come in, don't ask me for another nickel. After what went down this morning, if you told me the perp was in Jersey, I wouldn't pay your tolls for the trip over the George Washington Bridge."

CHAPTER 37

AS SOON AS Kylie and I broke the news to Corcoran and Fischer that they were the designated hitters to shadow the two suspects in the drone heist, we were able to pick up where we'd left off after our predawn meeting with Malique La Grande.

Thirty minutes later, we walked into the lobby of a forty-story green glass tower on Maiden Lane in the financial district.

"You know what I hate about this job?" Kylie asked as we stepped into an elevator.

"I'm sure you've got a list," I said. "But since we're only going to the twelfth floor, how about you just give me your bitch du jour?"

"Ass-kissing," she said as soon as the elevator door closed.

"Can you elaborate?"

"Nathan Hirsch came to us with his big confession about running drugs for Zoe Pound, but he left out the most important part," she said. "I mean, why tell us the whole truth when all he wanted us to do was arrest Malique?"

"The guy is a slimeball with a wife and kids in Queens and a hooker on call in Jersey," I said. "Are you surprised that he *lied* to you?"

"No. They all lie, Zach. But if Hirsch were a run-of-the-mill asshole, we'd drag him into an interview room and scare the crap out of him. But since he's a privileged asshole, we're heading upstairs to his office, and we've got to smile politely, pucker up, and kiss his butt while he keeps lying to us."

"I believe you just summed up the mission statement of our unit," I said. "To protect and serve the privileged assholes."

"Thanks for reminding me," she said. "I'll give it a shot. Let me do the talking."

The elevator door opened on twelve. There were five names on the wall, one of which was Hirsch's.

We went through the standard meet and greet with the receptionist. No, we didn't have an appointment, but tell Mr. Hirsch that Detectives Jordan and MacDonald are here, and we're sure he'll find the time.

In less than a minute, we were sitting in Hirsch's office, where the familiar aroma of cigar smoke and flop sweat permeated the air.

"Did you arrest La Grande?" he asked.

"He said he didn't do it," Kylie said.

"There's a shocker," Hirsch said. "A drug dealer who lies to the cops."

"Was he lying about Geraldo Segura?" she snapped, neither smiling nor puckering up.

"Is that why you're here?" he said, raising his voice. "La Grande told you about Segura, and I didn't, so you've come to the erroneous conclusion that I have something to hide."

"Do you?"

"No. But the fact that Segura is in prison is irrelevant."

"Not to us," Kylie said. "According to La Grande, Segura was innocent. You brought him along to take the fall if the drug run went south."

"*I* brought him along?" Hirsch said, his fists clenched, his face turning red. "The entire operation, start to finish, was Princeton's. He set up the deal with Dingo, he provided the plane, and the rest of us didn't even know Segura was coming along for the ride until he showed up at the hangar. I was a kid, I was stoned half the time, and if Segura was set up to take the fall, blame Princeton Wells. He was the mastermind."

"And what if Segura doesn't know that?" she said.

"What do you mean?"

"What if he blames all four of you? Wouldn't that make him a prime suspect?"

"No. It makes him someone who might *want* to kill us, not someone who can actually pull off the bombings. In case you forgot, Detective, Geraldo Segura is serving fifty years in a prison in Thailand."

"You know who else is doing time in a prison in Thailand?" Kylie said. "The man who designed the bombs that killed Del Fairfax and Arnie Zimmer."

Hirsch sat there, mouth open, head cocked, eyes squinting. "What...what do you mean?"

"Bombs have signatures," she said. "The ones that killed your partners are the handiwork of a man named Flynn Samuels, who is also locked up in Thailand, and who may have taught Segura the tricks of his trade."

Hirsch's pasty-white face turned an even ghostlier shade of pale. "But...but Geraldo is in *prison*."

"That might slow him down, but it won't stop him.

If Geraldo Segura has the motive *and* the method, the only thing he would need to *actually pull off the bombings* is an accomplice in New York."

"Like who?"

"We don't think his grandmother infiltrated The Pierre hotel, but you'd be amazed at the kind of free-lance talent that's available for the right price."

"Segura is dirt-poor, and his family…" Hirsch stopped. "Oh my God."

"What?"

"Silver Bullet has been sending the grandmother money. It was Princeton's idea. He told her it was a privilege to be able to help Geraldo's family, but in reality, it's just blood money."

"How much?"

"Fifty thousand a year…for the past twenty years."

"So let's see," Kylie said. "Fifty thousand times twenty—wow, you better hope that Granny isn't the vindictive type. Because a million dollars would buy her a hell of a lot of firepower." She nodded to me. "Let's go, Zach."

"Wait!" Hirsch said. "What do I do?"

Kylie handed him her business card. "Call us if you think of something. We can't help if we don't know what's going on."

She turned, and the two of us left his office and walked to the elevator.

"So how'd I do?" she said.

"A refresher course in sensitivity training couldn't hurt," I said, "but one thing's for sure: Nathan Hirsch is never going to lie to you again."

CHAPTER 38

EVEN WITH LIGHT traffic on the FDR Drive it took us more than half an hour to get to Princeton Wells's mansion on Central Park West.

"You realize he knows we're coming," Kylie said. "Hirsch probably called him the minute we left, so he's had more than enough time to rehearse his answers."

"Since when do people need time to rehearse the truth?" I said, ringing the front doorbell.

"Since when have any of these people been remotely truthful?"

I could see that Wells had a change in attitude as soon as he opened the door. The preppy billionaire was wearing jeans, a faded work shirt, a perfectly wrinkled hunter-green cashmere V-neck sweater, and bright red Nikes. But not a trace of a smile.

"I spoke to Nathan," he grumbled, leading us up the stairs to his office. "He's out of his mind."

"Understandable," I said. "He's afraid he's next on the killer's hit list."

"I didn't say he's out of his mind with *fear*," Wells snapped. "I'm saying the man is out of his fucking mind. What was he thinking, sending you off to accuse Malique La Grande of those murders?"

"You don't think Malique is responsible?"

We entered Wells's office. "No," he said, slamming the door shut. "I have no doubt that if Malique were in charge twenty years ago, he'd have killed us all. Luckily for us, Dingo called the shots. But I knew Dingo wouldn't be around forever, so I reached out to Malique—quietly, privately—and over time we reached a peaceful accord. A détente, if you will."

"So are we talking about a handshake agreement here?" Kylie asked.

Wells finally cracked a faint smile. "I didn't so much shake his hand as grease his palm. Regularly."

"You pay him not to kill you."

"It's basic street economics—the same as the local pizza parlor paying the mob for protection. It was an insurance policy in case Malique ever got to be the boss."

"And now that he is, do you think he kept his word?" I asked.

"Yes. I don't think he killed Arnie or Del, but now that Nathan has gone and sicced the cops on him, I hope he doesn't go off the deep end and kill us for lack of respect. The Zoes are bad to the bone. They don't *resolve* problems. They *eliminate* them. Malique's son killed a total stranger in a bar just for looking at him funny."

"Tell us about your friend Geraldo Segura," Kylie said.

"Friend," Wells said, spitting out the word. "More like a hustler, but none of us knew it at the time. He was the scrappy little scholarship kid from El Barrio, and we were the hot shit Upper East Side rich kids. You'd think that he'd idolize us—that he'd want

what we had—but that's not the way it played out. It wasn't long before we all wanted to be him."

"What do you mean?"

"When you're nineteen, being rich and white with your future all planned out for you is like a death sentence. Geraldo lived on the edge. He was a street fighter, fast on his feet, and even faster with his fists. The girls loved him. When he was fifteen he was banging this eighteen-year-old, and her two brothers jumped him. They both wound up eating breakfast, lunch, and dinner through a straw for the better part of a year."

"And you wanted to be him?" I said.

He nodded. "I'm guessing you were never a big fan of gangsta rap, were you, Detective?"

"Not my kind of music," I said.

"It was mine—N.W.A., Tupac, Wu-Tang. It's about struggling against life in the ghetto, and I identified. Geraldo and I just came from different ghettos."

"Tell us about the drug run for Dingo Slide," I said.

"We were coming up on Christmas break. I told Geraldo we were going to Bangkok on my father's plane and asked if he wanted to come along. He said no. I said we're gonna get drunk, we're gonna get stoned, we're gonna get laid, and he said, 'Me too, and I don't have to go halfway around the world to do it.' The next day, he went from no to maybe. He knew Dingo was our dealer, and he told us he knew how we could get three, four months' supply of coke free. All we had to do was bring back a small package from Thailand."

"And you knew what was in the package."

"Hell, yeah. That's what made it exciting. I wouldn't pick up somebody's laundry for free cocaine.

But smuggling heroin from Thailand? Do you have any idea what kind of a rush that was?"

"Malique said you're the one who cut the deal with Dingo."

"Dingo knew me. I was a good customer. I guess he trusted me as much as any Haitian drug lord can trust a rich white kid. It was all Geraldo's idea, but I got to be the front man. I loved it."

"How come he's in prison, and you're not?"

"My father paid the Thais a fortune to let us go. But they would only release four of us. They needed someone to stay behind. It's their perverted way of showing their justice system works. The last thing I did before I left Geraldo was make a promise that we'd take care of his family. We have."

"Did Nathan Hirsch tell you that Segura may have crossed paths with the man who designed the bombs?"

"Yes, but Nathan is an idiot if he thinks Geraldo's *abuela* is funding these bombings."

"Can you think of anyone here in the States who might be acting on his behalf?"

"No, but I'm not the right person to ask."

"Who is?"

"Geraldo Segura."

"That's impossible."

"Bullshit. Two of my partners are dead, and I'm starting to believe Nathan that he and I are next on the list. So do me a favor: get your glorified supercop asses on the next plane to Bangkok, and keep that from happening."

"I don't know what that would cost," I said, "but I'm pretty sure the department isn't going to shell out the kind of money it would take to fly us to Thailand."

"You never know till you ask, Detective."

"I wouldn't even know who to ask."

"Then we're in luck," Wells said. "Because as it turns out, I do."

CHAPTER 39

I WAS BACK in the office when my cell phone rang. The caller ID said Silvercup Studios. I picked up.

"Zach, it's Bob Reitzfeld. How's your day going so far?"

I looked at my watch. It was 3:00 p.m. "Let's see: I've been at it for twelve hours, and so far I've had to suck up to a Haitian drug lord in the back room of a supermarket in Brooklyn, been chewed out by a billionaire, lied to by a lawyer, and wait...I know there is one more thing. Oh yeah: despite the fact that I had a six-man backup team, I managed to lose a hundred thousand dollars of the DA's money. On the plus side, I got to spend some time on the High Line. It's quite spectacular. I'm hoping next weekend I can go back there with Cheryl. And how's your day going, Bob?"

"I need your help."

"Why? Did someone zip-tie you to another water pipe?"

"I think I know who hired those two lowlifes who pulled off the poker game robbery."

I inhaled sharply. "Hold on a minute."

Kylie had gone to the break room for coffee, but

she'd be back any second, and this wasn't a phone call I wanted to have with her sitting at the next desk. I took the stairs up to the fourth floor, found an empty interview room, and shut the door.

"Bob, I'm sorry if I sounded like a jerk. It's what happens when you ask an overworked cop how his day is going. Who do you like for the robbery?"

"Is Kylie within earshot? I don't want her to pick up on your reaction."

"No, we're good. I'm alone."

"I'm pretty sure it's her boyfriend who planned the whole operation. His name is C. J. Berringer. Do you remember meeting him the other night?"

Did I remember meeting him? I'd dug deep into Clyde Jerome Berringer's past, hoping to find something I could use against him, but since Reitzfeld had told me to mind my own business, I couldn't admit to him how much I knew. "Yeah, I met C.J.," I said. "Tall guy, professional poker player—what makes you think it's him?"

"Because it's clearly an inside job. At first I thought it might be someone connected to the hotel—a desk clerk, someone from room service, a bellman—but I interviewed anyone and everyone at the Mark who knew about the game, and they all come up clean. So I decided to focus on the people in the room."

"Uh-huh," I said, leaving out the fact that I'd gone down the exact same road two nights ago. "And how did you land on Berringer?"

"Zach, the man sticks out like a boner in a Speedo," Reitzfeld said. "Everyone else is a regular— same faces month after month, year after year. This Berringer character starts dating Kylie, gets her to introduce him to Shelley, plays twice, which is all it takes to get the routine down pat, and bingo—

the third time he's in the room, the game gets hit by a couple of bozos who couldn't organize a two-car funeral if you spotted them a hearse and six pallbearers."

"Can you prove anything?"

"Probably—if Shelley would let me."

"What do you mean *if*?"

"When I told him I thought Berringer could be the brains behind the hit, he told me to back off. I love the old man, but he just doesn't think like a cop."

"That's why he made you head of security at Silvercup Studios."

"It's a great title, Zach—very impressive on my business card. I've never seen Shelley's business card, but it should say *Control Freak*. He doesn't want me to follow up on C.J. because he doesn't want Kylie to get hurt. He says her husband has caused her enough pain, and he would rather protect her than recover eight hundred thousand dollars."

"That's insane," I said. "I know Kylie: if her boyfriend is guilty, she'd want you to nail him."

"That's why I'm calling you. You're her partner. Shelley won't listen to me, but he'll listen to you."

"I'm not so sure."

"It can't hurt to ask him."

"Yes it can. If I tell him to go after Berringer, and he says no, I can't then turn around and do it anyway. But if I don't say anything…"

"Don't ask permission; ask forgiveness," Reitzfeld said. "But you'd have to investigate on your own. Do you mind?"

Did I mind proving Kylie's latest was a crook? I grinned. "I can deal with it. Give me a few days."

"Thanks. So tell me about losing the DA's hundred thousand dollars."

"How about I tell you over a beer at my retirement party, which will be coming around a lot sooner than I planned if I don't find the money?"

He hung up, and I sat there, staring at my phone. I was planning my next move when a text message popped up on the screen. It was from Kylie.

Where R U?

I tapped out an answer.

I was meditating. Thanks for harshing my zen.

She texted back.

Your zen can wait. Cates wants us.

I let her know I was on my way, then hit Q's number on my speed dial.

He answered on the first ring. "Detective Jordan," he said. "Rumor has it that you and Judge Rafferty had quite a costly adventure on the High Line."

"The good news is His Honor no longer thinks you're blackmailing him."

"For which you have my undying gratitude," Q replied. "If you ever need any—"

"Forget 'If you ever.' I'm collecting now." I filled him in on the poker game robbery that went down at the Mark.

"So you want me to be on the lookout for two gentlemen of dubious earning power who are spending money like a couple of scratch-off winners."

"Yes," I said. "And Q…this one is between me, you, and nobody else."

"Please, Detective," he said. "You know my

reputation. I'm as discreet as a whisper in a windstorm."

"And you know my partner," I said. "If she finds out, I'll be as dead as a flounder in a frying pan."

I hung up and headed for my meeting with Cates. As I double-timed down the stairs, I realized I was smiling. I know it's not healthy, but for me, there's something gratifying about proving to the woman who dumped me for another man that once again, she'd made the wrong choice.

CHAPTER 40

"UH-OH," KYLIE said as the two of us walked down the hall to Cates's office.

Her door was shut, the privacy blinds on the glass wall were down, and there were two large men standing directly outside her office. I knew them well: Mayor Sykes's bodyguards.

"Well if it isn't Cagney and Lacey," Kylie said, never missing an opportunity to bust balls. "Glad to see that the taxpayers were smart enough to pay *two* of you to protect the mayor from the evils that lurk in the halls of an Upper East Side police precinct."

"Ah, the ever delightful Detective MacDonald," the larger of the two large men said, putting his hand on the doorknob. "Let's see if you're still smiling when you come back out." He held the door open, and Kylie and I went in.

Cates was behind her desk. Sykes was sitting across from her. "He's taking hostages," the mayor said as soon as the door closed behind us.

"Ma'am?" I said. "Who's taking hostages?"

"Princeton Wells. The Silver Bullet Foundation was supposed to break ground on Tremont Gardens next month." In case we hadn't been paying attention to the speeches on the night of the hotel bombing, she added, "It's the city's permanent housing project for homeless people that Del Fairfax designed. But Wells is putting it on hold until the person or persons responsible for the deaths of his two partners are brought to justice."

"That's emotional blackmail," Kylie said.

"But that's how billionaires work the system, Detective."

"Madam Mayor, we're doing everything we can."

"Not according to Wells. He told me the whole story of this drug deal he and his cohorts got caught up in when they were kids—"

"Excuse me, ma'am," Kylie said, "but he probably only gave you *his* account of the whole story. There are other versions."

"Don't waste my time asking if I believe a drug dealer or a philanthropist," Sykes said. "All I know is that the bomb maker is in a prison in Thailand, and this Geraldo Segura, who has a deep-seated grudge against Wells and the others, is also incarcerated in Thailand. Captain Cates has just confirmed that."

"But we don't know if the two men ever met," Kylie said.

"Mr. Wells refuses to wait for the Thai government to be forthcoming with that information. He tells me he suggested that the two of you fly to Thailand and find out for yourselves. Your response was that the city would never pay your travel expenses."

"Not the *city*," Kylie said. "The department."

"MacDonald," Cates said, "stop talking and start listening."

"Captain," Kylie said, "after what happened this morning on the High Line, we were under the impression that the department wouldn't pay for—"

Cates stood up. "Stop. Talking. Now."

"Thank you, Delia," the mayor said. She turned to the two of us. "First, I assured Mr. Wells that this administration would go to the ends of the earth to hunt down the people who murdered two of our city's most generous benefactors, and that cost was definitely not a factor.

"He then pointed out to me that he knows exactly how our system works. You can't just jump on a plane to Bangkok without jumping through a lot of bureaucratic hoops. It would take days for the pencil pushers and the number crunchers to approve your travel expenses. I told him I could cut through a lot of that red tape with one phone call to the police commissioner, and that you'd be on your way within twenty-four hours. He laughed and said he could cut through *all* of the red tape and have you wheels up by seven thirty tonight."

"Ma'am," Kylie said, "Wells talks a good game, but how is that even possible?"

"Anything is possible when you own a fleet of corporate jets. Wells will have a plane and a flight crew waiting for you at Teterboro."

"Isn't that…" Kylie stopped herself.

"Isn't that what?" Sykes asked.

"Nothing, ma'am. It's not important."

"It's important to me, because once you get on that plane, I want you to have no other concerns besides tracking down Geraldo Segura. Now ask the question."

"Zach and I are city employees. Aren't we bound by the law that prohibits us from accepting gifts for anything valued over seventy-five dollars?"

"Yes. But as mayor of this city, I can issue an

executive order waiving that law due to the dire emergency of the situation. Any more questions?"

"No, ma'am."

"Then dust off your passports and pack your bags, because in three hours the two of you are leaving for Thailand."

CHAPTER 41

I WENT STRAIGHT to Cheryl's office. "Something came up," I said.

"Judging by the hangdog look on your face, I'm guessing it's something that's going to screw up our dinner reservations at Paola's."

"Sorry. I have to cancel."

"I've been looking forward to her *carciofi alla giudea* all day, so you better have a good reason for bailing on me."

"Kylie and I are going to Thailand."

She laughed. "No, seriously."

"I'm not kidding. We're leaving tonight."

"Tonight?"

"The Silver Bullet bombings. All roads lead to Thailand."

"Oh, Zach," she said, picking up her cell. "What's your flight number? At least I can follow you on FlightView."

"Actually," I said, knowing that there was no way to sugarcoat what I was about to say, "we're not going commercial. We're flying out of Teterboro on Princeton Wells's corporate jet."

"You, Kylie, and Wells?"

"I doubt if Wells is going to go to Thailand. Ever. I think he only flies into countries he knows he can fly out of."

"So it's just you and Kylie on a private plane."

"And the crew," I added lamely.

"Do you realize that as a city employee it's against the law for you to accept—"

"I know, I know. It's a long story. I don't have time to give you the details. My flight leaves at seven thirty. I've got to go home and pack." I put my arms around her. "I just came to say good-bye."

"Not here," she said, backing off. "Let's go. I'll help you pack."

She grabbed her purse, and I followed her out of the office.

My apartment was a short cab ride away, but four thirty in the afternoon is not the best time for finding a taxi, so we snagged a ride uptown with a couple of uniforms. It was fast and cheap, but it's impossible to have a personal conversation when you're riding with two chatty cops in a squad car.

I waited till we got in the elevator. "Look, Cheryl, I know this sucks. I'm really sorry."

"For what? You didn't do anything wrong."

"No, but Kylie and I are going to be flying God knows how many hours on this luxury airplane, and…"

"So, then, is this another one of your famous prophylactic apologies? Or are you just projecting that I'm jealous?"

"None of the above, but—" The elevator stopped on the tenth floor, and we got out.

"But what?"

"*Are* you jealous?"

"Zach, you're a cop. Kylie is your partner. You

spend sixty hours a week with her in the same office, the same car, on stakeouts together, eating meals together—it's what you do. So what's the difference if you do it on a private plane? What's the difference if you do it eight thousand miles and eleven time zones away in an exotic country with gorgeous beaches, exciting nightlife, and luxurious hotels? Why would I be jealous? If I trust you here, I trust you there."

I wasn't a hundred percent sure I could wade through the subtext, so I took the high road. I said nothing. I unlocked my door, and we entered the apartment.

As soon as we were inside, Cheryl grabbed me, pressed me against the wall, and kissed me hard. "You realize I'm not here to help you pack, don't you?" she said, pulling her sweater over her head and dragging me toward the bedroom.

"Packing is highly overrated," I said, shucking my clothes along the way, my libido kicking into overdrive.

One of the things I love about my sex life with Cheryl is that she has never once been hesitant to let me know what she needs. There are times when our lovemaking is practically puritanical—sweet, slow, gentle. Skin to skin, heart to heart, soul to soul.

This was not one of those times. This was raw sex. Frenzied, loud, primal. I doubt if we lasted more than ten minutes, but they were ten of the most incredible minutes of my adult life.

I lay there on my bed, wrapped in her arms, completely spent, deliriously happy. "That," I said, still breathing heavily, "was the best going-away present I ever got."

"Wait till you see the welcome-home present I have planned for you," she whispered, her tongue teasing my ear, her fingertips making small circles against my nipple.

I felt myself stirring. "You keep that up, and I may not wait till I get back home to collect."

She kept it up. I collected.

This time the sex was unhurried, sensuous, tender, each of us caught up in the act of making love, neither of us racing to the finish line.

"You're getting pretty good at this," she said as we curled up for the second time.

"Thanks. I'd be even better if I'd had any sleep last night. I've been up since three."

"Don't worry. You'll sleep on the plane."

"I hope so. I don't sleep well on airplanes."

"You'll sleep like a log on this one." She pressed her body closer to mine, and I could feel her warm breath on my ear. "Trust me," she said. "I'm a doctor."

CHAPTER 42

PRINCETON WELLS THOUGHT of everything. At five thirty I got a call from a man named Matéo, who asked me what I'd care to eat en route.

"I'm easy," I said. "Whatever you've got on the plane."

"At the moment the cupboard is bare, but I'm about to call our in-flight catering service," he said. "They feed some of the world's most demanding clientele, so please tell me what foods you enjoy, and they will be on board."

I gave him a few of my favorites.

"Is that all?" He sounded disappointed.

"I'm sure my traveling companion will give you a much more challenging shopping list," I said.

"She already has," he said. "A car will pick you up shortly. I'll meet you on the tarmac."

The *car* turned out to be a custom-built stretch Bentley complete with the obligatory bar in the back. Kylie had already popped the cork on a cold bottle of champagne, and a crystal flute of golden bubbly was waiting for me as soon as I got in.

"To police work," she said, raising her glass in a toast. "Somebody's got to do it."

Traffic was heavy, and we arrived at the airport in Teterboro, New Jersey, about fifteen minutes before flight time. A no-no in real life, but perfectly acceptable when your limo pulls up to the nose of your Gulfstream G650.

Matéo gave us a grand tour of the aircraft. I'd been on corporate jets before. Comfortable reclining leather seats, highly efficient tables that can be adjusted for work or for meals, a well-stocked bar, and a number of available options for in-flight entertainment. Very corporate chic.

This was not that. This was Princeton Wells's fantasy bachelor pad with wings—decadence on a grand scale, high in the sky at six hundred miles an hour. The main cabin was a sumptuous living and dining area with some of the same decorating influences I remembered from Wells's apartment in The Pierre. At the rear of the plane, hidden from sight by a sweeping frosted-glass bulkhead, was a large master bedroom with a king-size bed, and behind that a spacious bathroom with polished marble countertops, a heated floor, and a shower big enough for two.

"What do you think?" Matéo asked.

"Mind-boggling," I said.

Kylie shrugged. "It'll do."

I could see in his eyes that Matéo, like men everywhere, was dazzled by her.

"Your flight will be approximately seventeen hours," he said. "We have three pilots on board. Captain Dan Fennessy is in command. Normally there would be only two in the cockpit, and a second team would be flown commercially to relieve them when we set down to refuel. But Mr. Wells pulled this together in such a hurry that there was no time to get a relief crew in place."

"Pretty sloppy way to run an airline," Kylie said.

"I'll make a note to management," Matéo said, half smiling, half drooling. "Can I get you anything to drink before takeoff?"

"A glass of water," I said, clearly disappointing him again.

"I'll stick with champagne," Kylie said.

We sat down, buckled up, and Matéo brought our drinks.

"Water?" Kylie said to me. "You're an embarrassment to freeloading cops everywhere."

Cheryl had given me an Ambien, and I popped it.

Five minutes later, we were airborne, and Matéo invited us to make ourselves comfortable in the main cabin, where he'd set out platters of cheese, caviar, and seafood.

"This looks great," I said, "but I could use a before-dinner nap. Do you mind if I stretch out back there?"

"This is your airplane, Detective Jordan," he said. "Think of it as a hotel at fifty-one thousand feet. There are fresh linens on the bed, and there's an assortment of nightwear in the closet."

"Zach, you are no fun at all," Kylie said, spooning caviar onto a toast point.

"Wake me in half an hour," I said. "I promise to be more fun then."

I went to the bedroom and found a supply of men's silk pajamas, all black. I changed, donned an eye mask and a pair of Bose noise-canceling headphones, and crawled into bed under a thick comforter.

People actually live like this, I thought as I drifted off. The next thing I knew, I was jolted awake. It took a few seconds to remember that I was on an airplane, and I figured that the bump I'd felt was turbulence. I took off the headphones, and I could hear the hum of the tires on a runway. We'd landed. I had no idea where or why.

I peeled off my eye mask and got hit by a second jolt. There was a body, also wearing black silk pajamas, lying next to me in bed. Kylie.

She put her hand to her head. "I think I drank too much."

There was a knock on the glass bulkhead, and Matéo called our names.

Kylie muttered something that sounded like an invitation for him to come in. He did.

"Good morning, Detectives," he said. "Welcome to Helsinki. Can I start you off with some coffee and fresh-baked *korvapuustit?*"

I didn't answer. I was still staring at the woman in my bed.

CHAPTER 43

"GIVE US A few minutes, Matéo," Kylie said.

Without a word, he backed away and eased the door shut with all the grace of an English butler who knows that what happens in the master bedroom stays in the master bedroom.

Kylie sat up, leaned back against the headboard, and drilled her eyes into mine. "And what are you staring at, Papa Bear? Goldilocks is sleeping in your bed? Is that a problem?"

Of course it was a problem. But not one I wanted to discuss with Kylie. "No," I said. "More like a surprise."

"What was your last partner's name?" she asked. "Shanks, right?"

"Omar Shanks."

"So if you were making this trip with Omar, and you rolled over and saw him asleep next to you, would you give him that same what-the-hell-are-you-doing-in-my-bed look?"

"It depends. Did Omar and I bang our brains out when we were in the academy together? Because if we did, I might give him a weird look if he suddenly hopped back into the sack with me twelve years later."

"Oh please, Zach. Get over yourself. Don't dredge up what happened a lifetime ago. Plus I didn't exactly *hop* into your bed—excuse me—*the* bed, the *only* bed, which technically makes it *our* bed. I tried to wake you after a half hour, then I gave you another half hour, but you were lying there like a dead mackerel. So I had dinner and more wine than I should have, and I crashed. Remember, you're not the only sleep-deprived cop on this airplane."

And just like that, I'd been sucked into the exact high school, soap opera dialogue I'd wanted to avoid. I knew Kylie. She never met an argument she didn't like to win. And now, here we were once again, all cozy in bed, tempers flaring, passions rising, and if I'd learned anything during our torrid affair, it was that this wasn't a fight. It was foreplay.

Sex with Kylie had always been a twelve on a scale of one to ten. But some times were better than others. One was mornings. Especially if she woke up with her hair tousled, her eyes at half-mast, looking like a drop-dead gorgeous lost waif who'd wandered into my bed during the night. Our other best time was make-up sex. This was starting to feel a lot like both.

The black silk pajamas clung to her in all the right places, but she'd left the top three buttons open, and despite the fact that I knew every inch of her naked body, undressing her with my eyes was driving me crazy.

I was completely turned on.

If I were in New York, I'd have gone running to Gerri Gomperts at the diner, but I was a continent away from my quasi therapist. I was on my own, and

I might not have handled the situation all that well so far, but I knew the exact right thing to do now. *Stop eyeballing your ex-girlfriend's awesome cleavage and get the hell out of bed before you do something you'll regret.*

I swung my legs over the side. "You know what?" I said. "This is dumb. Sorry if I stared at you funny. Feel free to crash in *our* bed whenever you want. I'm going to take a shower."

I stood up and headed straight for the lav.

"Don't forget to lock the door, Sugar Pants," she chirped.

I didn't respond. Letting her have the last word—and the last laugh—was the best way to convince her she'd won.

I turned on the shower and stepped under the hot water. I would also need a blast of cold before I stepped out, but at least the moment had passed.

I dressed, then checked my cell phone. It was the middle of the night in New York, but Cheryl had texted me before she went to bed.

Hope you slept well. Love you.

I texted back, thanking her for the Ambien and all the other contributions she'd made toward tiring me out, but I left out the part about waking up with my ex-girlfriend curled up next to me.

Kylie was in the main cabin enjoying the breakfast feast Matéo had laid out. "Sink your teeth into this," she said, handing me a warm cinnamon roll. "And check out the DVD collection. We could fly around the world ten times and not run out of movies." She winked. "It'd be a lot of fun—assuming we could work out the sleeping arrangements."

It was classic Kylie. Always happy to get in one more dig. Knowing her, it wouldn't be the last.

Our pit stop was fast and efficient. We left Helsinki at 9:15 a.m. and flew through half a dozen time zones. It was the shortest day I'd ever experienced and one of the most relaxing. Kylie and I watched movies, catnapped in our respective seats, and ate like royalty.

We touched down at Suvarnabhumi Airport shortly after midnight. A black Lincoln with an American flag mounted on the fender was parked on the tarmac. A tall young man in jeans bounded toward us. "David Hinds, U.S. Embassy," he said. "Welcome to Bangkok."

He whipped us through customs and immigration, and within minutes we were on the road to our hotel.

"When do we get to interview Segura and Samuels?" I asked.

"Who?"

"We're here to meet with two prisoners. When do we get to see them?"

"Sorry, Detective, but I don't know anything about that. I work in the mushroom division of the embassy. They keep us in the dark and shovel shit on us. All I know is that tomorrow you're scheduled to meet with Pongrit Juntasa, head of the Department of Corruption."

"The what?"

"Department of *Corrections*. That was embassy humor. You'll be his honored guests at the Muay Thai matches."

"That's lovely," Kylie said, "but we didn't come here to watch boxing."

"Muay Thai is not *boxing*. It's an ancient fighting

style known as the art of eight limbs—fighters use their fists, feet, elbows, and knees. It's practically a religion in this country."

"David, tell Mr. Juntasa we're flattered by the invitation," Kylie said, "but we're here on a homicide investigation."

"Detective, did anyone teach you anything about Thai culture before you got on that airplane?" Hinds said.

"You mean like remove your shoes before entering someone's house or don't sunbathe in the nude?"

Hinds laughed. "You are *so* New York," he said. "But that won't cut it in Bangkok. Thais don't do business—wham, bam—on the first date. They have to get to know you. He's aware of why you're here. Just don't jump into it until you've spent quality time together."

Kylie rolled her eyes. "Define *quality*."

"Small talk, some laughs, break bread, and, most important, be seen together. Pongrit Juntasa is a high-ranking government official who wants everyone to know that two *esteemed* New York City police officers flew halfway around the world to bask in his aura. To put it in diplomatic terms: the more you kiss his ass, the more likely you are to get his blessing to meet your prisoners."

Kylie shook her head and looked at me. "Zach, you know what I hate about this job?"

"Ass-kissing," I said. "But on the plus side, you're getting very good at it."

CHAPTER 44

WE CHECKED INTO the Plaza Athénée Bangkok at two in the morning. Separate rooms. By the time David Hinds picked us up at 4:00 p.m., my body clock felt like it was ticking on Bangkok time.

"Sorry about the wheels," he said, opening the back door to a red Toyota Yaris. "This is my roommate's car. The embassy Lincoln is in the shop."

"If you're going to work for the State Department," Kylie said, getting in the front seat and relegating me to the back, "you've got to learn how to lie better."

I could see the panic in the kid's eyes. "Ma'am?"

"Don't *ma'am* me like you don't know what I'm talking about. You're low man on the totem pole, David, so I get why you were the one stuck picking us up at the airport at midnight. But it's a bright new day; we're meeting with some Thai honcho, and not only is there nobody here resembling a career diplomat, but now there's no embassy car. And it's not *in the shop*. What's going on?"

Hinds got behind the wheel and started driving. He cleared his throat. "Gambling is illegal in Thailand."

"Cut the bullshit and get to the point," Kylie said,

"or I'll dump you on the side of the road and leave your roommate's car in downtown Bangkok with the doors open and the motor running."

"The embassy fucked up," Hinds said. "They thought Juntasa was taking you to a sanctioned Muay Thai match in an arena, or even in the prison. But we just found out the fights are in the Khlong Toei district."

"Bad neighborhood?" Kylie said, poking at him.

"The fights are in a shithole gym in a back alley in shantytown. It's an illegal gambling operation run by the Thai Mafia, and the First Secretary doesn't want anyone from the embassy near it—including our car."

"But they don't mind sending you."

"I'm a peon driving his roommate's Yaris. Besides, I know my way around there."

"You're a *fan* of the sport?" Kylie asked.

"You mean do I like being invited to Lumpinee Stadium and watching two *nak muays* bow, and scrape, and pray, and do ritualistic dances around the ring, while my host recounts the legend of Nai Khanom Tom, the father of Muay Thai? I did it once, and once was enough.

"But I'm an action junkie. Where I'm taking you today—that shit is raw, brutal, but they draw the best boxers in the world. The matches are all fixed. The judges are bribed. The fighters are doped up, and some of the wannabes will get in the ring with anyone. I watched a young kid get beat to a pulp by a seasoned pro with twenty pounds on him. And the crowd—they're insane: drinking, screaming for blood, and betting on every punch, every foot thrust, every knee strike. Money is flying everywhere. One night I walked away winning twenty-seven thousand baht, which is like seven hundred and fifty dollars."

"How'd you make out on all the other nights?" Kylie asked.

He laughed. "The only ones guaranteed to make money are the promoters, and I'll give you one guess who runs the operation in Khlong Toei."

"Pongrit Juntasa from the Department of Corruption," I said.

"Oh, so close, but no cigar. Juntasa is the puppet master, but his sister Buppha runs the ring."

"A woman?"

"More like a world-class hustler. She weighs about ninety pounds, and she's the most dangerous person in the room. You still want to go?"

"More than ever," Kylie said.

We drove through slums, past a slaughterhouse, and then through winding, fender-scraping streets dotted with tiny shops that were shuttered or hidden behind rolling corrugated metal doors.

"And here it is," Hinds said after twenty minutes. "The no-name gym."

Technically it had a name. There was a sign over the door, but with most of the letters shot out, No-Name Gym would have to do.

One of Juntasa's men led the three of us into a smoke-filled cavern thick with the musky smell of sweat and testosterone. Nobody noticed us. There was a fight going on. The spectators, almost all men in work clothes, were in a frenzy, some screaming at the two fighters in the ring, some waving fists full of paper money at anyone who would take their bet.

There were about twenty tables at the front of the room, and men in white shirts weaved adeptly through the melee of fans, carrying trays of drinks to those privileged patrons who could afford seats and waiter service.

The bell clanged, signaling the end of a round, and our escort delivered us to our host, who was sitting at a primo ringside table.

I've met my share of corrupt government officials. They tend to be a smarmy lot, and Pongrit Juntasa lived up to type. Even as he extended a hand to welcome us, his body language cried out "Dangerous. Not to be trusted."

"You are just in time," he said. "The boy in the red trunks is Kob Sook Meesang, my protégé. He is fighting for his freedom."

"I'm not sure I understand," I said.

"He killed a man who raped his sister. A noble act, but foolish. He is in prison for forty years. But as a Muay Thai fighter, he can bring honor and glory to his country. In exchange, we will reduce his sentence."

"By how much?" Kylie asked.

"Today I have promised him six months off for every fight he wins. So far he has won three."

"And now he's fighting his *fourth* match?"

Juntasa smiled. "He's young, he's smaller than his opponent, and he's fatigued, so the crowd is betting against him, but they have no idea that he is fierce. He can rip the heart out of a lion."

The bell rang, and Juntasa turned toward the ring.

Our young guide from the embassy leaned close to us and whispered, "The fix is in. We should get in on the action. The crowd is hungry for anybody who will put money on this kid."

Kylie put her arm around him. "You pull a single baht out of your pocket," she said, "and I will rip *your* heart out, personally deliver it to your ambassador, and tell him to stop hiring idiots."

The crowd suddenly erupted. The fighter in the red trunks had just slammed a roundhouse kick into his opponent's head. The man went down hard, the referee counted him out, but he still couldn't get up. His cornermen jumped into the ring and dragged him off.

Kob Sook Meesang had just knocked another six months off his sentence.

CHAPTER 45

JUNTASA'S GOLDEN BOY won two more fights, both by decision. The fact that the losers were both foreigners and the judges were all locals was not lost on the crowd. So when Kob Sook Meesang stepped back into the ring for the seventh time, the room went wild.

The betting was frenzied and totally lopsided. Everyone wanted a piece of the new hometown hero, the scrappy little man with the wide smile, the big heart, and the judges in his back pocket. Correction: almost everyone. In the back of the arena, a wisp of a woman wearing black pants, a black tunic, and a Bluetooth called the shots as her minions circulated through the mob, covering the bets.

To her credit, Juntasa's sister Buppha gave the suckers their money's worth. In the first round, Meesang kicked his opponent right through the ropes. The man grabbed a tray from one of the waiters, jumped back in the ring, and smashed Meesang over the head with it.

It wasn't quite up to the entertainment level set by the WWE, but it was pure theater, and the crowd reaction was earsplitting. Meesang came back strong the next round, and per the script, he took a dive thirty seconds into round three. Hinds, who had whispered the outcome to me before the fight started, shook his head like the loser on a TV game show who knew the answer but didn't buzz in fast enough.

We sat through six more matches. Finally, Juntasa stood. "I would be honored if you would dine with me in my home," he said.

We assured him that the honor would be all ours.

We drove to the gated community where Pongrit Juntasa lived. The homes were opulent, and his was bordering on palatial. Clearly the bureaucrats in Bangkok lived a lot better than their counterparts in the States.

Over dinner, he bombarded us with questions about crime and punishment in New York, and he was completely entranced by the concept of a police unit dedicated to the needs of the city's rich and powerful.

"We, too, are a city of economic extremes," he said. "It seems to me that our wealthiest citizens would be extremely grateful to feel so well protected."

"I'm sure they would," Kylie said. "Perhaps you could schedule a visit to New York. We'd be glad to show you our model. There's no reason why the same principles couldn't work in Bangkok."

I could almost hear the cash register in his head go *ka-ching*. He'd just demonstrated how effortlessly he could scam money from the unsuspecting poor. And now it seemed like we were offering to show him how to bleed even more money from the ridiculously rich.

"That would be very generous of you," he said. "So, I understand you're here in Thailand to question two of my prisoners."

"With your kind permission," Kylie said, laying it on.

"I would need a formal request."

I was about to ask him what the hell he was talking about, when David Hinds stepped in. "I have the documents right here, Mr. Minister," he said, taking two envelopes from his pocket. "These were prepared by the embassy and signed by the First Secretary."

Juntasa opened the first envelope. "Flynn Samuels," he said. "Fascinating man. Permission granted. Please tell him I asked for him."

"I'm very impressed," Kylie said. "Considering the size of your prison population, I would hardly expect you to know any of them by name."

A cryptic smile crossed Juntasa's lips as he opened the second envelope. "Geraldo Segura?" he said. "I'm afraid the American Embassy is sadly out of touch. Mr. Segura changed his name years ago." He handed the document back to Hinds.

"My apologies, sir. We must not have been notified. I can redo the paperwork and be back in an hour. What is his name now?"

Juntasa grinned. "Rom Ran Sura."

Hinds stared at him, dumbfounded. "Rom Ran Sura?" he said, slowly enunciating each syllable. "Geraldo Segura is Rom Ran Sura?"

Juntasa nodded. "It's a fitting Thai name for such a warrior."

"Warrior?" I said, looking at Hinds for an answer.

"God, yes," Hinds said. "Rom Ran Sura is a Muay Thai legend. One of the best boxers in the country."

"One of?" Juntasa said. "He is the best to come out of our prison system in decades. How embarrassing that the American Embassy had no idea that our national hero was one of their citizens. Of course,

the man is now forty years old. His boxing days are over."

"Still, you must be very proud," Kylie said. "We look forward to meeting him."

"I wish I could help," Juntasa said, "but I can't."

"Why not?"

"I have no idea where he is."

"But you're in charge," Kylie said. "How could you not know—"

Juntasa held up a hand, cutting her off. "Detective, Rom Ran Sura has brought great honor to our country. The king pardoned him a month ago. At this point, nobody knows where he is."

PART THREE
SEX SLAVE

CHAPTER 46

AFTER DINNER WE adjourned to Juntasa's library, where he treated us to a verbal and visual tour of the things he loved most: his native Thailand and the story of his life.

We'd been warned to turn our phones off lest we offend our host, and by the time we were finally able to break loose from his nonstop hospitality, we each had a string of voice mails and texts.

"You'd think the man would be content running the prison system," Kylie said as soon as we squeezed our tired bodies back into the cramped confines of the Toyota Yaris. "But no: on top of that, the son of a bitch likes to take prisoners at dinner. I was ready to go three rounds of Muay Thai with him just to buy us a few hours of freedom."

Our first call was to Cates. We told her that Geraldo Segura had changed his name to Rom Ran Sura and had boxed thirty years off his fifty-year sentence.

"He's out?" Cates said.

"Pardoned by the king of Thailand," I said. "Odds are he's in New York."

"He'd need a passport to get back into the U.S.," she said. "He can't get one of those by royal decree. He'd have to go through the American Embassy."

"We can check tomorrow," I said, "but they operate with all the efficiency of the same federal government that runs Medicare, so don't get your hopes up. Segura wasn't on any watch list, and with two people dead, let's just assume he managed to slip in. He's well-known in Thailand, so I'm sure we can find a recent picture and email it to you. Have someone alert Homeland and get out a BOLO on him."

"When will you be back?"

"We just got permission to interview the bomb maker tomorrow morning. As soon as we're done, we'll be jumping on our private jet and flying home."

"What about Nathan Hirsch and Princeton Wells?"

"What about them?"

"Have you called them and told them Segura is on the loose?"

"They know somebody is after them, so hopefully they're lying low. We'll call them as soon as we finish talking with you."

"That would be now," she said, and hung up.

Kylie called Princeton Wells while I tried Nathan Hirsch. I caught him at his office. So much for lying low.

"Oh God," he said once I'd filled him in. "Geraldo? Geraldo killed Del and Arnie?"

"We have no proof," I said, "but he's at the top of the suspect list."

"And I'm at the top of his hit list."

"You and Princeton Wells."

"Now that you know who you're looking for, can't

you just put a shitload of cops on it and hunt him down?" he said.

"We will," I said, "but now that *you* know who we're looking for, can you pack up your family and head for an undisclosed location until we find him?"

He snorted a sound that was somewhere between a laugh and a scoff. "Do you know what I do for a living, Detective?"

"Yes, sir."

"No, you don't. You're thinking, *He's some kind of lawyer*. I'm not some kind of *anything*. I'm first chair on an eight-hundred-million-dollar class action lawsuit. Three years' worth of prep is coming to a head in the next few days. I can't just drop everything and go."

"Can you keep a low profile?"

"Detective, when there's eight hundred million dollars on the line, there are no *low profiles*."

"Do you want police protection?"

"You mean do I want to walk into the courtroom with a couple of cops and a bomb sniffing dog? How do you think that little tableau will play with the jury? Besides, police protection is bullshit. Del was surrounded by cops. Arnie rattled NYPD's cage from the commissioner on down. Fat lot of good that did either of them."

"It's your call, Mr. Hirsch. Just know that the department is ready to help in any way we can."

"You want to help?" he said. "Find Geraldo Segura, and let me get back to my fucking life."

He hung up.

Kylie's phone call had gone much faster than mine. "How did Wells take the news?" I asked.

"First shock, followed by acceptance, and finally he uttered those same four little words he said when he found out about the murders of his two partners: 'I need a drink.'"

Ten minutes later, we arrived at the hotel, and Kylie looked at her watch.

"Midnight," she said.

"Good," I said. "I've had enough assholes for one day."

CHAPTER 47

JUNTASA WAS A man of his word. Our interview with Flynn Samuels was set for 8:00 a.m. David Hinds picked us up at our hotel at seven thirty.

"Ah, the embassy Lincoln," Kylie said as we got into the spacious back seat. "Glad to see she's back on the road. I'll bet your roommate's happy about it, too."

Hinds wisely decided not to take the bait. "I'm sure you've been to prisons in the States," he said, pulling out onto Wireless Road. "Klong Prem is going to be a hell of a lot uglier."

"None of them are pretty, David," Kylie said.

"I know, but the Americans at least pretend that the inmates are there to be rehabilitated. In Thailand they're there to suffer. They sleep sixty, seventy men to a room. No beds, no mattresses—just a thin sheet on the cold, hard floor. There's one open toilet in the room, no medical, and not enough food. The State Department did a study that says every year spent in a Thai prison is equivalent to five years in a maximum security prison in the U.S."

"It's gratifying to hear that our government is finally spending our tax dollars on a study every

American will want to read," Kylie said. "Look, kid, we're not here to judge the Thai justice system. All we want to do is talk with Flynn Samuels. What can you tell us about him?"

Hinds shrugged. "Never met him. I just know that he's in building five, which is where they house the hard cases—murderers, rapists, drug offenders— all of them sentenced to fifty years or more. A lot of them go stark raving mad after seven. Samuels has been there for fifteen. All I'm saying is, brace yourselves."

The prison itself turned out to be just what we'd expected: stone walls, barbed wire, steel doors, tight-lipped guards with sadistic eyes. Flynn Samuels, on the other hand, was nothing like what Hinds had prepared us for. He was neither undernourished nor crazy. He was a big outgoing bear of a man with a thick mop of graying reddish hair and a full gray beard. At about six foot eight and 350 pounds, he filled the doorway of the visitors' room. And like every Aussie I'd ever met, he was likable from the get-go.

"G'day, mates," he boomed, plopping down on a bench on the other side of a thick steel-mesh divider. "You're the first visitors I ever had from New York." He laughed. "Hell, you're the first visitors I've had from anywhere."

"Thanks for seeing us," I said.

"Happy to take time out of my busy two-hundred-year schedule," he said. "Besides, I'd do anything for my boy P.J."

"P.J.?" I said.

"Pongrit Juntasa. He's my man."

"We had dinner with him last night. He certainly speaks highly of you."

"He's a big fan. Sends me special little gifts from time to time: food, booze, smokes, a hooker for Christmas. He made sure I have a private cell with a bed and a blanket. In this hellhole, it helps to have friends in high places."

"You're lucky," I said. "He didn't seem like the type to have favorites."

"Well, it doesn't hurt that I helped him get his job. I blew his predecessor to kingdom come. So what can I do for you?"

"We're looking for Geraldo Segura, also known as Rom Ran Sura."

His face lit up, and he let out another laugh. "And since you're NYPD, I'm guessing that little bugger is blowing up people on your side of the pond. Hot damn, I'm proud of that boy. I taught him everything he knows."

"How?" Kylie said. "How do you teach someone to build bombs in a place like this without getting caught?"

"Rolling paper."

He paused. The man was in no hurry to tell his tale. He had two hundred years to kill. I stared at his hands while I waited. They were just as big as the rest of him. I tried to picture him manipulating the delicate mechanism of a bomb.

He caught me looking. "I know," he said, holding up his hands. "You'd think these giant paws would be a handicap, but no—not when you use jeweler's tools. Nobody can build a shaped charge bomb like me. I can put one in the middle of a symphony orchestra, take out the piccolo player, and leave the entire string section intact. I never shared my technique—figured it would die with me. Then one day Rom Ran asked if I could teach him the tricks of the trade. I thought,

Hell, it can't hurt to be buddy-buddy with the toughest motherfucker in the prison. So I diagrammed the first step on a piece of rolling paper, gave him five minutes to study it, then rolled a cigarette and smoked the evidence."

"And then what?"

"Then I told him to redraw it for me. Of course he couldn't. It took him weeks before he could commit that first step to memory. When I was sure he had it, I moved on to step two."

"How many steps are there altogether?"

"Nineteen. I probably gave myself lung cancer waiting for that wanker to commit every step to memory, but I guess all that studying paid off. The kid gets an A plus."

"We need to find him," Kylie said. "Do you know where he is?"

"Sorry, but he didn't leave a forwarding address."

"Is there anything you can tell us that might help? We'd really like to tell your pal P.J. that you were cooperative..." Kylie's voice trailed off, the quasi threat dangling in the air.

Samuels rubbed his thick beard. "How many people has he killed so far?"

"Two," I said.

"Two," Samuels said, repeating the number. "If I were you, I'd hurry on home, mate. He ain't done yet."

CHAPTER 48

SUVARNABHUMI AIRPORT WAS only a thirty-minute drive from the prison, and after spending less than a day and a half in Thailand, we were, as Samuels had suggested, hurrying on home.

Captain Fennessy and his crew were on the tarmac, waiting for us, and once again I was reminded that the rich really do live differently.

I spent the next eighteen hours flying back to the woman I love, and the twelve hours after that reconnecting with her. First physically, then emotionally. After a good night's sleep, we gave *physically* another shot.

At 7:00 a.m. Cheryl and I walked to the precinct. It was mid-May, one of those perfect spring days in New York when Central Park looks like it was Photoshopped by the man upstairs, and most New Yorkers on their way to work have full-blown smiles on their faces.

And then I was back to reality: Captain Cates's office. Kylie and I had identified the prime suspect in the Silver Bullet bombing case. Now came the tough part: catching him.

"Did you release Sura's picture to the press?" I asked.

Whenever there's a citywide manhunt, the brass debates whether or not to enlist the public's help by releasing a photo of the suspect to the media. Most of the time we don't. The standard reasoning is, *Why let the perp know that we're onto him?*

"Absolutely not," Cates said. But this time the logic was different. Cates spelled it out for us.

"Sura is Guatemalan. His mama could pick him out of a crowd, but if you flash a picture of a dark-skinned, dark-haired mad bomber on a TV screen for five seconds, you know what's going to happen."

"Chinese waiter syndrome," I said. "They all look alike."

Every year, thousands of witnesses identify the wrong person—especially when the felon and the witness are of different races. In a city with four million white people it was smarter to circulate Sura's picture to trained police officers.

"Next order of business," Cates said. "A hundred thousand dollars of the DA's money flew off into the sunset last week. Would you like to know how many times he's called me since you left for Thailand?"

"No, Captain, but did you tell the DA that we have two suspects?"

"Yes, and he doesn't give a shit about suspects. Nor is he interested in the fact that Detectives Corcoran and Fischer have been tailing them. All he wants to hear is that he's getting his money back. Where are you on finding it?"

"We're meeting with Corcoran and Fischer as soon as we're done here."

"In that case, we're done. Go—and don't come back empty-handed."

Danny Corcoran and Tommy Fischer were parked outside the precinct. "We've been tailing Troy Marschand and Dylan Freemont since Friday," Danny said as soon as we got in the car.

"Who's watching them now?" Kylie said.

Danny pulled out. "These boys don't need watching at this hour. They sleep in till around noon."

"Don't they work?"

"Marschand, if he's still employed, is the assistant to a dead woman. Not very demanding on his time. Freemont is an actor-slash-waiter. We followed him to a burger joint on Second Avenue on Saturday. He went inside, came out fifteen minutes later, and hailed a cab. We checked with the manager. She told us he quit. Came in to pick up his money."

"You think he landed an acting job?"

"More likely he's found a new career as a blackmailer. The two of them have been dining at some of New York's finer restaurants, and they spent yesterday shopping on Madison Avenue. Paying cash."

"The tips must be good at that burger joint," Kylie said. "So now what?"

"You remember Jerry Brainard, the dispatcher who worked the new mobile command center? Jerry knows drones. We showed him the chopper video of the one that scooped up the ransom money, and he ID'd it as a DJI Phantom 3."

"Get a court order for their credit card records," Kylie said. "See if they bought one."

"We did. Nothing came up, but that doesn't prove anything. There are third-party sellers all over the lot. Or they could have bought a used one. Jerry checked with the FAA. You're supposed to register these things with the Feds, but there's nothing under either of their names."

"We can get a warrant to search their apartment for a drone with a grappling hook dangling from the bottom," I said.

"The hook was homemade. I doubt if they'd leave it on. But even if we found a drone on their kitchen table, the ADA said she couldn't make a case that they committed the crime. We were about to give up on the drone connection and wait for them to hit another victim, but Jerry texted me last night, said he had an idea, and asked if we could meet him at the fire academy on Randall's Island."

"What's he doing out there?" Kylie asked.

"Teaching cops to fly drones," Fischer said.

Kylie's eyes lit up. "Now you're talking."

Fifteen minutes later, we rolled up to a huge training facility where the streets are lined with buildings that are set on fire regularly. There was a bombed-out city bus with mannequin arms and legs sticking out of the charred remains, and there were more plastic bodies—civilians and fallen firefighters—lying in the street.

Jerry Brainard was waiting for us in front of a row of mock storefronts. "I'm really sorry to drag you all the way out here, guys. There's almost no place in the city where you can legally fly, so the FDNY lets us use their space."

"No problem," Kylie said. "I heard you're the man to see if a girl wants to lose her drone virginity."

I jumped in. "Before we get to the fun and games, can we focus on the mission at hand?"

Jerry Brainard has the unflappable temperament of a man who sits at a console fielding emergency calls all day. "Actually, a short lesson couldn't hurt." He showed Kylie his iPhone. "Your controls are all on your phone or your iPad."

Thirty seconds into the tutorial she grabbed his phone. "Got it," she said.

Kylie flew like she drove. Total cowgirl.

"Pretty good," Brainard said. "But aren't you the same cop who ran a million-dollar Mercedes into a—"

"Exigent circumstances," she yelled. "I was completely exonerated."

He gave her another few minutes in the air, then had her bring it in.

Brainard took the phone, tapped on the glass a few times, and handed it back to her. "What does this tell you?" he said.

"Holy shit," Kylie said, staring at the screen. "It tells me we're about to make the DA a very happy man."

CHAPTER 49

"SO WHAT DO you think?" Kylie said on the way back to the precinct. "Did Marschand and Freemont murder Aubrey Davenport?"

"I know Cates told us not to rule them out," I said, "but what's their motive?"

"That sex tape of her and the judge is probably the tip of the iceberg," Kylie said. "Who knows how many there are? Troy Marschand found them, told his boyfriend, and they decided to go into the extortion business. But first they had to kill her."

"Oh, I can picture that conversation," Danny said. "Troy says, 'Hey Dylan, let's get a gun and whack my boss.' And Dylan says, 'No, I have a better idea. First we convince her that the two of us want to have autoerotic sex with her, then we take her out to this deserted smallpox hospital on Roosevelt Island, where she and Janek go to do all their kinky—'"

"Stop," Kylie said. "I get your point."

"I think Danny's right," I said. "Janek Hoffmann killed her. Troy and Dylan found the sex tapes on Aubrey's computer after the fact. Like Cates said: the blackmail was most likely a crime of opportunity."

"Fine. We'll nail them on extortion and see where

we can take it from there," Kylie said. "All I know is that these two assholes think they're smarter than we are, and we're about to show them they're not."

"Technically, they *are* smarter than we are," Tommy Fischer said. "They're just not smarter than Jerry Brainard."

Danny dropped us off at the precinct, and we stayed just long enough to pick up a car. Then we headed downtown to ADA Selma Kaplan's office to tell her what we had on Marschand and Freemont.

"Do we have a case?" I asked.

"If you find what you think you're going to find, you'll have a slam dunk," she said. "But I doubt if it'll ever come to trial. Judge Rafferty would be crazy to go public with his sexual hijinks, and the perps would be even crazier not to plead out."

"We need a couple of warrants," I said.

"There's not a judge in the building who wouldn't be happy to sign off," Kaplan said. "The only one who can't is the aggrieved party, the Honorable Michael J. Rafferty."

It was the fastest warrant we'd ever gotten.

Troy and Dylan lived on Franklin Street in Tribeca, which was only a five-minute drive from the courthouse. Corcoran and Fischer were parked outside their building.

"Marschand did a Starbucks run about twenty minutes ago," Danny said. "Right now they're both in the apartment sipping lattes and thinking about where to spend the DA's money next."

"Let's go upstairs and ruin their day," Kylie said.

We instructed the doorman not to ring up, and the four of us took the elevator to the fifth floor. Kylie knocked on the door, and Troy opened it.

"Remember me?" she said. "Detective MacDonald.

My partner and I are working on the Davenport murder."

"Of course I remember. But I thought you arrested Janek Hoffmann."

"We did. You've been so helpful already. Sorry to keep bothering you. We just have some loose ends to tie up. Can we come in?"

"Sure." He gave a yell. "Dylan, the two homicide detectives are here."

We walked in, followed by Corcoran and Fischer.

"And they brought reinforcements," Troy said with a laugh.

Dylan Freemont joined us, and once again I was weirded out by how much alike they looked. More like brothers than lovers. They were both wearing jeans and T-shirts. Dylan's was black; Troy's was lavender.

I nodded at Corcoran and Fischer, and they took out their cell phones.

"How can we help?" Troy asked.

"Well, here's the thing," Kylie said. She stopped, interrupted by the familiar thrum of the bass and the *doot-didoot-didoot* beat of Lou Reed's "Walk on the Wild Side." It was the ringtone on Troy's cell.

Seconds later, another phone rang. The ringtone on this one was Madonna singing "Vogue." Dylan answered his phone.

"Like I started to say," Kylie boomed, "we've got a search warrant for your cell phones and your iPads. Hand them over, boys."

The two of them were dumbstruck. Troy handed his phone over immediately. Dylan balked.

"Thank you," Corcoran said, yanking Dylan's phone out of his hand and giving it to Kylie. "Now, which way to the iPads?"

"I don't have a fucking iPad," Dylan said.

"Then have a seat," Danny said, grabbing him by the shoulder and forcing him to the floor.

Troy was more cooperative. "I don't have an iPad. I have a Kindle. Is that okay?"

"Let's just start with Dylan's phone," Kylie said, thumbing through his apps. "I heard you're an actor. Have I seen you in anything?"

Dylan spit in her direction.

"Son of a gun...Dylan must have a drone, because he's got one of those DJI apps. Let's take a quick peek at your flight history."

"You have no right to look at my shit, bitch."

"Read the warrant, dude. I've got plenty of rights. Hey, Zach, take a look at this. Friday, May twelfth. Dylan was flying his bird over the High Line at the exact same time we were there. He loses altitude around Twenty-Fifth Street, then takes off again and heads for Penn Station."

I leaned over her shoulder. It was all there. "You know what the cops call this, Dylan?"

He scowled.

"Hard evidence," I said.

"And speaking of rights," Kylie said, "Dylan Freemont and Troy Marschand, you're under arrest. You have the right to remain silent." She finished the Miranda warning and asked if they understood. Troy, tears streaming down his face, said a meek "Yes."

"Dylan," Kylie said. "Do you understand?"

"Yes! What's the fucking charge?"

"Conspiracy."

"Conspiracy for *what*?"

"Well, we've got you cold for extortion," Kylie said. "But we're looking to put murder on the table."

Troy made a loud retching sound and vomited down the front of his lavender shirt.

"We didn't kill her," Dylan said. "I swear to God."

My phone rang. It was Cates. I held up my hand. "Hold that thought, Mr. Freemont."

I answered the phone. "Yes, Captain?"

"I don't care what you're doing," she said. "Drop it now, and get your asses over to Foley Square."

"What's going on?"

"Nathan Hirsch is sitting on the courthouse steps handcuffed to a bomb."

CHAPTER 50

"**YOU TAKE THE** happy couple," I said to Corcoran and Fischer. "We're out of here."

Kylie followed me out the door. As we ran down the stairs I told her all I knew. "Nathan Hirsch. Handcuffed to a bomb. Foley Square."

We jumped in the car. I hit the light bar but kept the siren off. I still had Cates on the phone. I put her on speaker.

"We're on the way," I said. "What have you got?"

"Ten minutes ago Hirsch was on his way to court. A male Hispanic comes up behind him, cuffs a briefcase to his wrist, shoves a burner phone in his hand, and says, 'Don't do anything stupid, or I'll blow you to kingdom come.'"

"Segura," I said.

"We have a positive ID," Cates said.

"Then what happened?"

"He called 911."

"What?" Kylie yelled. "Segura tells him not to do anything stupid, and the first thing he does is call 911?"

"You're not tracking with me, MacDonald," Cates said. "Hirsch didn't do anything, except probably piss his pants. *Segura* called 911. Then he patched it into a three-way call: the victim, the perp, and the 911 operator."

I heard what she said, but I couldn't make sense of it. "Why?" I asked.

"My best guess is that Segura wants Hirsch to confess all his sins, and calling 911 guarantees that it's all going to be recorded and released to the press."

Kylie made a hard right onto Lafayette.

"Right now Hirsch is spilling his guts out," Cates said. "He owned up to the Thailand drug run twenty years ago, he admitted he's got this hooker set up in a condo in Jersey, and he just confessed to bribing a witness in a libel case he won last year. That alone will get him disbarred."

"Segura spent twenty years in a Bangkok prison because of this asshole and his friends," I said. "Do you think he's going to be happy with Hirsch losing his law license and doing a Martha Stewart in a minimum security country club?"

"Almost there," Kylie said, making a left on Duane.

"I don't care how good a lawyer Hirsch is," I said. "He's not going to be able to argue for his life. Segura wants him dead, but first he wants to completely humiliate him—destroy whatever legacy this weasel may possibly have. And I'll bet that as soon as Hirsch coughs up every smarmy, slimy thing he ever did, Segura is going to blow him up the same way he killed the other two."

We turned left onto Centre Street, and Kylie hit the brakes. The New York County Supreme Court building at 60 Centre is directly across the street from Foley Square, an iconic landmark in lower Manhattan steeped in history and the site of the sculpture *Triumph of the Human Spirit*.

Kylie and I had just been there, all pumped up about getting the search warrant that would bring down Troy Marschand and Dylan Freemont. I'd barely taken note of my surroundings, but I vaguely remember that the air was crisp and clean, the traffic was flowing, and all was right with the world.

Now, less than an hour later, men and women in uniform were scrambling to set up barricades three hundred feet from the courthouse steps, where a lone man in a dark suit sat with a cell phone to his ear and a bomb chained to his wrist.

"We're at the scene, Captain," I said. "We've got cop cars, fire trucks, and media vans up the ass. Where the hell is the bomb squad?"

"Bay Ridge, Riverdale, Ozone Park, and Harlem. We got a rash of school bomb threats just before this one came in. I'm sure Segura is behind it, but we can't take a chance until we evacuate every one of those kids and have the dogs canvass the buildings. The Emergency Service Unit is on the way, but right now, it's on you."

"The uniforms are working on crowd control. What do you want us to do?"

"Stay on this phone," Cates said. "Nine one one will patch you into the conversation between Hirsch and Segura."

"Patch...? Why?"

"Why the hell do you think, Jordan? You've been to Bangkok. You know the players better than anyone. This is your case. I want you to talk with Segura and keep him from detonating that bomb."

Kylie looked at me and shook her head. She knew what I knew. Segura had spent half his lifetime planning for this moment. There was no way on earth he was going to settle for an apology and a couple of confessions. But that's not what Cates wanted to hear.

"All right, Captain," I said, opening the car door. "I'll try my best."

"There's no *trying* on this one, Jordan," she barked. "Suit up and get it done. This department and this mayor cannot afford another dead New York City millionaire on the front page of every paper in the country."

I heard a click, and then I was listening to a man speaking. I recognized Nathan Hirsch right away.

"Hello," I said.

"Hello," Hirsch said. "Who is this?"

"This is Detective Zach Jordan. I'd like to join this conversation."

"Detective," a second voice said. "Do you know who this is?"

"I do."

"Nathan tells me you flew to Bangkok to pay me a visit."

"Yes, sir."

"So sorry I missed you," he said. "Why don't we catch up now?"

CHAPTER 51

"YOU'RE QUITE THE hero in Thailand," I said. "I had dinner with Pongrit Juntasa, and he told me that Rom Ran Sura brought great honor to—"

"Rom Ran Sura is dead."

"But I thought you were—"

"I am Geraldo Segura. It's the name my Guatemalan parents gave me when I was born, and it will be my name when I die. Rom Ran Sura was part of the artifice, a tool I used to dig my way out of prison thirty years ahead of time."

"Whatever your name is, you're a Muay Thai legend."

"There are no legends in hell. Except for Satan himself. You should be honored that he dined with you. I subsisted on a single bowl of rice in watered-down soup every day while Nathan got fatter and richer."

"I know what you went through," I said. "I visited Klong Prem. I saw the deplorable conditions you were subjected—"

"Will you shut the fuck up, Detective?" It was Nathan Hirsch. "What the hell are you doing on this phone call, anyway?"

"You have a bomb attached to your wrist, sir. I'm

trying to negotiate a peaceful resolve to a volatile situation."

"By agitating the man? By rehashing the life he just escaped from? Geraldo and I were having a meaningful discussion. We all make mistakes when we're young. He and I were both seduced by Princeton Wells. Wells made the drug deal with Zoe Pound. Wells bought the heroin. And it was Wells who made sure that if we got caught, Geraldo would pay the price. My only crime was not mounting a campaign to free my friend."

"Don't be modest, Nathan," Segura said. "That's not your *only* crime. You've already admitted to several, and we were just getting started."

"So I'm a lawyer who broke the law. They'll disbar me. They'll fine me. They'll put me in jail. They'll give me what I deserve. But I don't deserve to die."

"That's exactly what I wanted to say to Mr. Segura," I said.

"Do me a favor, Detective. Don't say anything. Butt out."

"I'm sorry, Detective Jordan," Segura said. "It appears Nathan doesn't want your help. But feel free to listen."

I muted the phone as Hirsch launched into another mea culpa.

I scanned the street on the far side of the square. In the few minutes since I'd arrived, it had mushroomed into an armed camp packed with first responders ready, willing, and able to take on whatever disaster befell their city.

Behind them were the media vans, gobbling up the human drama and spitting it out to cyberspace, the airwaves, and the printed page to satisfy the bloodlust of their loyal followers. Nathan Hirsch had woken up this morning with a head full of secrets. By nightfall, they would belong to the world.

Kylie came running toward me with a large pair of bolt cutters in her hand.

"If you're thinking about cutting the chain to the briefcase, forget it," I said. "Segura is watching from somewhere. If you get within a hundred feet of Nathan Hirsch, you'd better be wearing earplugs."

"Zach, I know, I know, but listen to me. Remember what Howard Malley told us about the code name Interpol gave Flynn Samuels?"

"They call him Sammy Six Digits."

"Right. He taps a six-digit date into his cell phone to detonate the bomb. *Cell phone,* Zach. Segura can't blow up anything without a cell signal, and guess what they have on the ESU truck? A cell jammer."

"And guess what NYPD can't use without a warrant?" I said. "If you want to run across the street to the courthouse, maybe you can get one."

"There's no time for a goddamn warrant. This is a life-and-death situation."

"How many thousands of people do you think live and work in this area? What if one of them has a life-and-death situation and can't call 911 because you jammed the airwaves to save Nathan Hirsch? Kylie, cell jammers are like search warrants. Judges get to make the decision. Not cops."

"Fine," she said. "The bomb squad is ten minutes out. Maybe they can do something. How are you doing on your hostage negotiations?"

"I'm persona non grata. Nathan Hirsch doesn't want my help. All I can do is listen."

"Hold on to these," she said, handing me the bolt cutters. "I know what Segura looks like. I'm going to work the crowd and see if I can spot him."

Kylie took off, and I set the bolt cutters at my feet and put the phone to my ear. Nathan Hirsch had been wrong to tell me to butt out. I may not have been an experienced negotiator, but I wasn't some random cop jumping on to the phone call. I knew a hell of a lot about Geraldo Segura. I hadn't been agitating him. I'd been empathizing with him. Saying what I had to say to get him to trust me.

As far as I could tell, Nathan wasn't doing such a great job of winning Segura over. I thought about unmuting my phone and jumping back into the fray. I'd start off by hitting him with that quote from Abraham Lincoln: "He who represents himself has a fool for a client."

"And the fifty thousand dollars a year we paid your grandmother," I heard Hirsch say. "That was my idea. Wells was against it. I remember one year I wrote the check, and he started arguing with me about—"

My phone went dead. I looked up at the crowd, almost every one of whom had a cell phone in their hands. Their phones were dead, too.

Then a bullhorn cut through the air. "Zach. Zach." It was Kylie. "Do it, Zach. Do it. Do it. Do it."

I wanted to scream at her. I wanted to lash out and tell her she was the most infuriating, irresponsible, uncontrollable partner a cop could possibly have. And then when I was finally finished ranting, and railing, and venting my spleen, I wanted to have incredible make-up sex with her.

But, of course, I didn't do any of that.

Instead I grabbed the bolt cutters and raced toward the man chained to a bomb on the courthouse steps.

CHAPTER 52

I SPRINTED ACROSS the empty square. By the time I hit Centre Street the crowd erupted, picking up Kylie's chant. *Do it, Zach. Do it, Zach. Do it, Zach.*

Do what? Get myself killed because my partner, who spent a few minutes talking to some guy in a Thai prison, suddenly decided she was an expert on when bombs can go off and when they can't?

The clamor grew more raucous as the mob egged me on.

And then out of nowhere came the music. Some crazy son of a bitch in the horde of well-wishers had a saxophone, and I heard those stirring opening notes to "Theme from Rocky."

Dum, dum, da-da-dum, da-da-dum, da-da-dum.

Hero music. But I didn't feel heroic. I felt like an idiot. Kylie's words raced through my brain. "Segura can't blow up anything without a cell signal, and guess what they have on the ESU truck? A cell jammer."

My gut reaction when she said it was to try to stop her from using the jammer illegally. What I should have said was, "How do you know Segura can't blow anything up without a cell signal? What if he has a computer rigged with a backup detonator? What if he has a high-powered rifle, and he shoots me for trying to save the man who cost him twenty years of his life?"

But I hadn't questioned her logic, and now I was putting my ass on the line to save one of the biggest dirtbags on the planet.

Nathan Hirsch sat staring at his dead cell phone, probably wondering if Segura was going to call him back or blow him up. He was a dozen steps up from street level, dead center between two massive Corinthian columns. The towering temple of justice loomed behind him.

I wanted to bound up the stairs two at a time, but as soon as my foot hit the first step, everything seemed to slow down. It was like that recurring dream where you're running, running, running, but you feel like you're barely moving.

Maybe it was the jet lag. Maybe it was the abject fear fucking with my head, but it seemed to take a lifetime for my foot to touch the second step.

Someone had found a way to amp up the sound of the sax, and with the music blaring and the crowd chanting, I made it to the third step. And the fourth.

Days later, I would watch some of the many videos of my climb up those courthouse steps. On film it only took seconds, but in real life my entire world was in slow motion.

"Nathan—don't move," I called out as I got closer.

He looked up when he heard me. Cates had guessed right. Hirsch had pissed himself. And he was crying.

Please, God, I thought, *don't let this fat bastard be the last thing I ever see during my time here on earth.*

"Hold still," I said, lowering his cuffed wrist so I could rest the briefcase on the steps. I took a look at the bolt cutters I'd been dragging along like an appendage. They were a flimsy government-issue piece of crap, and I remembered John Glenn's famous words: "As I hurtled through space, one thought kept crossing my mind: every part of this rocket was supplied by the lowest bidder."

Somewhere in my pocket was a key ring with half a dozen keys on it, one of which might open the cuffs. Or it might not. I hoped I didn't have to find out. I opened the bolt cutters wide, positioned the blades over two steel links, and, with every ounce of strength I had left in my travel-weary body, I slammed the two handles together.

The chain snapped.

"Run, Nathan, run!" I commanded.

He didn't. Or maybe he couldn't. He froze.

And he was too fat to carry.

I grabbed him by both arms, pulled him toward me, and put my mouth to his ear. "Listen to me, asshole. I've got a girlfriend I'm going home to. You either move or you can stay here and die."

He moved.

He navigated the steps like a pregnant sow, and I braced myself for the explosion that would hurl the two of us into the federal court building on the other side of Lafayette.

It never came. No *boom*. Just the whoops of the onlookers as I helped the gasping lawyer waddle across Centre Street toward the bedlam and finally passed him into the arms of a team of uniformed cops.

"Have the paramedics check him out," I said, "but don't let him wander off until he has a heart-to-heart with Selma Kaplan at the DA's office."

One of the cops put her hand on my shoulder. "What about you?" she said. "You okay?"

"I'm fine. Just get me away from these fucking cameras."

I followed her to a mobile command center that was parked on Worth Street, stumbled in the door, shut it behind me, dropped to my knees, and, half sobbing, half laughing, I thanked a God I hadn't been in touch with for longer than I care to admit.

CHAPTER 53

THERE WERE FOUR white-shirted cops in the command center. Brass. Two of them were barking into satellite phones. I'd picked the wrong place to duck into for quiet reflection. I took a few slow deep breaths, centered myself, and looked up.

One of the white shirts was looming over me. I recognized her immediately: Barbara O'Brien, a public information officer. I stood up.

"You've got balls, Detective Jordan," she said.

Coming from anyone else, that would have felt like a compliment. But not from her. I nodded, waiting for the other shoe to drop.

"You got a warrant to go with those balls?" she said.

"Ma'am?"

"You disabled the cell phone service for tens of thousands of civilians. The press is going to ask me if you came up with that little rescue mission on your own, or did you have a signed warrant?"

"I believe my partner was working on a warrant."

"*Working on?* For your sake, let's hope she got it."

"Lieutenant, I have to go. Captain Cates is expecting to hear from me."

"Tell her she'll be hearing from me, too."

I'd walked into the command center to the sound of a cheering crowd. I walked out a minute later at the top of somebody's shit list.

Within seconds after I stepped back outside, the crowd let out another joyful roar. But this one wasn't for me. Their cell phones had come back on.

"I see that you restored their cell service," I said to Kylie as she made her way toward me.

"It's more like I restored their lives," she said. "Another few minutes without a dial tone and these people would have gotten ugly."

"So now the bomb is hot again."

"No problem. The guys in the bomb squad live for that shit. They'll be fighting to see who gets to disarm it. Besides, Segura's not going to set it off without anyone to blow up. Now that he's got a cell signal again, he'll probably call back and congratulate you. As will I." She threw her arms around me. "You're a hero, partner."

"I don't think so," I said, "but I need the hug."

"*You don't think so?* Zach, just because people couldn't make phone calls doesn't mean they couldn't shoot videos. That hundred-yard mad dash of you running toward a bomb will be all over the internet. By tomorrow this time, you'll be a YouTube sensation. You risked your life to save someone most people wouldn't think was worth saving. Trust me: you're a rock star."

"Tell that to PIO O'Brien. I just ran into her in the command center."

"And what did that hard-ass want?"

"An inquiry into why two cops violated a federal law that prohibits police departments from operating a cell jammer without express authorization."

"And what makes you think we don't have authorization?"

"Because we don't."

"But we will in a minute."

"From who?"

"From the randy old coot who took me to dinner at the Harvard Club, and who after two glasses of wine said to me, 'If you ever need a favor, sweetheart, here's my cell number.'"

"Judge Rafferty," I said.

"I think the old boy has a crush on me."

"You're telling me you called him on his personal phone and got a warrant."

"Verbal. I'm going over to the courthouse now to get it on paper."

"You mean you're going over there hoping to *convince* him to give you a warrant after the fact?"

"Shut up and follow me. But we better go around the back way. That pesky bomb is blocking the front door."

Five minutes later, we were escorted into Judge Rafferty's chambers.

"Kylie," he said, coming around his desk and giving her a hug. "I've got your warrant right here."

"Ye of little faith," she said to me, grabbing the document that would exonerate us from the wrath of O'Brien and prosecution by the Feds.

"And you, young man," the judge said, shaking my hand. "I thought you were kind of a dolt at first, but I've come around."

"Zach Jordan," I said, hoping he'd eventually remember my name. "Thank you, sir."

"By the way, Your Honor," Kylie said, "we've just arrested the two scoundrels who were blackmailing you."

"That calls for a drink," he said, opening his desk drawer.

"We're still on duty, sir," Kylie said. "But we'll take a rain check."

"I'll hold you to it," he said. "But we'll have to have two drinks. One for the blackmailers, and one for Zach's masterful performance. I watched it on TV. It was textbook police work, son. I wouldn't change a thing."

"Oh, I'd definitely change one thing, sir."

"And what's that?"

"I'd have Wynton Marsalis on trumpet instead of that damn saxophone player."

CHAPTER 54

WE WERE ON our way back to the precinct when Cates called. I put her on speaker. "I just got off the phone with Barbara O'Brien," she said.

"What does she want?" I said. "My badge or my balls?"

"She told me she tore into you, but she's changed her tune now that the bomb is disabled and you somehow magically came up with a warrant. Now she wants me to put you both up for a commendation."

"We'll settle for a day off," Kylie said.

"It's not in the cards. I need your asses back here. Your two drone bandits lawyered up. ADA Kaplan is trying to cut a deal with them now."

"A deal?" I said. "Those smug bastards blackmailed a judge."

"Kaplan doesn't care. They've got something she wants, and she's willing to give away the store to get it."

"Tell her to hold off. We'll be there in fifteen minutes," I said. Kylie hit the accelrator, and the car lurched forward. "Or less."

Seven minutes later, we walked into an interrogation room where ADA Selma Kaplan was sitting with the two blackmailers and a woman in her late thirties with curly red hair and a pleasant smile.

"This is Grace Marschand," Kaplan said, introducing us.

"I'm Troy's big sister," she said. "I'm a personal injury lawyer, but my brother can't afford an expensive criminal attorney, and he doesn't trust public defenders, so here I am. Good thing for him I watch a lot of *Law & Order*."

It was an act, and I didn't buy the fish-out-of-water routine for a second. If Grace Marschand were really out of her element, she'd be a wreck. This woman knew what she was doing, and I could see by the smirk on Dylan Freemont's face that she was doing it well.

Selma Kaplan stood up. "I need a moment outside with my detectives."

"Oh, take all the time you need," Marschand said. "But I just want to tell you both that Troy and Dylan are *really, really* sorry about what they did, and they're giving back all of the money."

"Is there any left?" Kylie said. "Because they went on a *really, really* big spending spree last weekend."

"I know. Shameful," Marschand said, looking at her brother like he was a naughty puppy who'd soiled the carpet. "But they still have eighty-four thousand left, and I'm going to make up the difference."

"I must have missed the episode of *Law & Order* where the penalty for committing a class D felony is *giving back the money if you get caught,*" Kylie said. "Your clients are looking at seven years, counselor."

Marschand smiled sweetly. "And yet Ms. Kaplan has just offered to drop all charges."

Before we could say a word, Kaplan herded us out of the room.

"Drop all charges?" Kylie said as soon as we closed the door. "Selma, what the hell have they got?"

"Thirty-two hidden-camera sex tapes, every one of them starring Aubrey Davenport."

"And who are her costars?"

"According to Ms. I Don't Know Anything About Criminal Law, they are the pillars of the community: the CEO of an international bank, a congressman, a newscaster, a university chancellor—a laundry list of New York City's boldest boldface names."

"So Troy Marschand had Aubrey's laptop all along."

"No. That's still missing. Troy says he was cleaning the office one day, and he stumbled on an external hard drive. He didn't know what it was, so he and Dylan screened the contents. Turns out that Aubrey spent over a year shooting this secret documentary. She wanted to expose these upstanding princes of industry as liars, cheaters, and sexual deviants."

"You mean she wanted to blackmail them."

"No. She was a dedicated filmmaker. She wasn't thinking about money. She wanted an Oscar. It was only after she was murdered that those two clowns realized they were sitting on a gold mine and went into the extortion business."

"That calls for some jail time in my book," Kylie said. "Offer them three years. They'll get out in eighteen months, but at least they'll have—"

Kaplan cut her off. "You think like a cop, MacDonald. The DA thinks like a politician. If those tapes ever saw the light of day, it would rock this city's establishment to the core. Forget about going to trial. I can't even charge them with anything, or it'll be on the public record."

"So the DA is willing to cut them loose just to suppress those tapes," I said.

"Zach, these are the people that Red is supposed to take care of."

"Protect and defend, Selma. Not cover up."

"It's not your call, and it's not mine," Kaplan said. "It's the DA's."

"No doubt with some input from our politician in chief, Mayor Sykes," Kylie said. "I bet every horndog on those tapes donated generously to her campaign."

"Sweetheart, you've been at this long enough not to sound shocked. The mayor and the DA are simply protecting the hands that feed them."

"Where is this external hard drive with all these damning videos now?" I said.

"Troy hid it in his mother's basement. We should have it in a few hours."

"Then maybe there's an upside to all this," I said.

"Please," Kaplan said. "I could use an upside."

"Most likely the external hard drive is a backup, and the original videos are still on Aubrey's laptop. Do you think Troy and Dylan have it?"

"Troy swears that they don't, and I believe him. He'd be too scared to hang on to it."

"And Janek Hoffmann didn't have it, either," I said. "But somebody does."

"The question is who."

"We know that Aubrey always had it with her, so my best guess is that somebody found out about this secret documentary, killed her, took the laptop, and has no idea there's a second copy. And I'm betting it's one of the thirty-two men on those videos."

"I guarantee you it's not the Honorable Michael J. Rafferty," Kylie said, a wide grin on her face.

"There you go," I said. "We've just narrowed down the suspect list to thirty-one of our fair city's most respected citizens."

CHAPTER 55

IT HAD TAKEN less than two minutes to cut Nathan Hirsch free from that bomb, and more than two hours to fill out the investigative work sheets that detailed the incident.

"If I'd have known that saving his life would involve so much paperwork," Kylie said, pushing her chair away from her desk, "I'd have thought twice about flipping the switch on that cell jammer."

"I doubt it," I said. "Since when have you ever thought twice before pulling one of your crazy-ass stunts?"

"It wasn't a stunt. I got a court order."

"Kylie, you can bullshit Barbara O'Brien, but don't bullshit me. I saw the signature at the bottom of that warrant. Rafferty's not a federal judge, so he must have sent his clerk across the street to the district court and had one of his cronies sign it. You couldn't possibly have gotten all that done before the fact."

"Well, aren't you the crafty detective? What's important here, Zach, is that we saved a man's life."

"Yes, and now that man is cuffed to a bed in Bellevue, his wife is filing for divorce, and the DA's office is charging him with half a dozen white-collar crimes. So I guess you're right. It sounds like a win-win all the way around. How do you plan on celebrating?"

"C.J. and I are going for dinner at the Mark."

"Are you serious? The same hotel where the robbery took place?"

"They have an incredible restaurant in the lobby. The hotel manager invited everyone at the poker game to be his guest, anytime. Hey, do you and Cheryl want to join us?"

"Thanks, but Cheryl took the Amtrak down to Philadelphia for a conference. My victory dinner will be a solo affair: sausage pizza, a six-pack of Blue Moon, and a Yankee game."

"That sounds dreadful."

It did. But it was a lie. Not the Cheryl part, but everything else. Q had texted me earlier in the day and told me he had a lead on the two thugs who had chloroformed Bob Reitzfeld, tied him up, and escaped with eight hundred thousand dollars. It was ironic that C.J. would be returning to the scene of the crime on the very same night that I was working hard to connect him to it.

As soon as Kylie left the office, I texted Q. Some of my informants like to give up the information they've got, take the money, and run. Not Q Lavish. He doesn't take money, and he enjoys turning our get-togethers into a social event.

An hour later, we were at Nom Wah Tea Parlor in Chinatown, sharing eight different kinds of dumplings. Halfway through the meal, the waiter brought us an order of boiled chicken feet with black bean sauce, which I happily pushed over to Q's side of the table.

"The two boys who hit the poker game are Tariq Jessup and Garvey Jewel," Q said, picking up a turnip cake with his chopsticks and taking a bite.

"You sure?"

"A hundred percent. I have a signed confession," he said, totally straight-faced. "They're waiting for you to cuff 'em and stuff 'em."

"Sorry. Dumb question. Let me rephrase. What makes you think they're the perps?"

"Jessup and Jewel are two bottom-feeder hip-hop promoters. They troll the streets and the internet looking for any wannabe Kanye or Nicki Minaj who can keep a beat and chant a rhyme. They put together a show, package it to any low-end club that will take them on, then beat the bushes for friends, family, and anyone else they can get to line up behind the velvet rope."

"So they're musical impresarios," I said.

"Impresarios who get paid in watered-down drinks and a small percentage of the gate if they're lucky. There's a ladder in the music business, Zachary, and these brothers barely have one foot on the bottom rung."

"And yet…"

"Are you familiar with Gansevoort PM? It's a club in the meatpacking district."

"I've heard of it." *From Kylie. She was supposed to meet C.J. there but called it off when Aubrey Davenport's body turned up on Roosevelt Island.*

"Now that's a club," Q said. "Their music rocks the roof off the building. And so do their prices. But guess who was seen there the past two nights?"

"Jessup and Jewel."

"Correct. They had their mitts all over two women who were totally out of their league, and they'd traded up from rack vodka to bottles of Dom. These mofos never had that kind of money in their lives."

"Is it possible they won it in a poker game?"

Q picked up another chicken foot. "You sure you won't try one of these?"

"No, I'm more of a breast man. Do you know where I can find Jessup and Jewel?"

"They move around."

"How about tonight?" I said.

He gave me a wide grin and sank his teeth into the chicken foot. Of course he knew. Q knows everything.

CHAPTER 56

AFTER DINNER WE polished off an order of sweet fried sesame balls and two pots of bo-lay tea while Q gave me everything he had on Jessup and Jewel. Then he helped me craft a cover story I never could have invented on my own.

"It's a little over-the-top," I said. "Can we make it more…I don't know…realistic?"

"You mean like the Nigerian prince scam? Zach, you know the old saying 'You can't make this shit up'? Sometimes the more unbelievable something is the more people are willing to believe it."

"You think they'll buy it?"

"You think you can sell it?" he fired back.

I shrugged. "Early on, I worked undercover for Narcotics. I remember my first day on the street. I hadn't showered or shaved for a week, my clothes were stained and raggedy, and I was totally convinced that I was the most authentic wreck of a junkie ever to try to make a buy. I approached the dealer, and the first thing he says to me is 'Take off your shoes.'"

Q started laughing before I even got to the punch line. "And I bet you had on a nice clean pair of socks," he said.

I nodded. "Dumbass rookie mistake. After a year I transferred out because I hated smelling like the inside of a Dumpster, but by the time I left I'd gotten pretty good at lying. I guess I'll find out if I still can pull it off."

"Drug dealers are hard to con because they think everybody's a narc. Jessup and Jewel are two-bit hustlers who have no reason to suspect you're undercover. You'll do fine. Just act like the guy in those old Westerns: you're Black Bart walking into the saloon."

"More like Caucasian Bart," I said, "but I get your point."

I paid the check and found a store in Chinatown that sold burner phones. Then I walked to Grand Street and took the D train uptown to the Bronx. It was a forty-five-minute ride, which gave me plenty of time to repeat my cover story to myself till it was second nature.

I got off at Bedford Park Boulevard and walked another eight blocks to Webster Avenue. The club was called Rattlesnake. If you could call it a club. It was more of a dive bar with a sandwich board on the sidewalk that said LIVE MUSIC TONIGHT.

There was no line, no velvet rope, just a guy in a muscle shirt sitting outside. He nodded at me and said, "Welcome to the Snake. Two-drink minimum."

It was relatively crowded for a Tuesday night. Close to a hundred people, most of whom checked out the white guy, then went back to what they were doing. I went to the bar, ordered a beer, and found a table near the back, as far from the music as possible.

Two minutes later, just as Q had predicted, a

good-looking man with shoulder-length dreads and a black beard flecked with gray pulled up a chair and flashed me a warm, gracious smile.

"Garvey Jewel," he said. "You with a label?"

I barely looked up from my beer. "No."

"You just into hip-hop?"

"Not a fan," I said.

"Then you in the wrong room," Jewel said, his smile morphing into a challenge. "And if you're here to cop some blow, you really in the wrong room. This place may look low-rent, but the old lady who owns it keeps it clean. Nobody underage. Nobody dealing. Just a bunch of people who come for the drinks and the music."

"I'm in the right room. But I didn't come for the music."

"Then why you here?"

"Same reason I go to the parking lot at Home Depot when I'm looking for day workers."

"What kind of day work you talking about?"

"Night work, actually. Not too dangerous, and it pays well."

"How well?"

I bent low and leaned forward, clasping my hands on the table. This was the moment of truth, and I dug down, hoping to channel the gravitas of Al Pacino and the psychological instability of Christopher Walken. I dropped my voice to a whisper. "More than you and your partner made last Wednesday night on the Upper East Side."

He pushed his chair away from the table, and his hand instinctively went to the waistband of his pants. "You a cop?"

I didn't flinch. "Answer me this, Garvey. Do you think the NYPD heard about your little blindman's bluff game at the Mark hotel, but there were no African American cops around, so they sent one lone white guy up to the Bronx to arrest you? Or do you think maybe you bragged to some woman who was sucking your dick, and she told her friend, who told her friends, who told their friends, and it finally got back to me?"

"Fucking Inez," Jewel said. "She got a big mouth."

Q had been right. "Guys like Jessup and Jewel won't be happy with a fat wad of money," he had told me. "They need to impress people with how they got it. Let him think the leak came from a girlfriend."

"What if he calls her on it?" I said.

"She'll deny it," Q said. "But he won't believe her. He'll believe you."

"Don't be mad at Inez," I said to Jewel. "She brought us together, didn't she? Now, would you like to hear what I have to say, or should I leave?"

"Wait here," he said, and walked toward the front of the room.

Two minutes later, he was back with his partner, who was wearing an Apple Watch on his wrist, just like the blind man in Reitzfeld's story.

"Twenty-five words or less," the new guy said. "And it better be good."

"Saturday night," I said. "Serious poker game in Jersey. The buy-in is a hundred and fifty grand. I'll be on the inside. I'm going to need some…"

"Some what?" Apple Watch said. He looked around, wondering why I had stopped. "Nobody's listening. Keep going."

"That was twenty-five words," I said. "I was counting on my fingers."

"You're a piece of work," he said, extending a hand. "Tariq Jessup."

I shook his hand and dropped my next whopper. "The name is Johnny Wurster," I said. "My friends call me Johnny Fly Boy."

"You a pilot?" he said.

"Back in the day, a couple of gorillas came over to my apartment and tossed me over a seventh-floor balcony. I bounced off an awning and landed on a three-hundred-pound doorman. I've been Johnny Fly Boy ever since."

The two of them laughed. "Okay, Mr. Fly Boy," Jessup said. "You just bought yourself a few thousand more words. Tell us about this poker game."

I told them all about it, and they hung on every word. I was their Nigerian prince.

CHAPTER 57

AT THREE IN the morning, Geraldo Segura put on his backpack and slipped out of his hotel on Sumner Place in Brooklyn. He stopped at an all-night market and bought a bottle of Poland Spring, two KIND bars, and the early editions of the *New York Post* and the *Daily News*.

He ate the energy bars and drank the water as he walked to the Flushing Avenue station. Then he climbed the stairs to the elevated subway platform, caught an eastbound J train, and scanned the papers.

A picture of the detective wielding a pair of bolt cutters to free Nathan Hirsch was on the front page of both. The *Post* headline said

HERO COP SAVES LYING LAWYER

He turned the page and read the banner above the lead story:

THAI BOXING CHAMP IS HOTEL BOMBER

There were two pictures of him: one from his high school yearbook, the other from his fighting days in

Thailand. At this point, he looked like neither. He'd come to New York with a bagful of professional disguises, and for this outing he'd aged himself twenty years, his head bald on top, with a fringe of mousy gray hair on each side. A matching beard obscured his face.

The details in the article were sketchy because the 911 tape had not yet been released, and Hirsch, who would have lied anyway, had been hauled off before the media could descend on him.

The *Daily News* coverage was the same as the *Post*'s, but the caption above his Muay Thai photo made him smile:

THE MOST WANTED MAN IN NEW YORK

He carefully tore the page from the newspaper, folded it, and put it in the pocket of his Windbreaker. He couldn't wait to show it to Jam.

He remembered the day he met her. She had come to Klong Prem prison not for the boxing but to watch her older sister parade around the ring in a bikini, holding up a card announcing the number of the next round.

"You're from America?" she asked him after he'd won four matches that day.

He smiled. She was cute. "Yes, ma'am."

"Who was your favorite president?" she asked.

"Abraham Lincoln."

"Then he's the one I'm going to read about," she said, flashing a bright smile. "Thanks."

He was twenty-two at the time. Jam was only twelve.

She came back for his next match and told him she'd read three books about Lincoln. "I cried when they shot him," she said. "What's your favorite book that you read when you were my age?"

"*To Kill a Mockingbird* by Harper Lee."

And so the friendship took hold. Soon Jam would start visiting between boxing matches, and the prisoner and the schoolgirl would talk about literature, philosophy, history, and her favorite subject, America.

"Whenever the girl comes," Pongrit Juntasa instructed his guards, "let her in. She makes him a better fighter."

That may or may not have been true, but by the time he was twenty-eight, Geraldo Segura had become Rom Ran Sura, the best Muay Thai boxer in Southeast Asia—with his sights set on the rest of the world.

Special prisoners are afforded special privileges, and one evening Segura was given a hot shower and clean clothes and driven to Juntasa's house. A guard escorted Segura to the dining room, where the head of the Department of Corrections was standing next to a table set for two.

"Rom Ran Sura, your most recent victory at the World Combat Games has once again brought great honor to the kingdom," Juntasa announced. "As a reward, His Majesty has graciously reduced your sentence by another seven years."

Segura silently did the math. He had been fighting for his freedom, and with this latest grant from the king, he would be out by the time he was fifty years old. He thanked his benefactor.

"I have one other gift," Juntasa said. He raised his hand, a door opened, and Jam Anantasu entered.

"It is her eighteenth birthday," Juntasa said. "The age of consent. Enjoy your evening."

He left the room, and Segura stood there, barely able to breathe. Jam was a vision, a goddess in a white-lace dress, her shimmering black hair cascading down to her bare shoulders, her lips parted in a shy smile, her smoldering eyes locked on his. She was no longer a child. She was a woman—the one he wanted to spend his life with. If only she was willing to wait.

They dined. They drank. They talked. They laughed. And then they adjourned to a bedroom suite, where the air was filled with soft music and the scent of jasmine, and they made love by candlelight.

The next morning, he returned to prison. He never lost another fight, and with each new achievement, the king rewarded him by taking more time off his sentence.

The conjugal visits continued, and over the next ten years, he and Jam had four children. As the dream of a life together slowly became a reality, she took a job working in the American Embassy in Bangkok. She was the one who secured his passports: one that gave him easy entry into the U.S., and a second passport with a new identity for his new life. Their new life.

He was too well-known in Thailand to go back, and as much as he knew Jam would want to live in America, that was impossible. The plan was to meet her and the kids in Adelaide, Australia. Flynn Samuels had given him contacts. After putting his life on hold for twenty years, he was ready for a fresh start.

But not yet. He still had two more people to see in New York.

Princeton Wells was no doubt expecting him. But first he had to pay a surprise visit to one of the most ruthless men in the city.

The J train stopped at Broadway Junction, and Segura connected to the L, took it six stops, and got off at the Rockaway Parkway station in Canarsie.

He tightened the straps of his backpack around his shoulders and started the mile-long walk to the Karayib Makèt on Rockaway Parkway.

He had a gift for Malique La Grande, and he planned to deliver it personally.

CHAPTER 58

"GOOD MORNING, HANDSOME."

I looked up from my keyboard. It was Cheryl. I checked my watch. It was only eight thirty. "Hey," I said. "What the heck are you doing here?"

"Well, I was thinking you'd be happy to see me," she said, "but I guess I thought wrong."

I jumped out of my chair and gave her a hug. "Of course I am. I just thought you were spending the day at that conference in Philadelphia."

"It was a total yawn. Then Captain Cates called this morning and asked me if I could come back. I caught a six-thirty train, and here I am."

Kylie was at her desk taking it all in. "I don't know about Zach," she said, "but I, for one, am thrilled you're here. It would have been even more fun if you'd been here last night."

"Why? What happened?"

"You know the robbery we caught last week at the Mark hotel?"

"Shelley Trager's poker game," Cheryl said. "Did you find the guys who did it?"

"Just the opposite. Shelley doesn't want us poking around. The hotel management is so grateful he's sweeping it under the rug that they offered us dinner at the Jean-Georges restaurant in the lobby. C.J. and I went last night. The place was packed, the food was incredible, and it was free. Guess who turned down an invitation to go with us?" Kylie pointed in my direction.

I looked at Cheryl. "Hey, you were out of town."

"I know. But the Mark restaurant? I'd have gone if you were out of town."

"Tell her what you did instead," Kylie said.

"I have a better idea," I said. "Instead of standing here rehashing every detail of my pathetic evening, I'd rather be alone with my girlfriend, so I can tell her how much I missed her. Excuse us." I put my arm around Cheryl and walked her to the stairwell.

"What's going on between you and Kylie?" she said as soon as we were alone.

"Nothing."

"Zach, I'm a cop and a shrink, so I get lied to every day."

"I'm not lying to you. I may be leaving out some of the details, but—"

"So you're sticking to your story that you had a *pathetic* evening last night?"

"I may have exaggerated that one."

"And when I asked 'What's going on between you and Kylie?' and you said 'Nothing,' was that an exaggeration, or were you just leaving out the details?"

"Maybe a little of both."

"I don't know what's going on, but I'm starting to understand why you weren't happy to see me this morning."

"Can I explain?"

"Go for it," she said. "They say the truth shall set you free."

Maybe so, but in this case, I was afraid that the truth would only dig me a deeper hole. So I started with a half-truth.

"I'm investigating Kylie's boyfriend," I said. "I think he may be involved in that poker game robbery."

"And this is something Cates asked you to do?" Cheryl said.

"Nobody *asked* me. I see a crime; I try to solve it. I'm a cop."

"A cop who's trying to put his ex-girlfriend's new boyfriend in jail."

"Bullshit. You think this is personal?"

"Zach, everything with you and Kylie is personal."

"She's my partner. If C.J. used her to get invited to that poker game, I think she'd want to know before he uses her again."

"Did she ask you to protect her from C.J.?"

"Of course not."

"Maybe that's because she's a grown woman who can take care of herself. She's also a smart cop, which means if *you* suspect C.J. because he's the new guy at the table, don't you think that thought might have crossed Kylie's mind as well?"

I opened my mouth, but nothing came out.

Cheryl kept going. "You say you're her partner, and you think she'd want to know if C.J. were using her. And yet you lied to her last night about what you were up to. What happens if you catch him? Are you going to arrest him?"

"No. Shelley has already said he won't press charges."

"So what do you think he'll do?"

"Knowing Shelley, he'll give the guy a chance to pay the money back and quietly slip out of town."

"So C.J. will be out of Kylie's life," Cheryl said. "Mission accomplished, partner. You just better hope she never finds out that you're the one who got rid of him."

Clearly the truth had not set me free. I'd only told Cheryl part of what I'd been up to, and all I'd managed to do was piss her off. The rest would have to wait.

"We'd better get back to work," I said. "Let's finish this up another time."

I opened the stairwell door, and we walked back into the squad room.

"Good timing," Kylie said. "Aubrey's hard drive is hooked up to a monitor. It's ready for us in the conference room."

I turned to Cheryl. "I'm glad you're back. I'll see you tonight."

"What do you mean *tonight*? I'm going with you now."

"With us? We're going to screen Aubrey Davenport's video files."

"I know. That's why Cates called me this morning. You're two cops working a homicide where the victim had deep-rooted psychosexual disorders. Cates thought it might help if an actual psychologist sat in and screened the videos with you."

"Great idea," Kylie said, giving me a thumbs-up.

I followed my ex-girlfriend and my current girlfriend into the conference room so we could watch sex tapes together. It was definitely not the threesome of my dreams.

CHAPTER 59

JASON WHITE, OUR resident computer genius, was waiting for us in the conference room. Normally, he's a high-energy guy with a passion for mountain bike racing, complex techno problems, and caffeine, but this morning he looked as joyless as a funeral director.

"Good morning, Detectives, Dr. Robinson," he said. "Brace yourselves. It's going to be a long day."

"What have you got?" I said, taking a seat.

"Aubrey Davenport was making a documentary. From what we could piece together, she video-ambushed thirty-two different men. She used code names, but some of them, like Judge Rafferty, are immediately recognizable. Given a little time, I'm sure our facial-recognition software can ID them all. We've organized the files according to date last opened. Every single one of them was opened after Aubrey's death."

"That would be our blackmailers' handiwork," Kylie said. "Can you tell if they edited anything?"

"They didn't," Jason said. "They just watched. The last file modified was Sunday, May seventh— the day before the murder. It's Aubrey's on-camera introduction to the film. It's only two minutes and twenty-four seconds long. The rest of the footage is Aubrey having sex with these men. None of it is pretty. It's still unedited and will take you about fourteen hours to screen. Less time if you high-speed through it. More time if you get sick to your stomach and have to walk away from it."

"Let's start with the introduction," Cheryl said.

Jason double-clicked a file, and the screen faded to a shot of Aubrey Davenport sitting on a tall director's chair. She wore dark gray pants and a soft dove-gray cashmere sweater. Her hair, which had been matted with dirt when I saw her on Roosevelt Island, was a rich chestnut and fell to her shoulders in waves. Her eyes were bright and intelligent, and she had just enough makeup on to make her camera-ready without looking made-up. She was attractive, intense, and very much alive.

She didn't introduce herself. She just started talking to the camera in a clear, confident voice.

"My sex addiction began at the age of twelve, when I found my father's stash of porn tapes. At that age I had a pretty good idea what sex was all about, but this wasn't that. This was much more interesting: bondage, discipline, dominance, submission. My fascination was instantaneous, and I wanted to be like the women in those videos."

The camera began to drift in slowly.

"By fourteen, I'd had several flings, but they were with clumsy teenage boys who wanted nothing more than to stick their dicks in a hole. And then I found Brad Overton. He was thirty-eight, a film producer, and I was sixteen, an unpaid summer intern. Brad was handsome, powerful, and when he came on to me, I couldn't say no. I didn't *want* to say no. Not to the drugs, not to the physical pain, not to the degradation. This was the sex I'd been dreaming of."

As I got drawn into her story, I realized the camera was pulling me in as well. It had moved to a medium shot and was continuing to drift closer still.

"When the summer was over, my job ended, and Brad replaced me with another girl. I spent the next twenty-three years trying to replace Brad. One man after another, raging sadists who hurt me physically and emotionally, and all I could do was beg for more. Until one day…"

She paused, and I held my breath.

"Until one day," she repeated, "I didn't just want them to *hurt* me. I wanted them to *kill* me."

At this point, the camera stopped moving. Aubrey's face filled the screen. Her eyes were moist.

"I am an addict," she said, her voice cracking slightly. "A slave to my sexual addiction. This documentary is about men who prey on women like me. It's all shot with hidden cameras. I don't have to tell you their names. You'll know them. Watch them hurt and humiliate me. They think they're in control. But I'm the one with the power. I'm the one doing the humiliating."

She took one more long pause.

"I've been hurt enough," she said. "This film is how I will heal."

The screen went to black, and white type slowly faded up onto it.

SEX SLAVE
A FILM BY AUBREY DAVENPORT

CHAPTER 60

NOBODY SAID A WORD.

Finally, Cheryl broke the silence. "That poor woman. What a tortured life."

"Jason, how many of the men in these videos have you positively identified?" Kylie asked.

"Nine," Jason answered, "but we've only had the footage for a couple of hours. Give us a day, and we'll ID them all."

"Do you know what Janek Hoffmann looks like?"

"The guy you arrested? Yeah. We looked for him. He's not in the mix."

Kylie looked at me. "Do you still think Janek killed her?"

"There is plenty of circumstantial evidence," I said. "Her car parked a block from his apartment is hard to ignore. Plus he doesn't have an alibi."

"He also doesn't have a motive."

"You don't need a motive when you have a history of 'roid rage. Kylie, he beat her up bad in the past."

"But this time she wasn't beat up. And the murder wasn't the result of a flash of rage. It was too well planned and executed. Aubrey caught thirty-two men on hidden camera, every one of whom had a better motive to kill her, steal her laptop, and make sure this documentary would never see the light of day."

"If they knew it existed."

"One of them did," Kylie said. "Our job is to find out which one."

"Or eliminate all thirty-two of them and keep trying to make a case that will convict Janek."

"Guys, it's going to be a long day," Cheryl said. "Can you save the detective talk until after you actually know what you're talking about?" She turned to Jason. "Play the tapes, please."

"She shot the first one fourteen months ago, Doc," Jason said. "The latest is dated two weeks before she died."

"Start with the oldest one first," Cheryl said. "There may be a narrative thread in there."

On the other hand, it seemed more likely that the killer was a recent victim who caught Aubrey taping him and wasted no time eliminating her. But I wasn't going to argue with Cheryl. I'd pissed her off enough for one day.

There was no thread. Just a theme: paraphilia. It's a shrink term for what most people would call really weird sex. Some of the men were much older than Aubrey—father figures. No big surprise. The rest of them were more age-appropriate, but they were all authority figures: a deputy police commissioner, a college professor, and of course Judge Rafferty.

The sex ran the gamut from standard fare soft-core porn, to the more exotic BDSM, to perversions I'd never heard of, much less seen. I'd have been uncomfortable watching it on my own, but sitting through it with my girlfriend to the right of me and my ex-girlfriend to the left made it excruciating.

By noon we'd waded through fifteen videos. "Should we send out for lunch?" Jason asked.

"I can't watch this and eat," I said. "Let's walk over to Gerri's Diner."

"Let's watch one more, and we'll be halfway through," Cheryl said.

"Good idea," I said.

The sixteenth film started like all the others. Aubrey had a pinhole camera in her shoulder bag that she'd turn on just before meeting up with her latest target. Then she'd give a brief cryptic introduction.

"This one may be the biggest hypocrite of them all," Aubrey said. She was in an elevator. The doors opened; she walked down a hall and rang a doorbell. A man opened the door, but the camera was so close that all we could see was his shirt and tie.

The two of them walked into a second room, and then Aubrey removed the bag from her shoulder and carefully set it down at table height so that the camera would pick up the entire room.

Kylie and I both stood up. The man was not yet on camera, but we didn't need to see him to make a positive ID. The curtained windows, the upholstered furniture, and the deep red Persian rug all looked familiar.

But the clincher was the giant poster of Dumbo the flying elephant hanging on the wall behind Dr. Morris Langford's desk.

Cheryl leaned forward and pointed at the screen. "Zach," she said. "I've been to that office."

"We all have," I said.

And then the man who told us how hard he had worked to help Aubrey overcome her addiction stepped into the frame, undid his belt, unzipped his fly, and let his pants drop to the floor.

"On your knees," he said.

CHAPTER 61

I WATCHED THE video with my fists clenched. Of all the men who had taken advantage of Aubrey, Langford was the most despicable.

"For her, sex had to be loveless and punishing," he had told us. He had analyzed her addiction, and then, privy to her darkest secrets, he made sure he gave her the high she was looking for.

"Sick son of a bitch," Kylie said. "It proves he lied to us, but we still have to prove he killed her."

Shrinks don't shock easily, but Cheryl looked nothing short of horrified.

"Are you okay?" I said.

She rolled her eyes. Of course she wasn't okay. Langford was a colleague, a highly regarded sex therapist. I could only imagine what she felt like watching him violate one of the basic moral principles set forth in the code of medical ethics.

"We're about to go all detective on this case," I said. "Do you want to stay?"

She smiled. "I'm fine, Zach. Well, maybe not fine. I'm sickened, but I'm not walking out on this."

"Let's start with his alibi," I said, flipping through my notebook. "Aubrey parked her car in the garage in Brooklyn at 4:52 p.m. on May seventh. I don't know how she got to Roosevelt Island, but most likely it was in Langford's car. It was rush hour, so she couldn't have gotten there much before five thirty. The body was called in shortly after nine thirty. When I spoke to Langford the following day, he said he had been at a medical conference in Albany. But was he there during that four-hour window when Aubrey was murdered?"

"Was there even a conference?" Kylie said.

"Hold on." Jason began tapping away on his laptop. It took him a few seconds to come up with an answer. "There was a substance abuse conference at the Albany Marriott on May seventh and eighth," he said.

"What's the number of the hotel?" Kylie asked. "We can call and find out when he checked in."

"We could do that," Jason said, "and hope that we could convince some hotel desk clerk to cooperate without a warrant. Or..." His fingers flew across the keys.

Thirty seconds later, he found what he was looking for.

"Or," he repeated, "we could check the good doctor's credit card charges and find out that he bought gas at the Plattekill rest stop on the New York State Thruway at 10:34 p.m. on May seventh, and he checked into the Albany Marriott at 12:10 a.m. on May eighth."

"It's a three-hour drive from New York," Kylie said. "I'd like to check his GPS and see where he started from."

I turned to Cheryl. "What's your take, Dr. Robinson?"

She took a deep breath and looked at the monitor.

The screen was dark now, but the memory was vivid. Then she turned back to the group. "I think we were wrong to assume that all the men on these videos had a strong motive for killing Aubrey," she said. "Judge Rafferty practically laughed it off. Most of the others would be subjected to public humiliation, but they'd bounce back. Men like that always do. People tend to be forgiving when politicians, sports heroes, and movie stars are caught up in a sex scandal. But they'd never forgive the one man Aubrey trusted to help her. Morey Langford's private practice, his hospital affiliations, his broadcast contracts, would all disappear overnight. He'd be ruined. If you need a motive for murder that will stick with a jury, you've got one."

"In that case," I said, "I'm skipping lunch and the other sixteen videos and paying Dr. Langford a house call."

"Let's do it," Kylie said, her adrenaline pumping—a fired-up female cop eager to race out the door to take down a repugnant male predator.

Cheryl, of course, shared none of Kylie's enthusiasm. "Good luck," she said, her voice barely above a whisper, her eyes unable to hide the disillusionment she felt inside.

"I'm sorry," I said. "I know how much you admired him."

"I did. And now I don't." She took another deep breath. "Great police work, Detectives," she said, her voice reenergized. "Now go get the bastard."

CHAPTER 62

"**IS HE GOOD** to go?" Kylie asked as we sped across the 79th Street transverse.

It was the classic question. Translation: do we have enough evidence to arrest him?

"No," I said. "The video doesn't prove he killed her, and the fact that his Albany alibi is full of holes doesn't put him on Roosevelt Island with Aubrey. All we can do is smile, be superpolite, and ask him if he'd be so kind as to come back with us to the station and help us with our investigation."

"*Superpolite* doesn't sound like me," Kylie said.

"Good call," I said. "Let me do the talking."

Kylie turned onto West End Avenue and parked the car in front of the same hydrant she'd blocked the week before. This time a doorman came running out of the building, waving his arms. He was about thirty, tall, with large bony hands and a thin-lipped scowl on his face that looked like it was painted on permanently.

"You can't park there, lady," he yelled.

"Wanna bet?" she said, flashing her badge.

"So what's the deal?" he said. "You two cops

are going to lunch for what—two hours? I need that space for people who are getting in and out of cabs."

"Relax, pal," I said. "We'll be out of here in ten minutes. We're going to see one of your tenants."

"Which one?"

"We'd rather not be announced," Kylie said.

"And I'd rather your car weren't blocking the front of my building. Life is full of disappointments, sweetheart. Which tenant?"

I'd never seen him before. He hadn't been on the door the night we first visited Langford. But I knew the type. Somewhere along the way he'd been soured on cops, and Kylie's in-your-face approach didn't help change his mind.

"Dr. Langford," I said.

He flashed a victory scowl. "Your names?"

We played the game and identified ourselves. He rang up.

"No problem, Doctor," he said after a brief dialogue. Then he turned to us. "He's with a patient. I'll let you know when you can go up."

"And what's your name, asshole?" Kylie asked.

"Eddy. With a y in case you're adding me to your Christmas card list. Now cool your jets outside. We have a no-loitering-in-the-lobby policy."

By the time he waved us in ten minutes later, Kylie was seething. "I'll be back for that punk-ass prick," she said as we rode up in the elevator.

"Calm down," I said. "Remember the deal. I do the talking."

I rang the bell, and Langford cracked the door open.

"Hate to bother you again, Doctor," I said, "but it would speed up our investigation if you came down to the station and helped us out with a few more questions."

"Could we do this another time?" he said. "I'm with a patient."

"We can wait downstairs," I said. "What time would work for you?"

"I have an impossible schedule," he said. "Plus I'm traveling this weekend. How about next Tuesday?"

"How about now?" Kylie said, shoving her way in front of me. "If that doesn't work for your schedule, how about five minutes from now?"

"Excuse me, Detective," he said, bristling, "but I've already told you everything I know about Aubrey Davenport."

"No you haven't. Take a ride with us, and I'll prove it."

The doorman had pressed all Kylie's buttons, and she was unleashing her anger on Langford. I tried to get the situation back under control.

"Dr. Langford, I'm sorry if we sound overly aggressive," I said. "It's just that some new evidence has come to light, and it would help if we could share it with you. Are you sure you can't spare twenty minutes?"

"No. If you've got new evidence, send me an email. I'll get to it when I can."

"How about if we just put it on YouTube?" Kylie said.

We had an ace in the hole, and Kylie was pissed enough to turn our cards faceup. If Langford was our murderer, he'd have known about the video. And now he knew that we knew. I was pretty sure he'd slam the door in our faces. But I was wrong.

"I'm sorry," he said. "I've been under a lot of

pressure. I very much want to help you catch Aubrey's killer. I'll go with you. Come in."

He opened the door, and we entered his waiting room. "I have a patient in my office. I can't just leave her there. We're in the middle of a hypnotherapy session."

"Does that actually work?" I said.

"Oh, goodness, yes. It's highly effective at helping people change behaviors like smoking or nail-biting. Also, a trained therapist can help people explore painful feelings and memories they may be hiding from their conscious mind. My patient is in a hypnotic state. Give me a few minutes to bring her out of it."

He stepped into his inner office.

"I don't get it," Kylie said. "Why is he suddenly being so cooperative?"

"Maybe it's because you threatened to ruin his career by going public with the video. Nice way to let me do the talking, MacDonald."

"And now you're bent out of shape because I got him to agree to come in for questioning? A hundred bucks says he cracks when we show him the video. Call Selma Kaplan. I want her behind the glass when he gives it up."

The inner door opened. "Detectives, please step in," Langford said.

We walked in. I didn't see the woman in the chair by the door until we were on the opposite side of the room. She was attractive, in her midthirties, sitting quietly with her purse on her lap.

"This is Karen," Langford said. "She had a horrific childhood. She was raped repeatedly by her mother's boyfriend, Lucas, and Mom did nothing to stop it. She was powerless then, but she's much stronger now. Aren't you, Karen?"

The woman nodded.

"Now that your mother and that evil Lucas are back in your life, what are you going to do if they try to hurt you?" Langford asked.

"Kill them," Karen said, taking a gun from her purse and pointing it at me and Kylie.

The shrink flashed us a devilish smile. "Oh, she will," he said. "I'm an expert at suggestion therapy. If you so much as move from where you're standing now, Karen will shoot you dead. Isn't that right, Karen?"

"That's right. I'll shoot them dead."

"Mom," Langford said, pointing at Kylie, "you've hurt your daughter enough, but now she has a new-found strength." Now he pointed his finger at me. "As for you, Lucas, don't even think about trying any of your old tricks."

He opened the door. "Good-bye," he said, and shut the door behind him.

My eyes scanned the room, stopping briefly on the flying elephant, who, according to Dr. Langford, symbolized the power of belief, and then they came to rest on the woman blocking the door.

Karen didn't blink. She stared straight ahead at the two of us, gun in hand, finger on the trigger.

CHAPTER 63

I'VE MADE SOME tough calls in my eleven-plus years as a cop. But I was face-to-face with the most excruciatingly difficult decision I'd ever had to make.

I wondered if Dr. Langford had any idea of the ethical, moral, and legal dilemma he had left me and Kylie in. Probably not. Most civilians don't have a clue about police protocol.

My partner and I were twelve feet away from a woman who had a deadly weapon pointed at us. But she wasn't a criminal. She was an average citizen who had been transformed into a killing machine by a man who got inside her head and rewired her brain.

By all accounts she was an innocent victim. You might think that two veteran police officers would do everything they could to help her out of this untenable situation. Most people would expect us to talk to her calmly until we could convince her to turn over the gun.

But that's not what we were trained to do. Our official response in a situation like this was clear-cut: *Shoot her dead.*

It's Police Academy 101. If a suspect points a gun, or reaches for a gun in a way that indicates they're going to shoot, police are authorized to fire. There's no debate. We are supposed to aim directly at the suspect's center mass and shoot to kill.

The aftermath of shooting this woman would be horrendous. People would scream police brutality and argue that a person would never do something under hypnosis that went against their personal code of ethics. Did I have any idea whether Karen's personal code would allow her to shoot a rapist and an abusive mother in cold blood? No. And I didn't care.

There was only one question on my mind. Could we kill her before she killed us?

I locked eyeballs with Kylie, and then I slowly let my gaze drift to the rug about four feet from Karen's left. Then I shifted and zeroed in on the corresponding spot four feet from Karen's right. The message was simple: Kylie would dive to the left, and I'd dive to the right. We'd roll, draw, and fire.

The odds were that Karen had no experience with guns, which meant that even if she pulled the trigger, she would do what most amateurs do and shoot the first round high while we were on the ground. She'd never have time to get off a second shot.

Kylie nodded. She understood the plan.

I angled my body to the right and shifted my weight to my left foot. Then I put three fingers to my face and counted down by tapping on my cheek. *One... Two...*

"Karen, I am so proud of you," Kylie said.

My head snapped in her direction, but she didn't look at me. She was focused on Karen.

"What?" Karen mewed.

"I'm proud," Kylie said. "Proud of you."

"For what?"

"For standing up," Kylie said. "All these years I stood by and did nothing. I'm sorry, Karen. I wanted to help you..."

"You did?"

"Of course I did. I'm your mother," Kylie said, taking a step toward Karen. "But now you're doing for yourself what I couldn't do for you. You're strong now, Karen. Nobody will ever hurt you again."

Kylie took another step forward. "I'm so very sorry," she said. "You're my daughter." Another step. "I only want the best for you." Then another.

It was insanity. The two women were squared off at point-blank range. "I love you," Kylie said, spreading her arms, begging her daughter's forgiveness.

Karen stood up. "Oh, Mama," she whimpered, tears rolling down her cheeks. She reached out for an embrace that was probably decades overdue. Without hesitation, Kylie went from loving mom to deadly commando, delivering a furious knife-hand strike to Karen's wrist.

Bone snapped, Karen yowled, the gun exploded, and glass shattered. Elephant down. The bullet hit Dumbo right between his eager-to-please baby-blue eyes. A fitting metaphor for Karen's sad existence.

"I'm sorry, kiddo," Kylie said, wrapping her arms around Karen and lowering her to the floor. "It was either this or blow your brains out. Mommy had to make a choice."

I retrieved the gun, which had fallen from Karen's limp hand. Then I called for backup and paramedics. "We have a white female, midthirties, in need of a doc to set a broken bone and a shrink to bring her out of a hypnotic state."

It's not a call Dispatch gets every day. "What kind of state did you say she was in, Detective?"

"Hypnotic. Like a medically induced trance. Call Dr. Cheryl Robinson at the One Nine. She may be able to help. My partner and I are leaving the scene in pursuit of a murder suspect, Dr. Morris Langford. White, male, midforties, reddish hair."

I dropped to the floor. Kylie had tucked a pillow under Karen's head and was about to cuff the dazed woman's ankle to the coffee table.

"Gosh, you're the best mom ever," I said.

"Sorry I couldn't shoot her, Lucas, but the paperwork's a bitch."

She took Langford's gun from my hand. "Now let's find Dr. Strangelove and give him his gun back," she said as we raced out the door.

"Maybe I better take it," I said.

"Thanks, but I'd rather hang on to it," she said, tucking the gun into her waistband. "There's a good chance I may use it on Eddy with a y."

CHAPTER 64

SHE DIDN'T USE the gun, but as soon as we got to the lobby, Kylie slammed the doorman against a wall. "Where did he go, you dickless bastard?" she screamed.

"Who?" he said.

Wrong answer. She jammed her forearm into his windpipe and drove a knee into his groin. He doubled over, gagging, fighting for air, but he was no match for a trained cop whose adrenaline was firing on all cylinders after a near-death experience.

I looked left and then right, hoping nobody was watching a high profile detective use excessive force on a civilian whose only crime was that he was a flaming asshole.

"Where did he go?" Kylie repeated as soon as Eddy caught his breath.

"Cab," the doorman squeaked. "Yellow...boxy cab...Nissan."

"Where is he going?" She dug hard into the pressure point on the webbing of his hand over his thumb.

He dropped to the floor, sniveling. "They drove south. That's all I know. I swear. Please stop. I'm sorry."

She cuffed him to a brass handrail just as the first squad car came to a screeching stop on West End Avenue.

"Officers," Kylie yelled, "make sure the lady in 7G gets immediate medical attention, then arrest this piece of shit for obstruction of justice. Take him down to Central Booking and make sure his paperwork gets the full bureaucratic monty. With any luck, he'll get lost in the Tombs for a week."

It was a bogus charge. But by the time Eddy got untangled from the city's clogged justice system, he'd never mouth off to another cop again. Hell hath no fury. We raced to the car and headed south.

"Call Natty," Kylie said, her spleen vented, her full attention on tracking down the fugitive psychiatrist.

Natalie Brown is a sultry-voiced singer with a progressive rock band. She has luxurious ringlets of red hair down to her shoulders and a kick-ass body down to her toes. But sexy and talented doesn't always pay the rent, so by day she works for the Taxi and Limousine Commission.

If a detective wants to know where a certain cabbie was at a certain time, the TLC can track down that information. But not right away. That's because they're also busy tracking down lost briefcases, cell phones, and umbrellas for the six hundred thousand passengers who hail cabs every day. Natty Brown is our go-to person when Kylie and I need answers in a New York minute.

"Hey, Red," I said as soon as she picked up. "Zach Jordan and Kylie MacDonald. This is a screaming emergency."

"It always is," she said. "Hit me."

"A yellow cab, probably a Nissan, picked up a

single white male on West End Avenue near the corner of Eighty-Fourth Street about five minutes ago. Passenger is a murder suspect on the run."

"Gimme a minute," she said, and I could hear the clacking of her nails on a keyboard. "Guys, I've got great news."

"What is it?" I said, raising the volume on the speaker.

"The band is going to be on the cover of *Prog* magazine in October."

"My cab, Natty! My cab!"

"Relax, Zach. I was just making small talk while I was waiting for the board to light up. Here we go. I've got two possibles. No, wait, this one is a Prius. I got your Nissan. License number is 8Y47. The driver's name is—"

"I don't care what his name is. Just tell me where he is."

"Central Park West. He just turned onto the Seventy-Ninth Street transverse."

"Seal off the other end," Kylie said, making a hard left onto 82nd Street.

I grabbed the radio and barked orders at the dispatcher. "I need all available units to block off the transverse at Seventy-Ninth and Fifth. Officers in pursuit of a murder suspect riding in the back of an eastbound yellow cab, license 8Y47. Suspect is white, male, midforties, and may be armed."

"Zach! Zach!" It was Natalie.

"We can take it from here, Natty," I said. "Thanks for your—"

"Don't hang up," she said. "This guy has a gun, and you're sending in the cavalry? You're putting my driver right in the middle of a shoot-out."

"Natalie, these cops are trained. They're not going

to start shooting with innocent bystanders in the line of fire."

"And how about the murderer in the back of 8Y47? Is he also trained not to shoot bystanders? Sorry, Zach, but I'm calling the driver and warning him."

"Wait: you can call him?"

"Of course I can. I started to give you his name and cell number, but you weren't interested."

"Change of plans," I said. "I'm very interested. But if a cop calls him, he's either going to freak out or he won't believe me. Does this guy know you?"

"I'm the hot redhead singer at the TLC. All the drivers know me, honey."

"Then tell him to stop his cab where he is, take the keys out of the ignition, and run as far from his passenger as he can. Tell him his life depends on it."

"His life and my job," she said. "Hold on."

Kylie ran a red on Central Park West and turned into the transverse. The entire stretch of road through the park is a little over half a mile. About a quarter of a mile into it, the traffic started to back up. And then it came to a dead stop. The roadblock was in place. No cars were getting in or out.

"Zach, the driver is out of his cab and running in your direction," Natalie said. "He's bought all of our albums, so don't shoot him."

Kylie and I jumped out of our car and started running down the roadway, badges on chains around our necks, guns drawn, yelling, "Police! Stay in your vehicles. Get down and stay down," as we ran. I could see the roof of the boxy yellow cab jutting up about a foot and a half above the passenger cars behind it.

A man ran toward us. It was the cabdriver. "He have *gahn,*" the man said in a thick Russian accent.

"Gone where?" I said.

"No, no, not gone. He have *gahn*." He pointed a finger at me. "Bang. You dead."

"He has a gun?"

"Yes. Small *vun*. Pistol."

"Are you sure?" Kylie asked.

"Am I sure? The man point *gahn* at me. He says tell cops I have *gahn*." The cabbie threw his hands up in the air. "You don't believe me? Go see for yourself."

CHAPTER 65

"**A BELOVED THERAPIST** with not one but two *gahns*?" Kylie said as we ran toward the cab. "Clearly there's more to Dr. Langford than his bio on Wikipedia would lead you to believe."

We closed in fast. A hundred yards, fifty, twenty, and then...

"Don't come any closer, Detectives." It was Langford. He was still in the back of the cab, crouched low on the floor. I could see the top of his ginger hair through the window.

"You're out of options, Doctor," Kylie said. "There's no place you can go."

"There are always options, Detective. Sometimes it just boils down to the lesser of two evils."

"Your best choice right now is to get out of the cab with your hands held high," she said.

"I don't think so. Not at my age, and certainly not in the state of New York."

"I'm not following."

"Don't play me, Detective. You know what I'm talking about. I'm forty-seven, I'm healthy, and there's no death penalty in New York. Dying is easy. It's on everyone's bucket list. But wasting away in a government-sanctioned dungeon until I'm seventy, or eighty, or ninety? Not an option."

"Shit," Kylie whispered to me. "He'd rather die than go to jail. You know what that means?"

I knew. Suicide by cop. It's a time-tested way to avoid a long-term prison sentence. Just come out shooting so the cops are forced to shoot back and kill you.

"Keep him talking," she said. Then, using the line of backed-up cars for cover, she made her way east toward the roadblock.

"Dr. Langford," I called out, trying to keep my tone as friendly as possible. "Aubrey was blackmailing you. It doesn't get you off the hook for killing her, but it means you were also a victim. A good lawyer could use that to negotiate a lighter sentence with the DA."

"News flash, Jordan," Langford yelled. "Aubrey wasn't blackmailing me. A few weeks ago I spent the night in her apartment, and she made the mistake of leaving her computer on with no password protection. I found the videos. Her introduction spelled it out. You saw it, didn't you?"

"Yes, sir. She had a backup of everything."

"Then you know she wasn't blackmailing anyone. She was making a documentary that would destroy as many men as she could, and I would be hurt the most."

"You're wrong," I said. "Having sex with a patient wouldn't have hurt your career."

"Maybe not if Aubrey were the only patient. But there are others. Dozens. They've been silent till now, but going public with that film would have opened the floodgates. I had to kill her. It was a smart plan. I told her to meet me for dinner at a restaurant that just *happened* to be near Janek Hoffmann's apartment. Then I picked her up, told her I changed my mind, and we drove out to Roosevelt Island together. You should have seen the look on her face when she realized I wasn't going to release the choke hold."

My cell rang. It was Kylie. I picked up. "I don't think I can keep him talking much longer," I said.

"Tell him to come out," she said. "*Make* him come out."

"I've been involved in a lot of homicides, Dr. Langford," I said. "You'd be amazed at how easy some of them are to solve. This one was genius. If Aubrey hadn't backed up those videos, I never would have caught you. But you couldn't know she did that. You may wind up in jail, but I know the media. They're all going to want you: *60 Minutes,* the *New York Times, Time* magazine."

The cab door opened, and Langford stepped out, gun in hand. "Did they teach you that at the academy, Jordan? If you're negotiating with a narcissist, get him to give up by convincing him he can become a media darling, a rock star inmate. I told you: rotting away in prison is not an option."

He pointed the gun in my direction and started walking toward me. "You or me, Detective. And trust me, I won't hesitate to shoot."

I raised my gun. "Don't make me do this," I said.

"One of us is going to pull the trigger," he said, still advancing. "Your choice."

And then Kylie stepped out from behind the far side of the yellow Nissan. Her shooting stance was textbook. Feet shoulder width apart, the firing-side foot slightly behind the support-side foot. Her knees were flexed, arms extended straight out, head level.

She fired.

The two barbed darts flew from the Taser gun, one hitting Langford in the back, the other in the right hamstring. The pistol dropped from his hand, his body pitched forward, and he let out a prolonged agonizing scream as Kylie unleashed fifty thousand volts into his body.

Two uniforms poured out from behind the cab. Within five seconds, Kylie killed the power, and the cops pulled Langford to his feet.

She walked up to him and squared off. "Morris Langford, you're under arrest for the murder of Aubrey Davenport. You have the right to remain silent."

When she finished reading him his rights, one of the cops holding Langford said, "Would you like to do the honors and cuff him, Detective?"

Kylie slapped her hand to her belt and smiled. "I'm afraid one of you will have to do it, officer," she said. "My partner and I are out of cuffs. It's been a busy day."

CHAPTER 66

AT FOUR THIRTY, Mayor Muriel Sykes did what she does best. She showed up at the precinct unannounced.

Well, almost unannounced. Before she could get up to the third floor, I got a heads-up call from Bob McGrath, my eyes and ears at the front desk.

"Your prom date is here, Detective," he said.

"Thanks. How does she look?"

"Ravishing as always."

"I'm serious, Sarge. Pissed? Happy? What?"

"I've never seen her happy, and if you're wondering did she bring a box of doughnuts to reward you for your takedown in Central Park, the answer is no. She just blew right by me and headed up the stairs like a heat-seeking missile."

"Thanks, Sarge. I owe you one."

"Everybody owes me at least one, Jordan," McGrath said. "And you and your wackadoo partner owe me more than most."

"Shit," I said, hanging up the phone.

"What now?" Kylie asked.

"The mayor is on her way up."

"Shit," Kylie repeated. "Attaboys come by email. Personal appearances are never a good sign."

There was no time for further discussion. The stairwell door opened, and the mayor's heels clackety-clacked across the floor until she got to my desk.

"Congratulations on breaking the Davenport case," she said. "It was a home run."

The words were there, but the look on her face didn't match. If we'd hit a home run, how come there was no joy in Mudville?

"Thank you, ma'am," I said. "Is something wrong?"

"Everything is fucking wrong," she said. "Morris Langford is a celebrity shrink—talk shows, news programs, magazines. Even people who never met a psychiatrist can tell you who he is. And now he's going to be the focus of a murder trial where the key piece of evidence is a collection of videos that will give new meaning to the phrase 'New York society's most prominent members.'"

"Madam Mayor," Kylie said, "we know for a fact that the DA will do all he can to keep those tapes from seeing the light of day."

"Oh, I'm sure Mick Wilson can get a judge to rule them inadmissible at trial," Sykes said. "But once the press becomes aware of their existence, they will stop at nothing to get their hands on them. Or at the very least get the name of every man who got caught with his pants around his ankles. To an investigative reporter, those videos are a Pulitzer waiting to happen."

If there's one thing I've learned in my job it's this: never get in the way of a person who outranks you when they're blowing off steam. Kylie and I didn't say a word.

"Where are you on finding this mad bomber, Segura?" the mayor asked.

"We've got thirty-five thousand cops out there looking for him," Kylie said.

"And I've got eight and a half million people looking over their shoulder, wondering if he's going to cuff an exploding briefcase to their wrist," the mayor said. "Find him. Fast."

She turned and started to walk away. Then she stopped and came back. "One more thing," she said.

It was bullshit. She didn't have *one more thing*. This was the *only* thing. The mayor of the city of New York doesn't drive over to East 67th Street to congratulate two cops on closing one case and bitch at them for not cracking another. She came because she needed something. But instead of straight out saying "I'm here because I need a favor," she decided to make it look like it was an afterthought to our little heart-to-heart chat.

"When was the last time either of you spoke to Princeton Wells?" she said.

"I called him from Thailand to give him a heads-up about Segura," Kylie said. "I think it was Sunday night New York time, so it's been about three days."

"I've been trying to get hold of him, but he seems to be off the grid."

"Considering what happened to his partners, that kind of makes sense," Kylie said.

"Remember that little black-tie dinner at The Pierre hotel?" the mayor said. "A lot of powerful people donated a lot of money to build permanent housing for the homeless. Tremont Gardens is important to those donors and to this administration. We're scheduled to break ground in two weeks, and I can't get in touch with the man who is supposed to make it all happen. Someone has to tell Princeton Wells that just because the podium exploded doesn't mean the entire project gets blown up with it."

"Would you like us to reach out on your behalf?" Kylie said.

"Excellent idea, Detective. Just don't make it sound like I have NYPD running political errands for me. He's holed up at his place. Pay him a visit. Reassure him that you're close to catching Segura. Offer him police protection. Tell him we have to go back to business as usual, or the terrorists win. I don't care what you say to him—just get him to call me."

This time she turned and left. She got what she came for and made it sound like it was Kylie's idea to help.

"I guess we're going to Wells's place," I said. "You ready?"

"I just need a minute to update my résumé," Kylie said. "I'm going to add 'Personal flunky to the mayor.'"

CHAPTER 67

GERALDO SEGURA SMILED as he watched Carlotta step out of the front door of Princeton Wells's mansion on Central Park West. He didn't have to look at his watch to know exactly what time it was: 4:30 p.m. On the dot. Not a minute earlier, not a minute later. Carlotta was a creature of habit.

Her key ring was already in her hand, and she double-locked the front door with a practiced twist, tossed the keys in her purse, and zipped it up.

He raised the binoculars to his eyes. She had aged well over the years. She was in her sixties now. Her face was rounder, fuller, but her dark eyes were just as alert and intense as ever as she lifted the flap on the keypad at the front door and carefully punched in the security code.

He trained his gaze on her fingers. Eight. One. One. Seven. Five. *Gracias, Carlotta.*

He knew where she was going. She'd follow the same path she took every day, five days a week, for thirty-six years: a block and a half to the subway station at 72nd Street, catch the uptown C train, take it ten stops to West 155th Street, and walk another block and a half to her apartment on St. Nicholas Avenue.

He and Carlotta had bonded from the very first day he set foot in Princeton Wells's house. She was Salvadoran; he was Guatemalan. They had an almost identical coppery skin tone, a shared culture, and a mutual distrust of rich white people.

He remembered asking her once why she didn't ask Princeton's mother to have the family chauffeur drive her home, or at least pay for a cab.

"Mrs. Wells, she offered," Carlotta said. "But I say 'No thank you very much.'"

"Why would you turn down a ride in a limo?" he asked.

"A ride in a limo is wonderful," she said. "But getting out of a limo in my neighborhood is not so smart. When you take the subway, nobody notices you."

And Carlotta definitely did not want to be noticed. Thanks to the Wells family, she was a permanent legal resident of the United States, but her husband, Milton, his two brothers, and three of her cousins were not.

He watched her walk purposefully toward the station. When she was halfway down the stairs, he stepped out of the shadows and followed her. God, how he wished they could reconnect. If she saw him, she'd scoop him up in her arms and insist on taking him home and cooking up a big platter of *pupusas*.

If only, he thought as he came up behind her and wrapped his left arm around her neck and pushed her head forward with his right hand, putting enough pressure on her carotid artery to cut off the blood flow to her brain.

She went limp immediately, and he lowered her to the ground. He unzipped her purse, removed her keys, and went back up the stairs. She'd regain consciousness in a few minutes, check her purse, and breathe a sigh of relief when she saw that her wallet and her money were still there.

She'd be home before she realized her keys were missing. But she wouldn't call the cops to report the attack. Even though she could produce a green card, Carlotta would never invite *la policía* into her apartment when there were that many undocumented skeletons in her family closet.

Segura walked back toward Wells's home, tapped the digits 81175 into the keypad, and unlocked the door. As soon as he stepped inside, he heard the *beep-beep-beep* of the alarm system asking for yet another security code that would prove he was not an intruder.

That was easy. He'd learned it years ago, and he was sure it would never change. The password was 36459, which spelled e-m-i-l-y on the keypad.

Emily Gerson Wells was Princeton's great-grandmother. Her singular sense of design and elegance permeated every corner of the mansion. Her portrait, painted by the renowned John Singer Sargent, hung over the mantel in the great room. And lest anyone forget their heritage, her name had to be spelled out every time one of her heirs wanted passage into the grand home that was her legacy.

Segura tapped in Emily's name, and the beeping stopped.

Back in the day, Princeton's father had an imposing office on the second floor. The old man had died a few years ago, so the office would be Princeton's now. Segura trod silently up the stairs, put his ear to the mahogany door, and heard the soulful voice of Mary J. Blige coming from inside.

He opened the door and stepped over the threshold. Princeton was stretched out on a leather sofa, a book in one hand, a drink on the table at his side. He looked up at the bronze hard-bodied ghost from his past, and he froze.

"Hello, Princeton," Segura said. "I see you're still a reader. Is it a good book?"

"Hello, Geraldo," Wells said. "Yes, I'm enjoying it."

Segura nodded. "Too bad you're not going to live long enough to finish it."

CHAPTER 68

"**WOULD YOU CARE** for a drink before you kill me?" Wells asked.

"No thanks. But feel free to finish yours."

Wells sat up on the sofa and downed his drink. "Do you mind if I have one more for the long journey ahead?" he said, getting up and going to the bar.

"You're taking this rather calmly," Segura said.

"Geraldo, it's not like I didn't expect you. Even so, I'm rather in awe of how you slipped in the way you did."

"It helps to have a history. I'll leave these here for Carlotta." He dropped her key ring on the desk. "So tell me something: if you knew I was coming, why didn't you get out of the country? You have a plane. You have money. You could have gone anywhere."

"I didn't want to go anywhere," Wells said, pouring from a bottle of Balvenie thirty-year single malt. "New York is my home. My work is here. My charity is here. My whole life is here. I decided I'd wait for you to show up and try to do what I do best."

"And what's that?"

"Negotiate."

Segura laughed. "You mean beg for mercy like Nathan did."

"Give me a little credit, will you? I'm not begging. I'm trying to increase the value of my life."

"It's like old times, Princeton. You've totally lost me."

"Right now I'm worth nothing to you. You kill me, and I'm dead. End of story. But what if I said I'd give you a hundred dollars not to kill me? Now I'm no longer worth nothing. Now it's going to cost you a hundred bucks to kill me."

Segura laughed. "And worth every penny. Pour me a little of that Scotch, will you?"

Wells took a clean rocks glass from the bar, added three fingers of the single malt, and handed it to Segura.

"You trying to get me drunk, mate?"

"I don't think that would help my case. Now, where were we?"

"It was costing me a hundred dollars to whack you, and I happily paid the price."

"Now what if I said a million dollars? You'd probably still kill me, but you'd walk out of the room knowing that revenge cost you a million dollars. You see where I'm going with this?"

"You're very good at these high-finance shenanigans, aren't you? So now you're going to try to come up with a number that would make me think, *I can't kill the fucker. It's going to cost me a fortune.*"

"That's the plan," Wells said. "It's a gentleman's game. Very civilized. All I have to do is make me worth so much money alive that you realize you can't afford to kill me."

"You took twenty years of my life," Segura said. "Do you think I can put a price on that?"

"I think you already have, Geraldo. That's why you're here. Del, Arnie, and Nathan all paid for what we did to you. If you kill me, you'll have exacted revenge. But what about justice? Shouldn't one of us compensate you for your twenty years of pain and suffering? Shouldn't one of us pay for the forty or fifty years you have left ahead of you? I'm the only one with those kinds of resources. That's why I'm still alive, and you're here drinking my single malt."

Segura grinned. "You're right. In the beginning, I wanted to mow down the four of you with an AK-47. But as I got closer to freedom, I realized that while four dead former friends would make me feel good for a few brief moments, three dead and a shitload of money would keep me happy forever."

"Hallelujah," Wells said, tossing down half of his drink. "So tell me the number you have in your head, and we can both get a second chance at life."

"Five million dollars—"

"Done," Wells said quickly.

"A year," Segura said. "Five million dollars for every year I spent in that rat-infested shithole wearing leg-irons and shackles in the stupefying heat, choking on the stench from the communal latrine, while you got fatter and richer, never once lifting a finger to rescue me from the hell you subjected me to."

"A hundred million dollars," Wells said, making it sound partly like a statement, partly like a question.

"Take it or leave it."

"Clearly you're very good at these high-finance shenanigans yourself," Wells said. "I'll take it."

"You can wire it to my offshore account. I'll give you the number."

Wells sat down at his computer and began to type.

"One question," he said. "How do I know you won't wait for me to wire the money and then kill me?"

"You took my youth, my dream years, but my honor is still intact. If I take your blood money, I swear on the graves of my parents that I won't kill you. Not now. Not ever. And once I walk out that door, you'll never see me or hear from me again."

Wells nodded and went back to typing. Segura walked to the bar and was about to pour himself another drink when the doorbell rang.

The video camera at the front door flashed a picture of the visitors on Wells's screen.

"It's those two goddamn detectives," he said. "What should I do?"

Segura removed a gun from his waistband. "Take off your clothes. All of them."

CHAPTER 69

KYLIE HAD NO patience. She rang Wells's doorbell a second time.

"Who is it?" he responded over the intercom.

"Detectives MacDonald and Jordan, NYPD," she said. "We need to talk. It won't take long."

"It's rather inconvenient right now," he said. "I'm in the middle of something. Can you come back tomorrow?"

"It's rather inconvenient to have a mass murderer wandering around our city, Mr. Wells," she said. "Since you're at the top of his hit list, maybe you could drop what you're doing and spend a few minutes with the people who are trying to get to him before he gets to you."

"Point well taken, Detective," he said. "I'll be right down."

She stepped away from the intercom and threw her hands up in the air. "This is the same bullshit we got from Langford. Nobody wants to talk to the cops."

"Langford didn't want to talk because he was guilty of murder," I said.

"So what's Wells's excuse?" Kylie said. "Do you

think he knows that we're the mayor's stooges, and he's not in the mood to talk about building housing for the homeless? Or do you think he's totally in denial about Segura, and he figures if he makes us go away, then the problem goes away?"

"Or there's a third possibility," I said.

"Like what?"

"Like maybe he's in the middle of something, and we came at a really inconvenient time."

The front door opened and Princeton Wells stood there, his hair wet, his feet bare, and a towel around his waist. He reeked of booze.

"Sorry to keep you waiting," he said. "Kenda and I were in the hot tub."

"We apologize if we caught you at a bad time," I said.

"Bad time? Hell, you caught me at a great time. And if the two of you want to join me and Kenda in the hot tub, it could be a fucking fantastic time."

"Mr. Wells, I know you've turned us down before," I said, "but in light of what happened with Nathan Hirsch, NYPD is prepared to offer you police protection. Do you want it?"

"Sure. You can protect me from that blonde in the hot tub. She's insatiable. I swear to God that woman will be the death of me."

"Sir, have you been drinking?" Kylie said.

"Nonstop, Detective. It's my go-to coping mechanism. As far as I know there's no law against it, so if there's nothing further..."

"There's one other thing. The mayor would like you to call her."

"Tell Muriel she's on my list," he said. "No, no, wait: Tell her the truth. Tell her Princeton Wells is on a bender, but he's safely locked up in his great-grandmother's mansion, which is like the Fortress of Solitude, only with better decorating. Also tell her that the Tremont Gardens project will go on as scheduled. It's Del Fairfax's legacy, and I'll be damned if I'm going to let it die with him. I'm a little sauced right now, but tomorrow morning I promise I will be sober, and I'll start writing checks, making phone calls, and moving heaven and earth to get it done. I swear."

"Mayor Sykes will be happy to hear that," I said.

"Then we're good," he said.

"Yes, sir."

"Thanks for coming," he said, and shut the door.

"I don't get it," I said as Kylie and I walked back to the car.

"What don't you get, Zach? That rich people are assholes? That Princeton Wells would rather get drunk and get laid than get out of Dodge?"

"No, it's not that. It's just that he never asked us where we are in the investigation. With Nathan Hirsch it was always, 'Did you find Segura? Did you arrest La Grande?' For a man who is the killer's next target, Princeton Wells seems remarkably uninterested in how the manhunt for Geraldo Segura is going."

"Which just reinforces my rich-people-are-assholes theory."

I looked at my watch. "I've given the city enough of my life today," I said. "I'm going to punch out and go home."

"What are you doing tonight?" Kylie asked.

"Probably have dinner with Cheryl, catch something on Netflix."

It was true. I just left out the part about my plan to trap her boyfriend into helping me rob a high-stakes poker game.

CHAPTER 70

TRYING TO HIDE the truth from your girlfriend is a risky proposition. And when said girlfriend also happens to be a shrink, a cop, and a hot-tempered Latina, the risk factor goes up exponentially, and secret-keeping becomes more of a death wish.

So I decided to do a one-eighty from where I was that morning. As soon as I got to Cheryl's apartment, I told her everything. She might not approve, but she couldn't slam me for withholding information. I started with my dinner with Q.

She stopped me immediately. "Q points a finger at these two guys, Jessup and Jewel, and you believe him?" she said. "He has no evidence."

"Cheryl, this is not a jury trial. Q is a world-class snitch. He said, and I quote, 'These brothers are spending money like the sultan of Brunei died and named them sole beneficiaries.' Unquote."

"That's specious logic."

"It's street logic," I said. Then I launched into the details of my undercover meeting with the two hip-hop promoters at Rattlesnake. She didn't say a word until I got to the name of my alter ego.

"*Fly Boy?*" she said, laughing.

"Johnny Fly Boy Wurster," I said. "Funny how I got that name." I told her my story about being thrown off a seventh-story balcony and walking away without a scratch.

She shook her head. "Those two guys actually bought that?"

"What's not to buy? It's like Freddy No Nose or Sammy the Bull. It's a nickname with a story behind it."

"And they believe you've recruited them to stick up a poker game at a private home and get away with a million dollars."

"A million two," I corrected. "Eight players at a hundred and fifty K a pop."

"So now what?" she asked.

"At this point, they've had twenty-four hours to think about the score. They figure it's a piece of cake, and they're already spending the money in their dreams. So now I'm going to throw a monkey wrench into the deal. Do you want to watch?"

"Of course I want to watch," she said, adding some more white wine to her glass and sitting down on the sofa with her legs curled underneath her. "As long as you understand that my fascination should in no way be misinterpreted as an endorsement of your actions."

"Understood," I said, taking it as a small victory. "Jessup is the less trusting of the two. If the sting is going to work, I have to get him to take the bait." I got out my burner phone, put it on speaker, and dialed Jessup's number. He answered on the second ring.

"Tariq, this is Fly Boy," I said. "I got bad news. That sweet deal we had planned for Saturday night— I'm pulling the plug on it."

"What the fuck, man? You find someone who would do it for less money?"

"No, I was totally down with you guys. It's just that I've done this before. Always in a new city, always with new players. But I just found out that one of the guys in the room on Saturday is going to be someone who sat in on the game when I pulled this in Phoenix. He's not stupid. First thing he's going to think is, *What are the odds of being in identical robberies in two different towns, and both times Johnny Fly Boy is at the table with me?*"

"He'll make you in a heartbeat," Jessup said.

"That's why I'm moving on."

"Where you going next?"

"I'm thinking Dallas," I said.

"So that's a short plane ride. Me and Garvey will go with you."

"Not happening, bro. This is not a traveling circus. I'm a one-man show. I pick up local talent wherever I go. You were my Jersey boys, but I can't walk into that room, so the deal is off. Lose my phone number after I hang up."

"Wait a minute, Fly Boy," Jessup said. "Think this through before you bail. You already got the game lined up. You got the muscle in place. So if you can't sit in, all you need is someone who can."

"Don't you think I thought of that? I have a friend who I would trust to sit in for me, but he's in Europe for a few months making lonely wealthy widows a little less lonely...and a lot less wealthy."

"What if I can help?" Jessup said.

"No. You'd look like you were crashing the party."

"You saying I don't fit in because I'm black?"

"Hell, no," I said. "Black, white, brown, yellow—if your money's green, nobody gives a shit. But nobody sits down at that table unless they're a regular high-stakes player. That's not you, Tariq."

"What if I told you I got a guy who buys into six-figure games all the time? This dude would fit right in."

Cheryl looked at me, her eyes wide, her mouth open. The fish was nibbling at the hook.

"Do you trust this guy?" I asked.

"Hell, yeah. He was the inside man on the hotel job, and that went down like silk. He's going to want his cut, but with that much money on the table, I'm sure we can come to terms."

"I don't know, Tariq."

"Come on, Fly Boy. At least meet him."

"All right. Tonight at eleven. Houston Hall."

"Never heard of it."

"It's in the Village on West Houston Street, just off Varick. It's big, it's noisy, it's crowded, and I never have to worry about running into anyone who's ever played in a poker game where the limit was more than twenty bucks. You and Jewel bring your boy. If I like him, I'll stake him to the hundred and fifty grand, and then we'll move on to the next plateau. I'll see you at eleven."

I hung up. "And that, Dr. Robinson, is how it's done," I said.

"That was brilliant, Zach. You're a born con man. What happens when they show up?"

"Jessup and Jewel are small fish. Reitzfeld will toss them back into the pond and give C.J. a chance to pay back the money and get out of town. The guy's a poker player. He'll know that's the best hand he's going to be dealt."

"How do you feel about all this?" she asked.

"Pretty shitty. I feel good about cracking a case,

but I hate sneaking around on my partner. I just hope she never finds out."

"Aren't you going to ask how I feel?"

"Cheryl, I know how you feel. You don't trust my motives, and you don't approve. You told me that this morning."

"I changed my mind. At your core, you're a cop. I think your motives may be a little purer than I gave you credit for. Also…"

"Also what?"

"Watching you manipulate that guy into doing exactly what you want him to do was a bit of a turn-on."

"You're kidding."

She got off the sofa, took me by the hand, and started walking me to the bedroom. "Come on, Fly Boy. I'll show you if I'm kidding or not."

CHAPTER 71

HOUSTON HALL IS lower Manhattan's go-to watering hole for the under-thirty crowd. The cavernous building still has the exposed rafters, weathered brick walls, and nuts-and-guts architectural charm of the parking garage it was in a past life.

On weekends, the line to get in is around the block, but on a Wednesday at 10:00 p.m., Reitzfeld and I were able to walk right in and circulate among the raucous crowd of revelers who were hoisting steins of craft beer and munching on traditional fare like wings and sliders, as well as on the less predictable pastrami Reuben spring rolls and spicy sashimi tuna tacos.

"Christ," Reitzfeld said. "There must be five hundred people in here, and I'm old enough to be their father—every last one of them."

"I know," I said. "Did you see the red sign that flashed when you walked through the door? It said GEEZER ALERT."

"Kiss my ass, rookie. But thanks for doing this. Not everybody at the PD would go this far out on a limb for a retired cop."

"Then they're myopic," I said. "Eventually we're

all retired cops, and sooner or later we're going to need help from the inside. Let's get a couple of beers so we look like we fit in."

The vast wide-open beer hall had row after row of massive mead-hall tables and benches. I ordered two pitchers of lager and five glasses from the bar, and we found a spot that was midroom with a clear sight line to the front door.

The plan was simple. As soon as Jessup and Jewel identified C.J. as the mastermind behind the robbery, we'd let them go. Then I'd leave, and Reitzfeld could take it from there.

"You definitely can't be around when I ask for the money back," Reitzfeld said. "It's one thing for you to help me track down a couple of perps, but if you're in the room when I try to collect the eight hundred grand, IA will nail you for being a bagman."

"The funny thing is that Shelley cares less about getting the money back than you do."

"I've got more skin in the game than Shelley does," Reitzfeld said.

We nursed our beers and kept our eyes on the people coming and going. At 10:55, Jessup and Jewel walked through the front door and looked around. It was definitely not their world. More frat party than bar scene, and while there were black faces in the crowd, it was more East Hampton than South Bronx.

I dialed Jessup's number and watched him answer.

"On the right side," I said. "There are numbers painted on the wall over the light fixtures. I'm at the far end of the table under number nine."

"Are you sure you want to do this here?" he said.

"It's the only place I'll do it," I said. "If you don't like it, you're free to go back the way you came."

He hung up, and I watched him launch into an animated conversation with Jewel. Then they made their way cautiously to our table—actually, my table: by now Reitzfeld was standing off to the side.

"Thanks for coming," I said, filling two clean glasses.

They sat down. Jewel took a swig of the brew, but Jessup wasn't in a drinking mood.

"I counted maybe six brothers from the front door to here," he said. "Did we have to be so conspicuous?"

"First of all, none of the white people took a second look at you, and if you remember, I was in the minority last night at Rattlesnake. Suck it up. Now where's your inside man?"

Jessup looked at his Apple Watch. "It's four minutes shy of eleven, Fly Boy. I don't suppose that's enough time for the three of us to get in a round of darts with Biff and Chad over there?"

The joke caught Jewel middrink, and he did a spit take into his beer glass.

"Fun and games are over, fellas," I said. "It's time to get serious. Now listen carefully, and whatever you do, don't get up or even think about going for your piece, because there are four—count 'em, four—cops behind you."

There weren't four cops. Just one retiree who worked security at Silvercup Studios. But from where they were sitting, imaginary cops were as menacing as real ones.

"What the fuck?" Jessup said.

"And there's one cop in front of you," I said.

"Shit. I knew you were a cop," Jessup said.

"No you didn't, or you wouldn't have showed up. But here's the good news. Our beef isn't with you.

As soon as C.J. sits down, and you finger him for the Mark hotel robbery, you both win a Get Out of Jail Free card. Just walk out the door. No questions asked."

"Who's C.J.?" Jewel said.

"Don't be stupid, Garvey," I said. "All you have to do is point out your inside man at the poker game, and you're free to go."

"Happy to do it, officer," Jessup said, "but he didn't say his name was C.J."

"Fair enough. And my name isn't Fly Boy."

Jessup's phone rang. He looked at me. "He's here."

"Tell him where to find you, then stand up and wave. If you warn him and he bolts, you're in cuffs."

Jessup followed orders, and I stood off to the side with Reitzfeld until a man in a black Windbreaker and a black baseball cap walked over to the table and shook hands with his partners in crime.

Only it wasn't C. J. Berringer.

CHAPTER 72

"**THIS IS THE** dude who planned the whole operation," Tariq Jessup said, pointing at the newcomer. "He kept seven hundred thousand, and we got fifty thou apiece, which is not the kind of payday that fosters allegiance to your employer. So, I repeat, he did it. Do we get to go now, Officer Fly Boy?"

Reitzfeld stepped into the picture. "Don't move until I tell you," he said.

Jessup and Jewel recognized him immediately. "Dude," Jessup said, "sorry about the chloroform and tying you up and shit, but that was his idea, too. We were just the help."

Reitzfeld wasn't interested in them. He was focused on the man in the black cap. "Why'd you do it, Rick?" he said.

Rick Button, the stand-up comic, who until seconds ago had been one of the victims, shrugged. "Ah, the age-old question: why did the comedian steal the eight-hundred-thousand-dollar poker pot?" he said. "It was better than spending a year in a body cast, gumming my food, and shitting into a bag, which is what would have happened, compliments of a pair of Russian Neanderthals who work for the Bratva in Brighton Beach."

"Excuse us again, officers," Jessup said. "But Garvey and I break out in hives when we're in the presence of this many happy white people. You said we could go. Are you or are you not men of your word?"

Reitzfeld didn't look at me. It had to be his call. "Get lost," he said. "And if I were you, I wouldn't be telling tales about this evening around the hood, or it will come back to bite you in the ass."

"Have no fear," Jessup said. "We got played by a cop. It's not exactly something we plan to be tweeting about." He turned to Button. "I'm updating my résumé, boss. Can I count on you for a reference?"

Button laughed. "Good one," he said.

Jessup and Jewel left the beer hall.

"Sit down and don't move," Reitzfeld said to Button. Button sat.

Then Reitzfeld put his arm on my shoulder and walked me ten feet away from the table. "I got this, Zach. You better go, too," he said.

"Bob, this is a whole different scenario than the one we rehearsed," I said. "Shelley won't have the same compassion for this idiot that he did for Kylie's boyfriend. Do you think he's going to want to prosecute? Should I—"

"The only thing you should do, Zach, is get the hell out of here. Wash your hands of the whole affair. You helped me nail this weasel, and for that I am forever grateful. Whatever Shelley wants to do now is his call, but I can tell you that whatever it is, he'll make sure that your name isn't connected in any way."

"The only way for that to happen is for him to let

Rick Button walk. If he's arrested, there's no way to keep my name out of it."

"Don't lose any sleep over it, Zach. You didn't do anything wrong, and nobody is going to be asking you if you did. Thanks for the beer. Now go."

I went. Straight to Cheryl.

Her first question after I recounted the entire evening was right out of page one of the shrink's handbook. "So how do you feel about all this?" she said.

"Relieved," I said. "I know it looked like I was trying to remove C.J. from the picture, but I'm really glad it wasn't him. If it ever turned out that Kylie was dating a criminal, her career would be toast."

"And you would have lost the best partner you ever had," she said.

"And the most infuriating, and the most unpredictable, and the most unreasonable, and by far the most insane," I said. "I mean, yesterday she pulled the plug on tens of thousands of cell phones, and today she walked straight at a woman in a trance who was programmed to shoot her."

"It sounds like she'd be hard to replace."

I wrapped my arms around Cheryl, put my lips to her ear, and whispered, "So would you, Fly Girl. So would you."

EPILOGUE
HAITIAN JUSTICE

CHAPTER 73

GERALDO SEGURA WAS a man of his word. As soon as the cops were gone and the money had been wired to his account, he left Princeton Wells unharmed and in perfect health, except for the damage the expensive booze was doing to the man's liver.

He took a cab to JFK, and despite the fact that he was a millionaire a hundred times over, he had opted for a coach seat on Emirates to Adelaide, Australia, for $1,160. A first-class ticket with its own private cabin would only have cost another $23,000, but his logic was simple. Nobody pays attention to the people in the cheap seats.

He breezed through airport security with his new identity, and now at thirty-nine thousand feet he sat back in seat 58A, comfortably lost in the pack of 398 other economy passengers on the Airbus A380.

His mind flashed back to the start of his long day: a predawn visit to the Karayib Makèt in Brooklyn. The thugs at the door, all of whom towered over him, had no idea that he could have incapacitated them all. Two of them grabbed him, one on each arm, and asked what he wanted.

"I'm here to talk to Dingo Slide," he said.

"Dingo is resting with his ancestors," one of the goons said.

"Then who's in charge of this shit operation?" Segura demanded. "You fuckers owe me money."

The man drove a fist into his stomach. Segura doubled over and gasped for breath. But it was all an act. He had pulled back just before the moment of contact. Why let his attacker know he had abs of steel, and that nothing short of a kick to the gut from a mule could have brought him down?

They dragged him to the rear of the store, through a cold room, until he was face-to-face with the one man he had come to meet.

"My name is Geraldo Segura," he said defiantly.

"So…the martyr has returned to seek revenge," the leader of the Haitian cartel said. "I am Malique La Grande. I've been reading about your impressive accomplishments. Were you planning on killing me as well?"

"No. I'm here for compensation."

La Grande laughed out loud, and the others joined in. He waved his hand, and his men released their grip on their captive. "Prison has damaged your thinking," La Grande said. "Why would you think we owe you money?"

"Because it's the honorable thing to do. If Dingo Slide were here, he would agree. But I guess the Zoe Pound code of honor has deteriorated under new management."

"I know you're a fighter," La Grande said, taking a gun from his waistband. "This is how I win fights. Talk to me about *honor*."

"I was a kid. Zoe Pound drugs were planted on me. The least you can do is pay me for doing twenty years for your crime."

"So you lost twenty years," La Grande said. "I lost four kilos of heroin. We all pay a price."

"Bullshit!" Segura said, digging a hand into his jacket pocket.

The men at his side grabbed him and forced him to the ground.

"Emmanuel, you let him in here with a gun?" La Grande bellowed.

"No, boss. No, no," the guard said. "I searched him."

"What's in his pocket?"

One guard pulled Segura to his feet while Emmanuel dug a hand into the jacket pocket. "This is all, boss," he said, holding up a fistful of paper.

"And what is that?" La Grande said.

"My release papers from Klong Prem Central Prison," Segura said. "It's proof that you're lying to me."

La Grande tucked the gun back into his waistband and beckoned Emmanuel to bring him the papers. He read them carefully. Then he read them a second time, balled them up, hurled the papers to the floor, and erupted in a barrage of Haitian Creole.

Those who understood him looked shocked, angered.

Segura stood his ground. "English," he said calmly.

"Your papers say you were arrested for trying to smuggle a kilo of heroin out of Thailand," La Grande said. "What about the other three kilos?"

"What other three kilos? Your rich white mules planted the drugs in my bag. One kilo is all it took to put me in that hellhole for fifty years. I got out in twenty, no thanks to them. That's why I'm back. I killed two, ruined one for life, and by tomorrow morning, Princeton Wells's body will be in bits and pieces all over his bedroom. My grudge isn't against Zoe Pound, but the least you can do is pay me—"

"Where are the other three kilos?" La Grande said in a whisper that was far more menacing than a shout. "Where…are…the other…three kilos?"

"I don't know," Segura said. "Why don't you ask your partner, Mr. Wells?"

"Dingo asked him twenty years ago. Wells swore up and down that you were arrested with all four kilos."

"The paperwork states that the Thai government confiscated one kilo. Wells flies back home on his private jet and says, 'Sorry, Dingo. They took it all.' Who do you believe, Mr. La Grande?"

"I knew Wells was lying," La Grande said. "I wanted them all dead, but I was only a lieutenant. Dingo didn't have the balls to kill them. They bought us off with a quarter of a million dollars."

"Three kilos for a quarter million?" Segura said. "They cut it, sold it, and made a million dollars at your expense…and mine."

"Zoe Pound owes you nothing," La Grande said. "But I will give you a hundred large to walk away from all this."

"Why would you give me a nickel if you think you owe me nothing?"

"Because you're going to do me a favor."

"What's that?"

"Don't kill Wells," La Grande said.

"I have to," Segura said. "I've waited too long."

"You've got your revenge. Save a little for me, and I'll sweeten the deal by another fifty thousand."

Segura pondered the offer, then nodded slowly. "I accept," he said. "I can leave the country tonight. Don't do anything till I'm gone."

"Agreed," La Grande said.

"Once I leave I can never come back," Segura said. "So promise me you won't change your mind."

"Have no fear, Rom Ran Sura," La Grande said. "I am not my predecessor."

Segura left the market at five in the morning, his backpack stuffed with hundred-dollar bills. Then he went back to the hotel on Sumner Place, slept until noon, checked out, and made a surprise visit to his grandmother and his aunts to deliver the one hundred and fifty thousand dollars.

The next three hours were a chaotic hodgepodge of joy, tears, hallelujahs, and Guatemalan food. Before he left, he told his *abuela* and his *tias* that there would be no more money coming from his former school friends. From now on, he would send whatever they needed, including tickets to visit him and his family once they'd settled in.

By four thirty, he was on Central Park West, watching Carlotta lock the front door to the Wells mansion. And now he was flying across the Atlantic to his new life with Jam and the kids. First stop: Dubai, and then another twelve-hour flight, to Adelaide. He'd never been there, but after years of hearing Flynn Samuels talk about his hometown, Segura decided it was the best place in the world for a fresh start.

He closed his eyes, and just as he had done every night on a cold prison floor, he said a silent prayer asking God to help him forget the past and dream about the future.

And for the first time in twenty years, he fell asleep knowing his prayers would be answered.

CHAPTER 74

IT WAS FRIDAY NIGHT.

Morris Langford was in a jail cell on a suicide watch. Janek Hoffmann was out of jail, and no doubt pumping his body full of steroids and crack. Aubrey Davenport was finally reposing at the Frank E. Campbell funeral chapel on Madison Avenue, her internment scheduled for Sunday. Nathan Hirsch was charged with three counts of bribery and two counts of stock fraud, and was released on two million dollars' bail. Instead of a bomb handcuffed to his wrist, he was now under house arrest, a court-ordered electronic bracelet shackled to his ankle. I had no idea where Troy Marschand and Dylan Freemont were, and I didn't give a rat's ass. Princeton Wells had not called Mayor Sykes on Thursday morning as promised, and Captain Cates informed me that if Her Honor had not heard from Mr. Wells by Monday morning, Kylie and I were to pay him another visit. Hopefully by then he and Kenda would be out of the hot tub.

Most important, ten days after Del Fairfax's podium exploded at the Silver Bullet Foundation fund-raiser, Geraldo Segura was still at large, and the citywide manhunt for the bomber had been escalated to nationwide.

With that much law enforcement on the case, I was resigned to the unhappy fact that Kylie and I would not be the ones to collar him. But at least I could look on the bright side. It was Friday night.

A week ago, I'd had to cancel my Friday reservation with Cheryl at Paola's and fly to Bangkok. Tonight we were finally going to have the dinner date we had been looking forward to. With one difference. The reservation now said "Table for four."

"How the hell did this happen, anyway?" I asked Cheryl. We were in a cab on Madison Avenue heading uptown to Paola's.

"Wow," she said. "That's the tone of voice I'd expect if I ran your new car into a ditch. All I did was agree to have dinner with your partner and her significant other."

"Sorry about the tone of voice. It's just that I thought it was only going to be the two of us, and now it isn't."

"That's what happens when you stick your cop nose into other people's business. Apparently Shelley got his poker buddies together last night and told them how you and Bob Reitzfeld nailed Rick Button. There's about three hundred thousand still left from the money he stole, so everyone is getting about forty-three thousand back. C.J. is so grateful he wants to take us to dinner."

"We were already booked for tonight, and we're driving up to Woodstock tomorrow morning for the weekend," I said. "We had an ironclad excuse. You could have gotten out of it."

"Why would I want to get out of it?" Cheryl said.

"I've heard so much about Kylie's new boyfriend. I'm finally getting the chance to meet him."

Paola's son, Stefano, greeted us at the door and escorted us to our table, where Kylie and C.J. were waiting with a bottle of champagne and four glasses.

Kylie introduced him to Cheryl, Stefano poured the wine, and C.J. made the toast. "To Zach," he said. "You, sir, are an outstanding detective."

"And he's mighty good at keeping a secret, too," Kylie said. "Zach, I didn't know you were working the case."

"Reitzfeld asked me to help and to keep it under wraps," I said. "I couldn't say no."

Kylie grinned, and I could see she had me cold. Of the 275 recruits in our academy class, Kylie graduated number one. She was more than smart enough to figure out why I never told her I was helping Reitzfeld. And since I graduated number six, I was at least smart enough to know that she knew, and she was now going to bust my balls about it.

"So did you suspect Rick Button right from the get-go?" she asked, all wide-eyed and innocent.

I was groping for a passable answer when Cheryl came to my rescue. "I hate to be a hard-ass, guys, but Zach and I have a strict rule. No cell phones and no cop talk at the dinner table." She turned to C.J. "You, on the other hand, are *encouraged* to talk shop. I am totally fascinated with the psychology of being a professional gambler. When did you first know that's what you wanted to do?"

C.J. answered the question, but Kylie got Cheryl's message. *My boyfriend suspected your boyfriend. Get over it. Case closed.*

After that, the evening turned out to be a lot of fun. Paola fed us well, and Stefano treated us like rock stars. The biggest shocker of the night came just as we were about to order dessert.

Danny Corcoran and Tommy Fischer walked through the front door. I'd told them where I was having dinner, but I hadn't expected them to hunt me down. Stefano pointed to our table, and the two of them headed straight for us.

"Sorry to bust in on you," Danny said. "I know you guys are off the clock, but there's something we need to tell you before you hear it on the news."

"We tried calling," Tommy said, "but it just kept going to voice mail."

Cheryl's rules of dinner etiquette claim another two victims.

"What's going on?" I said.

"Princeton Wells is dead."

"Blown up?" Kylie said.

"Carved up," Danny said. "Haitian style. And in case we couldn't figure out who was behind it, his body was wrapped in a Zoe Pound flag and left in a vacant lot about three blocks from their headquarters."

"Do they want us on the scene?"

"Not now. The Six Seven is all over it," Tommy Fischer said. "Wells being who he is, it may float up to Red eventually, but we all know it was Malique La Grande. Proving it is a whole nother kettle of creole."

"We may never be able to prove who killed Princeton Wells," I said, "but we sure as hell know who didn't kill him."

"Geraldo Segura," Kylie said.

"Incredible," I said. "After all that, he didn't kill Wells."

"Why not?" C.J. said. "I thought he had a major vendetta."

"He did," Kylie said. "But when you blow some-one up with a bomb, they're dead in an instant. After twenty years in a Thai prison, I think Segura wanted Wells to die a long, slow, agonizing death. And no-body does it better than the Haitians."

"Excuse me," Cheryl said, "but I think it's time we got back to the no-cop-talk-at-dinner rule. Danny, we were just about to order dessert and coffee. Would you and Tommy like to join us?"

"Life must go on, Doc," Danny said, signaling a bus-boy to bring two more chairs. "And dessert is a great place to start. Let me take a look at that menu."

And then it hit me. With Wells dead, there was no reason for Segura to stay in New York. Or in the U.S., for that matter. In fact, since he farmed out the killing, he probably left the country while Wells was still alive.

I'd have liked to share my brilliant insight with my fellow detectives, but Cheryl runs a tight dinner table. No cop talk means no cop talk.

So I lifted my wineglass and drank a silent toast to Geraldo Segura, the one who got away.

ACKNOWLEDGMENTS

The authors would like to thank the following people for their help in making this work of fiction ring true: NYPD Detective Danny Corcoran, Under sheriff Frank Faluotico (retired) and Jerry Brainard of the Ulster County, New York, Sheriff's Department, retired NYPD Detectives Tommy Fischer and Sal Catapano, Dr. Lawrence Dresdale, Paul Aronson, Pam Herrick, Susan Brown, Gerri Gomperts, Victor Gomperts, Bill Neill, Oscar Ogg, Jason White, Dan Fennessy, Bill Harrison, David Hinds, Mel Berger, Bob Beatty, and Sarah Paris.

ABOUT THE AUTHORS

James Patterson is the world's bestselling author and most trusted storyteller. He has created many enduring fictional characters and series, including Alex Cross, the Women's Murder Club, Michael Bennett, Maximum Ride, Middle School, and I Funny. Among his notable literary collaborations are *The President Is Missing*, with President Bill Clinton, and the Max Einstein series, produced in partnership with the Albert Einstein estate. Patterson's writing career is characterized by a single mission: to prove that there is no such thing as a person who "doesn't like to read," only people who haven't found the right book. He's given over three million books to schoolkids and the military, donated more than seventy million dollars to support education, and endowed over five thousand college scholarships for teachers. The National Book Foundation recently presented Patterson with the Literarian Award for Outstanding Service to the American Literary Community, and he is also the recipient of an Edgar Award and six Emmy Awards. He lives in Florida with his family.

Marshall Karp has written for stage, screen, and TV, and is the author of five books in the Lomax and Biggs series. He is also the coauthor of the NYPD Red series with James Patterson.

JAMES
PATTERSON
RECOMMENDS

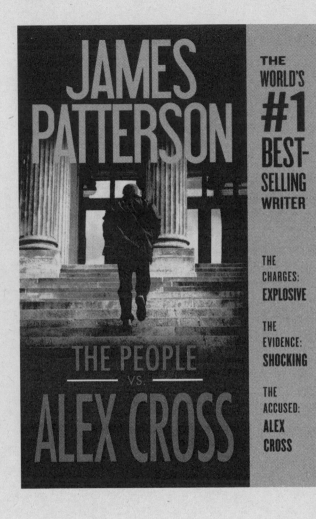

JAMES PATTERSON

THE PEOPLE vs. ALEX CROSS

THE WORLD'S #1 BEST-SELLING WRITER

THE CHARGES: EXPLOSIVE

THE EVIDENCE: SHOCKING

THE ACCUSED: ALEX CROSS

THE PEOPLE VS. ALEX CROSS

Alex Cross has always upheld the law, but now for the first time I've put him on the *wrong* side of it. Charged with gunning down followers of his nemesis Gary Soneji, Cross has been branded as a trigger-happy cop. You and I know it was self-defense, but the jury won't exactly see it that way.

When the trial of the century erupts with the prosecution's damaging case, national headlines scream for conviction and even those closest to Alex start to doubt his innocence. He may lose everything: his family, his career, and his freedom. Things couldn't possibly get worse—until they do.

As Alex begins the crucial preparation for his defense, his former partner John Sampson pulls him into a case linked to the mysterious disappearances of several young girls. The investigation leads to the darkest corners of the Internet, where murder is just another form of entertainment.

Alex will do whatever it takes to stop a dangerous criminal...even as his life hangs in the balance.

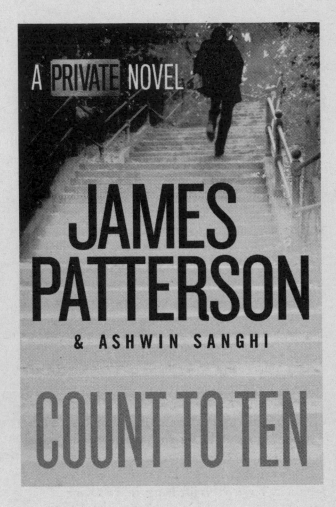

A PRIVATE NOVEL

JAMES PATTERSON

& ASHWIN SANGHI

COUNT TO TEN

COUNT TO TEN

I admit it: I put Private investigator Santosh Wagh through the wringer in his first outing. A combination of personal setbacks and a harrowing case almost did him in. Then I started wondering—is there something that can push him over the edge?

Santosh is ready to quit as the head of Private India. Except Jack Morgan, the global leader of Private, wants to open an office in Delhi, and Santosh is the only person he can trust. Still battling his demons, Santosh accepts and the agency takes on a case that threatens to destroy them. Plastic barrels containing dissolved human remains have been found in the basement of a house. But this isn't just any house. This property belongs to the state government.

With the crime scene in lockdown and information suppressed by the authorities, delving too deep soon makes Santosh a target to be eliminated.

"The plot twists will give you whiplash." —*Washington Post*

JAMES PATTERSON

THE BLACK BOOK

& DAVID ELLIS

THE #1 BESTSELLER EVERYWHERE

THE BLACK BOOK

I have favorites among the novels I've written. *Kiss the Girls*, *Invisible*, *1st to Die*, and *Honeymoon* are top of the list. With each, I had a good feeling when the writing was finished. I believe this book—*THE BLACK BOOK*—is the best work I've done in twenty-five years.

Meet Billy Harney. The son of Chicago's chief of detectives, he was born to be a cop. There's nothing he wouldn't sacrifice for his job. Enter Amy Lentini, an assistant state's attorney hell-bent on making a name for herself—by proving Billy isn't the cop he claims to be.

A horrifying murder leads investigators to a brothel that caters to Chicago's most powerful citizens. There's plenty of evidence on the scene, but what matters most is what's missing: the madam's black book.

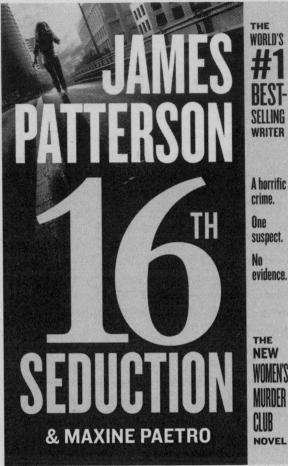

JAMES PATTERSON

16TH SEDUCTION

& MAXINE PAETRO

16TH SEDUCTION

Fierce. Determined. Smart. Unstoppable. That's Detective Lindsay Boxer in a nutshell. As the leader of the Women's Murder Club solving crimes in San Francisco, she's been tested time and time again. Now I've put even more pressure on her—as everyone she's ever relied on turns their back on her.

After her husband Joe's double life shattered their family, Lindsay is finally ready to welcome him back with open arms. And when their beloved hometown faces a threat unlike any the country has ever seen, Lindsay and Joe find a common cause and spring into action.

But what at first seems like an open-and-shut case quickly explodes. Undermined by a suspect with a brilliant mind, Lindsay's investigation is scrutinized and her motives are called into question. In a desperate fight for her career—and her life—Lindsay must connect the dots of a deadly conspiracy before *she's* put on trial and a criminal walks free with blood on his hands.

For a complete list of books by
JAMES PATTERSON

VISIT
JamesPatterson.com

 Follow James Patterson on Facebook
@JamesPatterson

 Follow James Patterson on Twitter
@JP_Books

 Follow James Patterson on Instagram
@jamespattersonbooks